RvPeck

HALLAPOOSA

Books by Robert Newton Peck

A Day No Pigs Would Die
Path of Hunters
Millie's Boy
Soup (a series)
Trig (a series)
Hamilton
Hang for Treason
Rabbits and Redcoats
King of Kazoo
Last Sunday
The King's Iron
Patooie
Eagle Fur
Basket Case
Hub
Mr. Little
Clunie
Secrets of Successful Fiction
Justice Lion
Kirk's Law
Banjo
Fiction Is Folks
The Seminole Seed
Dukes
Jo Silver
Spanish Hoof
My Vermont
The Horse Hunters
Hallapoosa

HALLAPOOSA

Robert Newton Peck

Walker and Company
New York

Hallapoosa . . .
is dedicated to the good and gentle people
who make a small town into a home town.

R. N. P.

First published in the United States of America
in 1988 by the Walker Publishing Company, Inc.

Published simultaneously in Canada by Thomas Allen & Son
Canada, Limited, Markham, Ontario.

Library of Congress Cataloging-in-Publication Data

Peck, Robert Newton.
  Hallapoosa.

  I. Title.
PS3566.E254H34   1988   813'.54   87-27921
ISBN 0-8027-1016-6

Printed in the United States of America

10 9 8 7 6 5 4 3 2

· *Prologue* ·

A giant cyclops eye pierced the night.

Behind it, a locomotive, coal tender and sixty-one freight cars steadily increased speed, leaving Jacksonville. Five hundred wheels of solid steel screamed and scraped along the rails.

Hauling its massive cargo of freight, the Florida East Coast Railway train gained momentum with every tie.

A mile ahead, two young Negro boys, brothers, were squatting on a sandy bank near a trash dump. An hour ago, the evening sky had faded to blackness, yet the two brothers waited as they so often did, hoping to watch a freight train go rolling by. Squinting down the track, they saw a distant pinpoint of light and heard a whistle, one intended to warn local residents of the unstoppable danger. Close to where the boys waited was one of several rural grade crossings where a dirt road humped up and over the tracks.

"Here it come," the older boy said. "Late, so she be moving along fast."

Below them, at the grade crossing, an electric switch had automatically been tripped, and two red lights alternately began to blink, coupled with a feeble dinging of a warning bell. The younger child pointed to his left, to a sand road. "Hey, here come a car too. Real quicksome. Maybe it fixing to beat the train."

The older brother chuckled. "Best he don't. Train be coming too soon."

As the car's headlights appeared larger, closer, both children noticed that the hurrying car was not approaching alone. Behind it, a second pair of headlights became visible. The speeding car was being followed by a somewhat larger and noisier vehicle, which appeared to the boys to be a dump truck.

"Car ain't going to make it."

The child had been correct. Previously, the car's driver had gunned the engine toward the grade crossing, but now displayed a sudden and prudent retreat from daring. With its wheels brake-locked, the car skidded to a stop as if in surrender, its tires spraying gravel, a few feet short of the railroad tracks to allow the onrushing freight to pass unchallenged. The car stalled. But the truck did not stop. It crashed headlong into the car's rear with enough force to nudge it onto the tracks.

A woman screamed, but a train whistle, shrieking as though in panic, bullied the scream into oblivion.

A breath later, the locomotive hit the car. Sparks scattered into the night as metal crunched into metal, followed by persistent sounds of crushing steel and shattering glass. Over and over the battered car rolled along the track, pounded again and again by the cowcatcher wedge of far greater mass. The collapsed car finally was bounced off the track to lie in a tangled smoking heap of gnawed wreckage. Freight car after freight car continued to rumble through the dust and the fumes of spilled gasoline.

As the ground trembled, the younger boy moved closer to his older brother.

"Look," the smaller boy said, pointing.

With a flashlight in hand, the truck's driver had leaped from the cab and was running through the darkness toward the mangled car. Whipping beams of light, the driver briefly studied the scene, examined the car's interior, and then removed something from his trouser pocket. Striking a match, the truck driver tossed the tiny flame at the car, and as it instantly began to burn brightly, turned, and raced back to his own vehicle.

Grinding the gears, the driver turned the dump truck around, and drove away in the direction of Jacksonville . . . using no headlights.

"You see that?" the younger boy asked, staring wide-eyed at the burning car.

The long freight train was beginning to slow, but it took over a minute to bring its momentum to a dead halt.

"Yeah, I see it all. Look like maybe somebody want somebody else to git dead. And stay deader."

"We best tell the train people."

"No." The older boy grabbed his brother's arm. "We ain't going to tell nothing, about nobody. What folks do secret in the night is maybe white business." Placing his hand over his brother's mouth, he said, "Don't say nothing, on account we wasn't watching. Hear?"

The younger child nodded. "I hear."

A trainman, swinging a lantern, was hurrying toward them. To avoid questioning, both of the Negro boys escaped quickly into the night. They would never discover how the horror they had witnessed, in August of 1931, would eventually stun the lives of many people, both young and old, Negro, white, and Seminole, in a small South Florida town in Collier County, three hundred miles away.

At a place called Hallapoosa.

· *One* ·

Hiram MacHugh stopped.
      Hooking a walking cane over his left forearm, he
pulled an already-damp bandanna from a right hip pocket to
mop his face. His white suit felt as rumpled as laundry.
August of 1931—a typical humid August, he thought, almost
wetter than rain, even when a Saturday afternoon sun hung
up there, baking a flock of clouds into dumplings.

A car honked.

"Another scorcher, High."

Even before turning his head, Hiram recognized the driver's
voice. As the veteran Justice of the Peace in Hallapoosa,
Hiram frequently had to tidy up legalities with Constable
Carney Ransom.

"Indeed so, Carney, indeed so. But I hardly imagine that
we'll be denied our later afternoon thunderboomer."

"No, reckon not. Maybe it'll cool us off. This dog-day weather
sure is tough on us fat folks. Meaning *me* as well as you."

True enough, Hiram silently agreed. His clothes always felt
tighter on a muggy day. To change the subject, he looked back
along Exchange Street, which was merely the local uppity
name for a dirt road. "Have you heard any news about the
turpentine mill?"

Constable Ransom shook his head.

"Nope, nary a whisper. Yet the gossip goes that possible
she's to close down. Up north, President Hoover even admits
the country's in for harder times."

Hiram stuffed the bandanna into his pocket. "So far, nineteen thirty-one hasn't treated any of us too kindly. We can hope next year will prosper us some."

"Maybe so." Carney made a face. "Trouble is, High, when the times turn sour, the jugs empty faster and it tends to twist good people into ornery. And back yonder, out amongst the pines, there's more than a few of them turpentiners that I don't guess I'm eager to swap knuckles with . . . even sober. And that goes for them Crickers too."

Quite so, Hiram was thinking. There were rough customers in the area. But, he and Carney had managed to clamp a lid on temper and to open up a clenched fist into a handshake. Carney Ransom was a good lawman, a fellow who possessed the grace to look the other way and allow people to live life as they doggone pleased.

With a flip of the key, Carney switched off the patrol car's engine.

"Well," he said, "it'll be Saturday night in a few hours, High. I s'pose you'll live up to your nickname and christen a fresh jug. Then kick up your heels." Carney's ruddy face twitched a sly wink. "And maybe elevate somebody else's."

There were few secrets, Hiram knew, in their small South Florida town of Hallapoosa. He'd been called High since early boyhood and later had earned the diminutive alcoholically as well. Carney Ransom was no doubt aware that every Saturday evening their Justice of the Peace had two visitors. One who brought the jug, then a second who stayed for a sporting. Anticipating it, Hiram MacHugh felt the dryness in his mouth, as well as his male eagerness for Glory.

Ah, only a few more hours, he was thinking, until sundown.

Perhaps, he thought, he should have taken himself a wife, years ago. But his shyness had stood in the way. His childhood illness, infantile paralysis, had resulted in a shorter and weaker right leg. No baseball, no dancing. Hiram MacHugh had enjoyed his books and his fantasies; later on, he sat in the bleachers to watch his younger brother, Bobby, play shortstop and steal bases. So, on Saturday nights, two suppliers knocked at his back door after dark. A man with a jug; later on, a young Cricker woman named Glory Callister.

Hiram MacHugh felt his face tighten because Carney Ransom was still smiling.

"Now don't get huffy, High. I was only joshing you in a friendly way. Ain't none of my business."

He knew Carney meant it. Sure, he was a needler, yet there was no malice in the remark, merely a passing comment that one man in a small town would make to another. Especially when the men had been boys together.

"No offense taken," Hiram said.

"Shucks," said the constable, "there ain't a soul in Hallapoosa who lives so pure and high-mighty that he'd deny you a slab of socializing. You got a right, High, same as the rest of us poondogs."

Hiram couldn't fault it. Carney, he knew, was a friend who might poke his ribs when they were face to face. Yet never knife his back.

"Just be careful," Carney warned, "that Glory's pa don't come calling. That ol' Kelby Callister is one brine-hearted critter. He'd piddle on a sick kitten."

Hiram laughed, but inside there was little joy in it, even though the constable's manner of phrasing had a way of amusing him. Any mention of the name Callister made Hiram MacHugh uncomfortable.

Carney started his engine. "High, between you and me, I always sort of been pleased that you'n that little gal feel kindly toward each other. Even though she's a Cricker. And you know certain that I wouldn't say such to nobody's ear except yours."

"I know, Carney. You and I have always enjoyed the luxury of being pie-in-the-face honest to each other."

"Hop in, I'll give your worthless carcass a lift home, if this car can haul our weight."

"Thanks, but I'll just stroll along on my own locomotion. Only exercise I take, walking down to the courthouse and back again. From the looks of you, Constable, maybe you might consider some athletics yourself."

"Amen. I probable ought. Oh, by the way, I hear they repaired the power lines and the local telephones are working once again. See ya."

Slapped into low gear, the Ford, Hallapoosa's only patrol car, eased away ahead of its dust, bearing its portly cargo.

With his cane now in his right hand, Hiram slowly turned in the direction of his house. A trio of three Negro women met

• 3 •

him and stepped aside to allow him to pass. With his left hand, he saluted them by touching the brim of his hat.

"Ladies," he said.

They smiled at him. "Good afternoon, Judge," one of them said to him. The other two merely nodded.

He recognized the largest woman who had spoken. Tally Thurman. A month ago, her boy, Elston, had gotten himself in a wisp of trouble by setting a fire. Nothing too serious. As the Justice of the Peace, Hiram had been rather lenient and had let the youngster go with only a reprimand. Even though no damage had been proved, Clemson Smather, the property owner, had demanded a stiffer sentence, a five-dollar fine.

How, wondered Hiram, does anyone who is sane ask people who have no money to cough up a fiver? Peace, he had long ago concluded, was more advantageous to the town of Halla-poosa than Justice. Smiling quietly, he recalled how Tally Thurman had verbally dressed down her son, making him apologize to Mr. Smather and then thank Hiram for his clemency. She had also vowed to keep Elston on the straight and narrow, promising that no offspring of hers would ever have to appear in the courthouse again. Hiram nodded as he walked. A straight woman, Tally Thurman. Her boy would become a good citizen.

His main problem was soothing Clemson Smather.

"Easy now, Clemson," he remembered telling him. "I know that when you and I were youngsters, right here in Halla-poosa, the two of us were absolutely perfect, twenty-four hours a day. So, saintly as we were and still are, it might be a strain for us to witness today's lads, who somehow lack our noble standards of deportment. However, you've heard Elston's apology and his mother's ironclad guarantee that he'll not be pesky again or flirt with matches. Therefore, I hereby impose upon your good nature, Clemson, to let loose of the matter."

Yes, thought Hiram, I could almost pat my own back, because Carney and I managed to cool off Clemson Smather's ire, which was burning hotter than the fire.

"Hello there, Hiram."

It was a relief, Hiram thought, to hear a voice speak his Christian name, and not call him High, regardless of the impressive number of jugs and Mason jars he had drained over the years. Removing his hat, he greeted the elderly

• 4 •

widow who, ever since he could recall, resided in the house next to his own.

"Mrs. Fulsom, good day to you." Even though Hiram was in his fifties, it had never occurred to him to call Mrs. Selma Fulsom by any other name. "My," he said, "your dahlia patch looks more fetching every season. And every one staked up straighter than a West Point cadet."

"Mercy," she pretended to scold, "how you carry on, Hiram MacHugh." Smiling, she shook a warning finger. "Just remember, you're still not too grown-up to take across my knee."

Each afternoon, their ritual was the same, always a friendly salutation, lauding her garden in return for a subsequent admonishing that he had come to welcome. She was known in town as Miss Sellie, thought to be eccentric by those who were kind, and an honest-to-goodness nuthatch by a few of the less charitable. Hiram viewed her with honor, as one of the most genteel senior residents in all of Hallapoosa.

Looking around her place, Hiram noticed that much of the debris resulting from last Monday's storm had been neatly piled.

"My, that Charlie," he said, referring to her gardener and general handyman. "He's certainly got your property looking tidy once again."

Charlie Moon Sky had come out of the swamp, about a year ago, looking for work. He lived with Mrs. Fulsom; not under her roof, as that would hardly have been condoned, but in a cowshed in the rear, a shelter without a cow, but now with a young halfbreed Seminole.

"That boy's a jewel," said Miss Sellie. "He works instead of gossips. Never talks. Wouldn't say *mud* if he had a mouthful. First off, I promised to pay him a dollar a week, plus keep. Then, after I took notice of how industrious he was, said I'd raise it a quarter. But would he take it? Shook his head, smiled, and held up one of his fingers, as if to remind me that a bargain was a bargain."

Looking at his own yard, Hiram said, "I wish he'd quit you and work for me. As you can see, my place is still all littery with twigs and boughs and leaves everywhere. Somehow, it doesn't appear as messy as it was."

Miss Sellie retied a dahlia. "That's because your housekeeper did some picking up. I reckon Vestavia put in at least a good hour on a rake. Maybe more." She pointed a trowel at Hiram. "If you ask me, that woman's more worthy than you deserve."

Hiram nodded. "Yes, indeed so." He truly valued Vestavia as a gem beyond measure. A black pearl.

Miss Sellie looked at Hiram's mailbox. "Say, I believe you got a letter today. Leastwise, I saw Mr. Goodwin shove something inside. Best you go and check."

With a respectful gesture of his hat, Hiram thanked her and moved toward his mailbox. "Needs painting," he said, pulling open the squeaky front flap, "and a lick of grease." Squinting through his glasses, he read the postmark and the return address on the white envelope's upper-left corner.

> Judge of the Court
> County of Duval
> Jacksonville, Florida

Slowly he read the letter.

Dear Mr. MacHugh: 10 August 1931
    I regret, sir, that it is my official duty to inform you of the deaths of your younger brother, Mr. Bobby MacHugh, and also his wife, Della.

Possibly due to the recent inclement weather in your area of South Florida, telephone lines were out of order, so I hereby resort to contacting you by this letter. Please allow me to express my deepest sympathy.

Our coroner's report states that both Mr. and Mrs. MacHugh died instantly, a result of a Florida East Coast Railway freight train demolishing their automobile at a grade crossing. Both bodies were mutilated and subsequently charred by fire, yet their human remains and their automobile have been positively identified.

As you may conclude, their two children are now legal orphans, to be housed as wards of the Duval County Orphanage, *or* sent to Hallapoosa to reside with you until majority.

Thane MacHugh is age twelve. His sister, Alma Lee MacHugh, is seven.

Prior to their being sent to Hallapoosa, this court must

receive your assurance that you are a gentleman of good moral character and responsibility, and that you shall afford your niece and nephew a home of adequate bed and board, seeing that they attend school, and otherwise providing for Thane and Alma Lee as wards of your guardianship until each child reaches an age of eighteen.

Your brother's will, which is now in probate, mentions that you, Mr. Hiram MacHugh of Hallapoosa (Florida), are the only living kinsman capable of assuming full responsibility for his progeny in the event of death of both parents.

His intent is quite clear.

A modest Metropolitan Life Insurance policy has been recovered and is being processed, and an amount of one thousand dollars ($1000) will subsequently be forwarded to you, to be divided equally between Thane and Alma Lee, but not until the age of eighteen years.

Other modest properties have been dissolved here, by authorities, to satisfy a number of outstanding debts to creditors. Your brother's financial situation was far from solvent. He was destitute, and unemployed.

Please give me your immediate answer by mail or telephone. Hearing not from you, sir, this court's only recourse is to place your nephew and niece in such local public institutions as I above stated.

Sincerely yours,
E. Wilfred Tabor
District Judge
County of Duval

As he leaned against a porch post, Hiram MacHugh stared silently at a letter that was trembling in his hand.

· Two ·

"Abercrombie . . . here's milk."

Bending down, Selma Fulsom placed her cat's lavender bowl on the rough floorboards behind the kitchen stove.

Her pet came at an eager trot.

"Tomorrow," she told him, "you shall get your Sunday-morning egg, to keep your fur silky. It's only Saturday, so don't you dare nag until church time. Hear?"

Slowly she left the kitchen, heading for her parlor and a rocker chair. Yet, prior to sitting down, she stared through her lace curtains at the MacHugh place.

A good man, Hiram MacHugh, she thought.

He's a bona fide gentleman, no matter how the town whispers about him. But some of the local tongues, even in her Methodist Missionary Society, would wag at Jehovah if given a chance. Especially someone such as Myrna May Singletary, who would find fault with Jesus and the Twelve.

Sitting, she rocked a few times and then stilled. August was too warm for rocking. Earlier, she didn't like the grim look on Hiram MacHugh's face as he was reading that letter. Maybe it was sorry news. Well, even if it was, the contents of a next-door neighbor's mail wasn't her concern.

"At my age," she said, "my opinion in Hallapoosa doesn't amount to knot on a sausage."

Still and all, Miss Sellie wondered about the letter. Only kin Hiram had were living up in Jacksonville, so far north they're dang near to being Yankees. Closing her eyes, Mrs.

Fulsom remembered all the MacHughs of years past. Good neighbors. Clarence and his wife Melba, then Hiram, and finally young Bobby. That hellion.

Bobby, she recalled, gradually became Hiram's dream. After the illness. My, how that little scamp could throw a baseball and run, climb my big old camphor tree and holler down to his older brother who was cripple-legged. And there stood Hiram, on ground, warning Bobby not to fall, claiming that he'd try best to catch him if he did.

"I salute you, Hiram," she said to the twilight. "I give you ample credit, after your folks passed on, for helping to educate Bobby the way you did. Even though it was *you* who loved your books like close friends."

Hearing a purr, she felt Abercrombie rubbing himself along her ankle.

"Precious," she asked him, "did you lap up all your milk so soon? Your old Miss Sellie adores you. Deed she does."

Crouching, he sprang into her lap, closing his eyes at the first tender touch of her hand along his spine. Kneading his claws into her brought a reprimand. "Paws," she warned him, "not claws. Nobody likes to be mangled, especially friends."

Selma imagined she heard Hiram's telephone ring.

Mercy, how she would cotton scooting next door to find out if Hiram's free of trouble. As he held that letter, his face had frozen to granite.

"*No*," she thought she'd heard him say as he was reading the letter.

Then he had walked slowly and disappeared inside his house, moving more thoughtfully than customary. Well, over the years, if any MacHugh ever needed her for solace, she was always here. Next door. In her dotage she mustn't turn herself into a spy, she thought. Yet, at the moment, Abercrombie's curiosity wouldn't hold a candle to hers.

She stamped her foot. "Sellie Fulsom, keep your nose where it belongs, right to home."

Hiram, she believed, would tell her if the news was really serious. Hadn't he always? Even when young Bobby finally went north for college schooling, then a job, and never came home again. Took himself a bride and sired a brace of children. Hiram had showed her their pictures. A boy and a girl, about four or five years apart, but with faces as alike as two peas.

Oh, she thought as she stroked her cat, how I wish Hiram had met up with some sweet gal, and gotten married. But when Clarence and Melba were alive, with them it was always Bobby they spoiled rotten. Hiram was reliable, sure enough, yet Bobby had become their shining star.

Abercrombie purred louder.

"Good cat," she said softly. "Naught to bother you in this world. Perhaps it's your fortune to be an animal, with nary a worry and free of care."

Lightly she scratched Abercrombie's head with her crooked arthritic fingers, trying her best to mind her own affairs and not be fretting about Hiram's news. With a nod of her white head, she decided that it was probable just a legal matter. Whatever it was, Selma concluded, Hiram MacHugh could handle it as he somehow managed to cope with all the tempers of the town.

"I'd wager our village council hasn't voted poor Hiram a raise in a decade. Finley Singletary, and that sister of his, wouldn't as much as toss a seed to a sparrow."

She heard voices.

Leaning an inch or two closer to the open window, Selma Fulsom caught herself doing so, and felt ashamed. Quickly she corrected her posture. "Land," she sighed, "have I so little in life that I'm trying to overhear what's being said at the MacHugh place?"

She did, however, recognize the high chirpy voice of Vestavia Holcum, the Negro woman who kept house and cooked for Hiram six days a week. Selma couldn't make out what exactly was being said, feeling grateful for this. Yet she could hardly help hearing that Vestavia was, as usual, doing most of the talking.

At the Missionary Society meetings, the quality of Negro domestics was sometimes discussed, and Myrna May Singletary had heatedly stated that Vestavia was an uppity nigger who hadn't ever learned her place.

"That's when I put in my two cents worth, Abercrombie. I told her straight out that Vestavia Holcum was probable in her late sixties, maybe more, and had sweated all her life long, sweeping, scrubbing, and tending the MacHughs. Vestavia also raised up her own children and grandchildren, single-handed, so had cause to hold her head up high."

Selma Fulsom chuckled.

She recalled the indignant expression on Myrna's face. Why, she wondered, was it so high-and-mighty important for Myrna May to remind everyone that she was a Singletary? Family this and family that . . . like Myrna was parading through life walking backward, so she could view all past glories. Listen to Myrna brag about *bloodlines* and you'd suspect she was a racehorse.

"Family background," Selma almost spat. "I declare, I often wonder how many times a day Myrna May Singletary employs that term. Most every breath."

Next door, Vestavia was speaking her mind to Hiram again. Well, as far as Selma Fulsom was concerned, Vestavia had a right. She'd helped to raise both Hiram and Bobby. She had whacked her hard little hand on that rascal Bobby MacHugh near to once a week, over her knee, on the place where it would do the most good. Yet she rarely touched Hiram. He was her favorite. Not that Vestavia ever admitted as much to Selma, possible never even to herself.

"But I knew, Abercrombie, because Hiram was always *my* favorite too."

Selma rocked back and forth, eyes closed, remembering the years past, still hearing young Bobby MacHugh and his Indian war whoop from up in her camphor tree. And down below, in a pool of shade, Hiram sat with his nose in a book. Night and day, those two. Opposites.

Opening her eyes, she looked out the window at the camphor. No child climbs anymore, she lamented. But there it stood, a lonely giant longing to hold a boy on his knee, or in the crook of a wooden elbow, and possible sharing his joy. The two of us, Selma was deciding, my tree and I don't stand as straight as once we did. Life is quieter now. A pity some young hellions in town don't kick up some mischief and paint an outhouse red.

"Help me," she chuckled aloud, "but I might even supply the paint myself, or lick a swipe with my own brush."

A shame, Selma was concluding, that Myrna May Singletary doesn't own a privy. *Hers* would certain be a nifty place to conjure a prank.

Selma scowled.

She could paddle that Bobby MacHugh for staying away so long and never bringing his family to visit Hiram. But Jacksonville was a devil of a trip by automobile, all the way here to Hallapoosa at the southern tip of the state, especially with two young-monkey kids in the back seat, fighting and yelling every Florida mile. Still and all, Bobby ought to come and see Hiram, or at least invite him up north some Christmas to meet his niece and nephew, two that Hiram's eyes never laid eyes on. It was Hiram who should have fathered children, instead of his impish brother. Yet it was Bobby who could charm the plaster off a wall.

Her eyes wandered to her dead husband's photograph on the mantel.

"May the Lord rest you, Dewey. And I'm regretful that I bore you nary a child. We'd have enjoyed them, you and I, even the fuss and the muss."

My, she thought, I'd almost give anything to see Bobby's children. I bet they're rascals too, like their father used to be, into deviltry. Well, maybe someday Hiram can go visit.

"That'd be real nice, Abercrombie."

I'm thankful, Selma was thinking, that I have my cat. Dewey's been gone so long, dead and buried. But now I have Charlie and he's sweeter than ripe fruit. He's honey, and bees don't know it. Charlie Moon Sky. Now that's a beauty of a name. Makes me almost wish I was a young Seminole gal. Or maybe a halfbreed like Charlie.

She looked out her window.

"I wonder where Charlie goes every night. Maybe he drifts down the slope to where the Crickers live, mostly upstream where Kalipsa Crick divides for the island. Those pitiful shacks of loose boards and vine rope. Makes one wonder how they stood the storm."

The crick must have been swollen high, Selma guessed, and perhaps washed away a shack or two. Dewey always said that the Crickers were best avoided, and left be. Ever since I was a girl, that Callister clan's been squatting there. Haven't paid a tax in their lives, on account even Carney Ransom wouldn't relish jumping from stone to stone, to reach the island and collect.

Selma smiled. And, she imagined, if their constable were to fall in, the crick would rise a lot higher.

"I suppose," she whispered to Abercrombie, "that there are people in Hallapoosa, some of the so-called respectables, that know about that Cricker gal's sneaking up-slope on Saturday evenings, to entertain Hiram." She took a hurried breath. "Shush, old woman. It's none of your affair. If anybody had a right to a little moonlight spooning, it's Hiram MacHugh."

A screen door banged.

Looking out her window, Selma Fulsom saw a familiar sight, one she'd witnessed for decades, six evenings a week. Hiram was walking home with Vestavia. The pair of them never walked side by side, for sake of appearances, because it just wouldn't look proper for a white man and a Negro woman to be out strolling together. As usual, Vestavia took the lead and Hiram followed with his cane, a respectable twenty feet to the rear, for propriety's sake.

Even with her eyes closed, Selma could envision their going as far as the broken fence at the rear edge of Darky Town, where Vestavia would turn her bare feet in the dirt and say, "Goodnight, Mr. Hiram," in her high fluttery voice. And he would say something like "Sleep well, Vestavia, and thank you."

Mornings, she came alone.

Evenings, when the hell-raisers were about and sometimes fortified with beverages possessing a bit more personality than lemonade, Hiram always made sure Vestavia got home safely. It had always been so, his custom, ever since boyhood.

"Jump down," she told Abercrombie.

Crossing the parlor, Selma Fulsom opened her screen door, closed it, and paced her front porch veranda to await Hiram's return. There were two chairs on her porch. Looking over to Hiram's, she saw only one chair on his, empty and alone, so like Hiram MacHugh himself.

She saw him coming, and waved.

"Hiram, come sit."

He stopped. Usually, she knew, he carried himself rather proudly despite his ample weight. But tonight his shoulders seem to sag beneath his white suit-jacket. Slowly he came up her front walk and the two sat together on the veranda. Selma saw him sniff the air.

"Mimosa," he said softly, a voice that sounded thin and almost frail, as if from a man half his considerable size.

"Something's wrong," she told him. "I just somehow sense it. I've known you too many years to apologize, Hiram, so just accept me as your old busybody neighbor." She paused, cogitating on how to ask. "I'm about to pry, Lord forgive me, and ask you if everything's all right."

Leaning forward in the chair, he buried his face in his hands, and took several seconds before he could speak.

"Bobby is dead."

"No."

Hiram nodded. "He and Della were both killed by a train, an automobile accident. An hour or so ago, a judge in Jacksonville telephoned, to confirm what his letter said. The funeral was yesterday."

Getting up, Selma crossed to where he sat, placing a hand on his shoulder. "You know how sorry I am about your brother."

Again he nodded. "Yes, I know. Thank you."

"If there's anything I can do, you have only to ask. Anything at all, dear boy."

"Well," he said, "just allow me to sit here for a moment or two, and try to collect myself." He sighed. "God, I need a drink."

Bending, she briefly leaned her face down to rest lightly on his hair. "No," she told him, "you only *want* one."

"You don't understand. I've done a tomfool thing. Judge Tabor in Jacksonville told me Bobby's children are now penniless and alone. He mentioned an orphanage. So I agreed to—to raise them."

She patted his shoulder. "I'm glad."

"But I'm fifty-two years old. Vestavia is seventy. It's too much to ask of her. God knows, I am the last person on earth qualified to serve as a guardian to young children I have never even met."

"You won't be a guardian, Hiram." She gently kissed his cheek. "The Lord has seen fit to favor you with a stewardship that's far more blessed."

"What shall I be to them?"

"An uncle."

· *Three* ·

"Lot!"

From the doorway of the island shack, Glory Callister looked downcrick. No sign of that child. Balancing with her bare feet on the wet rocks, she moved through the crick willows until she could spot her eight-year-old son.

"Lotty, your big sister's fixing to take herself a little walk tonight, so keep close to home, now it's darksome. Hear?"

"Can I come?"

Glory shook her head. "Not this time, honey. I sort of best go lonesome. But tomorrow be Sunday, so's us two might go ramble somewheres. Maybe throw some skipper stones to the pond."

"Promise?"

Touching his curls, she said, "Yes, I promise. And you recall I told you that a promise oughtn't to git broke if it's for somebody dear, like you."

"Okay."

"And if old Kelby wanders home, you fetch off and hide yourself quiet until I git back. Especial if he's loud yelling, or not steady footed."

"You're a good sister," Lot said. "If people say sorry about you, I tell 'em how sweet you be."

Glory Callister bit her lower lip, but only for a breath. Someday, she was hoping, she and her child would have a shack all to their own, without old Kelby, her father. Then perhaps she could tell the truth to Lot about matters . . . that she be his *ma*, not his sister.

"Stay close," Glory told him.

Returning to the shack, Glory ran a comb through her long blonde hair, then brushed to make it shine cornsilky. Doing so, as her head tilted to one side, she thought about soon seeing Hiram MacHugh. He wasn't like the others. Instead, he was gentle kind, needing more than her body.

"Someday," said Glory quietly, "maybe he'll git up the bowel to honest me and mine."

Leaving the shack, wearing her best three-dollar dress and some jewelry given to her by gentlemen friends, Glory still wore no shoes. If'n there was to be a *someday* for Lot and herself, she had decided, she would have to resist store-boughts. Each week a bit more money could be put by in her secret tobacco can. She and Lot might allow to become rich as Prince Albert.

Stone by stone, she crossed the crick, wading to her knees through the deepy part. Lifting her dress away up high, Glory felt the cool crick water rushing around her thighs, sucking at her.

"Feels goodsome," she said aloud.

As she danced through the low fan palms, avoiding the shafts and their curly prickers, Glory Callister felt happy to be going to visit Hiram. More than joyous, she felt rather wanting, eager to do for him and pleasure him with her loving. No other man made her hungry to touch or be touched. Plenty of them only grabbed. And took. They smelled too, like turpentine or pine pitch, and even week-old sweat. And their eyes didn't sparkle, they only burned.

Glory heard some leaves rustle.

The sudden slap across her face almost caused her to fall. Her cheek was stinging like a fury.

"You slut gal."

"Please don't, Daddy."

Kelby Callister drew back his arm, intending to strike her again. But she dodged away. Her father was wearing nothing except a torn shirt, his white legs looking dirty even in the moonlight.

"If you was a proper daughter, you'd give your old pappy some sugar too. On the house." His eyes narrowed as he stared at her belly. "You don't give me no sugar at all. No respect neither."

"Leave me be."

Kelby wiped his mouth with the back of his hand. "Unless you do me soon, I just might make your bastard kid perform. So best you take a choose. I git *you* . . . or I git to Lotty."

"He's hid. You won't find him nowhere. You trespass on him and I'll go fetch the constable. I'll sick Carney Ransom on you, and he'll foller you into the swamp with Mr. Blodgett's blood dogs, you hear?"

Her daddy, Glory could see, was close to being drunk. Even from a distance of ten feet, she could smell the corn on his breath. A sour smell, one that seemed to cut the air with its edge.

Kelby pointed up the slope. "I know where you be going. I know, to lay up with that fatty MacHugh."

"Ain't none of your business where I be going," Glory said, taking a short step forward. "And if you trail along behind, I'll ask my friend to telephone Carney and then he'll come and lock you so long in the courthouse basement that you'll rot. He's throwed you in jail before. Couple three times."

"I'll find Lotty . . . and tell 'im you ain't his sister, like he thinks. I'll say you're his whore mama. And he ain't nothing but a whoreson."

Fists on her hips, Glory looked her daddy in the eye. "There's no gentleman in you t'all. Can't you be a granddaddy to Lotty and play decent with him? No, you can't act thataway. He's your kin, old man. So be I." Glory pointed at him. "Best you do righteous to Lot, and treat him gentle . . . or else I bring hell's fire on you, Kelby Callister, on account I got me important friends in Hallapoosa. So you reason that, before you locate your skinny end in the jailhouse, or up to your neck in swamp water hearing dogs coming to rip your gullet."

Bending, he grabbed a handful of loose dirt and hurled it in her direction, but Glory anticipated his action and ran.

"Slut gal," he yelled after her. "I'll even the score on you. Hear? And on that judge too."

Her face was still smarting. "I won't cry," Glory told herself, trotting up the gradual slope that led away from the crick bed. "I'll just take Lotty away, really soon, and not never come back to Hallapoosa."

Perhaps, she thought, she could get work in Kalipsa Ferry, which was nearby. Or maybe all the way to Naples. In a new place, she could live respectable and nobody would know about her being a Callister, or a Cricker. Nor would they know she'd had Lot when turning fifteen. He was eight now, commencing to ask questions about the times when she went for walks during the evening, in a dress and beads, and smelling of perfume.

When she stopped walking for a moment, in order to listen to the evening whippoorwills, Glory could have sworn she heard a footstep. Only one. Was someone watching her, spying on her, trying to catch her visiting Hiram MacHugh? Perhaps, she thought, it was some of the other Callisters from down-crick.

Sometimes, Glory knew, her Callister cousins came sneaking up toward Hallapoosa on a Saturday night, to stir mischief.

Remaining motionless, Glory held her breath and listened, praying that the whippoorwills would pause too. They final did. Yet she heard and saw nothing. But the tingle feeling on the back of her neck seemed to nag at her, as a warning that she was being observed.

"Ain't nobody," she told herself, "except maybe a pesky old woodrat, or some other varmint."

She continued on.

Nearing the hedge behind the MacHugh house, Glory Callister kept herself well hidden in the shadows. Trunks of scrub oak, slender and twisted, stood all around her; beneath her feet, she felt the curly-brown live oak leaves crackling dry under her bare toes.

Hiram would be waiting, like usual, the way he had every Saturday night for a number of years.

"Once," she whispered to herself, "I'd like to saunter up a sidewalk and ring a front-door bell. Just one time."

Hearing voices, Glory squinted at Hiram MacHugh's rear door, seeing old Jason Yoobarr pocket his jug money and take his leave. Never did she want Jason, or anybody else, to see her arrive. No power on earth would make her compromise Hiram MacHugh. On tiptoe, Glory crept along the shrubbery until she gained the darkness beneath the rear roof's overhang. Then, at the door, she tapped lightly with a fingernail, three times.

The door opened. Hiram smiled.

"Welcome," he said to her.

No lights were on inside. None were needed. Closing the door, locking it, Hiram MacHugh turned to her as he always did, standing in the kitchen without a cane, opening his arms to her. Close to him, Glory felt his tenderness encircle her, and lips lightly kissing her hair.

"Saturday," he said, "is the only day out of seven that I'm fully alive."

Tightly she clung to him, eyes closed, feeling his strength and inhaling all his goodness with every breath, needing him more than he needed her.

"Glory," he whispered to her, "you are the only woman I have ever touched. *My only*." Words that made her regret that she could never say the same to him.

"Hiram . . . "

She loved this first moment, their initial embrace, like coming home, as she so raptured in just saying his name, over and over again. Hiram, my Hiram.

He was older than her father, she guessed, yet it mattered so little. With her he was boyhood, almost childhood. Yet all manhood. Strong, clean, sweet as *sugar*. Thinking of the word, her body fought a second or two of rigidity, then pressed against him, so wanting to be close, and closer. She felt him stagger and take a backward step.

"Careful," he said, "or you'll spill me over, and I'll fall, and splinter the floorboards."

"Oh, you're so . . . so . . . There just ain't a word nice enough to fit you proper."

Hiram laughed. "I seriously question if *proper* is my accurate description."

Again she hugged him, more tenderly, knowing that if the townfolk of Hallapoosa could see, they would point their mean fingers at the two of them, yet never understand how much they meant to one another. Perhaps, away off in the yonder of Heaven, she hoped, the Lord would bless their union. In Hiram's arms, Glory Callister felt like a person ought to feel sitting in church. It was holy to hold him.

"Now," she said, "you won't need no cane tonight. Lean on me, Hiram. I'm smallsome, but I be strong as a hymn."

Nonetheless, he brought his cane. Leaning on her, headed toward the only downstairs bedroom, he said, "That's so poetic. Strong as a hymn. It's a term of humble dignity."

"My mama said it once, long ago, before she passed on. How a woman so decent ever mated old Kelby, I don't guess I could ever understand."

Bending, he kissed her cheek. Something, Glory knew, was strange tonight. Hiram's breath smelled of corn. Not sour like her daddy's, yet it was certain there. He stumbled again.

"You never uncork your Saturday night jug until after I leave," she said. "Not ever once. Except tonight you've took a pull or two from it."

As she loosened his necktie, Hiram nodded.

"I confess. Guilty as charged."

"How come?" she asked him, removing her earrings to place on the nightstand.

"Because . . . things will be different now." He sat on the edge of his double bed, his weight squeaking the springs. "Something has happened. I have important duties to perform, Glory. I've agreed to a commitment." He looked at her in the moonlit room. "That means I've made a promise to someone."

Questions stuck in her throat. But when she could finally speak, Glory asked him if he was getting married.

Taking her hand, he held it for a moment. "Glory, I will never marry. I'm more than twice your age. You have your whole life before you. Now, before me, is another life too, in a sense. Equally challenging, a major step, perhaps far more than I have the right, or character, fully to assume."

"You're fixing to leave Hallapoosa." Silently, she was begging Hiram to take her too, and Lotty.

Hiram shook his head. "No, no, I'm staying right here in this house. Hallapoosa is my home." He paused to take a breath. "My brother Bobby and his wife are both dead. A freight train hit their car. His two children, a boy of twelve and a little girl of seven, are coming to live with me. I'm taking them in."

Oddly, she felt little sorrow in hearing that Bobby MacHugh was dead. Glory's mind was being flooded by too many other things to think about. In a way, knowing how lonely Hiram was, she honestly felt joyous for him. "Oh," she said, "I be so proud of you. And if you and Vestavia can't do all the tending, I can . . . "

Glory knew she could not. Though willing to help, it wouldn't look right for a young Callister woman to be seen in the MacHugh house. Especially not an unwed girl who had to entertain men to feed a child.

"Bless you, Glory." He touched her face. "There's more to tell you, my dear. It will be painful to say, and painful for you to hear."

Glory closed her eyes. "Don't say it. Please don't. I know you got to, but I can't bear you telling it to me. I won't come visiting you no more, on account of the children. You don't have to tell me, Hiram, you honest don't. I wouldn't be rightful company."

Placing both hands on her shoulders, he said, "You are so young, but so wise. Now you know why a cowardly old game-legged man thirsted for a drink, prior to your arriving. I didn't think I'd have the fortitude to tell you, or to order myself to stick to my decision. But we have no other alternative. No choice."

Glory covered her face with her hands. "If'n I didn't have Lot, right now I'd just run off somewhere and die."

"Please don't talk foolishly."

"Ain't fooly to care for somebody."

"No, you're right, it isn't foolish. Actually, when you add it all up, caring for people is what really matters the most."

"You cared all of your life, Hiram. Ever'body in Hallapoosa knows that. Why can't it be your turn to git, instead of give?"

He didn't answer. Reaching under his pillow, he pulled out some money. "It isn't much, Glory, and nowhere near enough. I want you to have it. Somehow, I'll support myself, Bobby's children, and have enough to pay Vestavia. Plus my salary as Justice of the Peace, I'm also a Notary, and for a fee I can . . . marry people." Hiram swallowed. "If things were different, Glory . . . oh, were I only younger, and whole. But I'm not any of it." He patted her hand. "I can't make love to you tonight. I'm too drunk. Instead, this is our goodbye."

"One final time?"

"I can't. It would hurt too much. Perhaps it's best if I be by myself, with my thoughts, and my jug of spirits." He tried to stand, his hand on a bedpost for support. "Please go."

Glory didn't want his money and told Hiram so. But, realizing that his mind was made up, tossed the bills on the bedspread and started to walk away. Then turned to face him as he still sat on his bed. Walking to him, Glory held his face in her hands.

"In a way," she said, "you're *my only* too."

· *Four* ·

Vestavia Holcum bowed her head.

As she sat erectly in the front row of the African Evangelical Church, her hands were folded inside white gloves, resting in her lap. Her ruffled dress was white too and she was wearing her one pair of shoes.

"Lord," said Reverend Fewsmith, "bless us one and all on this Sunday, this beloved day. Please bless our homes and our children . . . yes, and the people we work for. Bless our neighbors, bless our . . ."

Vestavia was usually devout and attentive during a prayer, but this Sunday was different. Times were about to change, Vestavia thought, and it was a possible turn for worse. Before her, Reverend Micah Fewsmith was blessing everybody and everything, including the mules. He could certain be a long-winded blesser.

Try as she might, Vestavia Holcum's mind couldn't seem to follow the stream of reverence that cascaded down from the unpainted pulpit.

Her hands locked fingers, feeling the softness of her gloves, white Sunday gloves which had once belonged to Mrs. Mac-Hugh. When his good mother died, Hiram had insisted that she have them to wear. For years now, Vestavia had worn them with pride, every Sunday morning. The other ladies had noticed, away back, when she had first worn the white gloves on Sunday. In fact, Tally Thurman had raised her eyebrows and said something.

"My, but ain't you a fancy nigger."

Using a white-gloved finger, Vestavia had pushed her own nose an inch higher, but couldn't maintain a sober face. Both she and Tally had busted out laughing. Life for both women had been arduous, yet too short for becoming upsome with one another.

Reverend Fewsmith was still blessing things, and would probable bless each pebble in the road, and every frog in the swamp.

"Put an Amen to it," Vestavia whispered to herself.

He final did.

The closing hymn was one she knew by heart, "What a Friend We Have in Jesus," and as Vestavia stood with her eyes shut tight, she truly felt blessed. It was a joy to sing on Sunday morning, she was thinking, because a sweet old hymn had a way of washing away all the dirt on a person, and healing all a body's hurt. It lifted you up, near enough to reach for the Lord's hand and worship His Lamb.

Patiently she stood and waited her turn, after the service, to follow the congregation to the front door and shake the preacher's hand. And to say how much she enjoyed his sermon on the sin of gambling. He had even rattled a pair of dice, which he'd called African dominos, and pointed a lean finger at young Elston Thurman and his older brother, Leeman.

"Reverend, you certain touched us all this morning," Vestavia told him. "Reached right into my soul with your prayer."

He smiled gratefully. "Why, thank you, Sister Holcum. It wouldn't be Sunday without your presence on that up-front bench."

In the churchyard, Tally waited in the oak shade with her two youngest, Leeman and Elston. People stepped aside to allow Vestavia to pass. She knew why, because it was well known in Hallapoosa that Vestavia Holcum worked for Judge MacHugh, and it might do some good to court a little favoring.

"Good morning, Tally."

"Good morning, Vestavia." Tally twisted her large body toward her sons. "You rascals both say a good day to this lady, and show off some manners. You heared our Reverend Micah this morning, about shooting dice. And how people who does oft-time wind up to be of little more account than hang-around street niggers."

"Yes'm," the boys responded quickly. "Good morning, Mrs. Holcum."

Tally Thurman was as large a lady as Vestavia was small, and she wasn't about to turn her youngsters loose just yet. Not from what Vestavia could observe.

"Good morning, boys," she answered.

"You might ask Mrs. Holcum how her poorly feet be," Tally demanded, "and if she still aching."

Dutifully, both Leeman and Elston inquired, and Vestavia said, "Better, thank you, now that all of last week's damp is past."

"Now then," Tally told her boys, "you two parade along home, and if'n you ain't there for Sunday dinner, Satan hisself won't stand to witness what I'll perform on you."

The boys walked slowly away, then broke into a trot and a let-out gallop. Tally watched them racing away. Turning to Vestavia, she said, "My, wouldn't it be joyful to have so much giddyap and bubble-up like seltzer."

Vestavia nodded to the younger woman.

"My," Tally said, "but isn't *you* the sober soul this Sunday. Nary a peep out of you unless I crowbar it out. Be a cat got your tongue?"

"I have thinking to do."

Tally grunted. "Ought nobody have to work or think on a Sunday." She nodded once, with emphasis, as if her pronouncement was Gospel. "Let's be going home."

Vestavia Holcum shook her head. "I won't be going home. Leastwise, not yet."

"Where you going?"

"For a walk. In church, I was deciding that I'd best look in on Mr. Hiram."

"Six days a week ain't enough?"

"Yes, it's aplenty. But I s'pect that the Judge might not be feeling so good lately. It's . . . his *leg*," Vestavia lied.

Little sense, Vestavia was thinking, in spilling the news to Tally Thurman. The people in Hallapoosa would learn soon enough.

"If you was to ask *me*," Tally said, "a Sunday noon ain't no proper time for a decent woman to barge in on Judge Mac-Hugh. You know why! Imagine what you stumble in on."

Vestavia stood very straight, looking up at Tally Thurman.

"Day or night," she said, "my Mr. Hiram is a well-bred gentleman . . . on account I help raise him to become so. And if'n he needs me *eight* days a week, I would attend him willing."

Tally shook her head. "Well, you never took yourself to the Judge's on a Sunday, long as I can recollect."

Recalling the subject of this morning's sermon by Reverend Micah Fewsmith, about dice, Vestavia held her head higher.

"I am gambling," she said.

As Tally Thurman watched her little lean friend heading for the white section of Hallapoosa, she snorted her final comment, loud enough for Vestavia to hear.

"You sure is."

Passing the broken fence that led out of Darky Town, Vestavia walked slowly, trying to decide what to do, and how to tell it all to Mr. Hiram. In her mind, she kept seeing the photograph of his niece and nephew, one she'd dusted near to every day. Two beautiful children. A boy of seven or so, and his little two-year-old baby sister.

Well, she thought, they're still young enough to handle and correct.

Vestavia stopped.

"You silly old nigger," she chastised herself. "Don't you know how long that picture's been sitting there?"

Continuing to walk, Vestavia was realizing that Mr. Bobby's children were older now. But how old? Perhaps only a year or two, possible three. Well, come tomorrow, she would know. Constable Ransom would be driving Mr. Hiram over to Kalipsa Ferry to meet the bus. And there would be tags hanging around the necks of the children, so's they wouldn't get lost or stray off.

Climbing the familiar front steps, Vestavia knocked at the front door. Usually, she used the back door, but not today. A back door might be useful to Mr. Hiram or to his . . . *company*.

There was no answer.

With her mouth set firmly, Vestavia knocked louder; and again when she heard no response, opened the door. "Mr. Hiram?" She heard a distant moan. Closing her eyes, she said, "Mr. Hiram, it is nigh to Sunday noon, and I apologize for disturbing your rest. But I would like to speak to you please. It's important."

After several minutes, he appeared, wearing a rumpled shirt and his white suit trousers and black stockings. He rubbed his eyes and tried to straighten his hair.

"Vestavia?"

She approached him. "Are you alone, Mr. Hiram, if you'll please pardon my asking?"

"Yes, I am alone." He paused to tap his cane on the floor, a gesture that Vestavia knew was one of annoyance. "May I remind you, Vestavia, that I am fifty-two years old, and no longer a child in your care."

His breath was foul. Nonetheless, she walked closer, noticing the rumpled bed. On the nightstand, there appeared to be a pair of earrings. Vestavia stiffened. How, she was wondering, do I say what ought to get spoke out plain?

"I'm not feeling too well this morning," he said.

"That's a pity. Would you like me to perk you some coffee? Or fix up some grits?"

He nodded. "Please. Just the coffee."

Hiram followed her into the kitchen, then sat at the kitchen table while she poked the stove awake. She rattled the shaker on the big black Acme American, lifted a griddle to check the embers, then replaced it none too gently.

"Must you make so much noise?" he complained.

She ignored his remark. In a few minutes, the coffee was ready and poured into a white mug. As he took his first sip, Vestavia stood and eyed him.

"Please sit down, Vestavia. Just don't stand there watching over me with your haughty disapproval."

"Thank you, but I will stand."

"You look very nice in your church clothes."

"Bless you, Mr. Hiram. I usual aim to look my best every Sunday morning, even if some people I know ought and don't."

His hand touched an unshaven chin. "All right, I did do some drinking last night. Go ahead and say it, I look like—like—"

"Trash," she mumbled.

He took another sip of coffee.

"Mr. Hiram, please excuse me. But in Hallapoosa, there's white trash and colored trash. There is trash that's poor and some highborn. Maybe I'm nothing except a skinny old woman who ought to tend her own. But I know *quality*, Mr. Hiram, be it nigger or white. I ain't worked in this house all my years to wind up seeing a child I help to raise turn out sorry."

Hiram nodded, holding the mug of coffee in both hands to steady it.

"I'm fixing to quit, Mr. Hiram."

He stared up at her with red eyes. "*Quit?* But I need you, Vestavia. You know what tomorrow means to me."

She paced the kitchen floor. "Deed I do." Leaving the room, she returned holding the photograph of Mr. Bobby's children. "But it's today, Mr. Hiram, that you best do a deciding . . . about corn . . . and about the company you keep."

Her hand flew to cover her mouth. I always kept my place, she thought, and here I be telling off Mr. Hiram like he mean nothing to me. I can't let all my years in a MacHugh house end like so. Yet I got to stamp my foot about matters before the whole town turns on him.

"You ain't never been trashy, Mr. Hiram. Not to me, not to nobody else neither. You act polite to well-off people and to shack folks." She pointed a finger at him. "But look at you this Sunday. You look like trash and stink worse. God forgive me, Mr. Hiram, for speaking such to you. But I got cause." She placed the photograph on the table before him. "Like you got reason to hear me. Two reasons."

"Tomorrow," he sighed.

"And you is about ready to embrace your new children like Tally Thurman can fly. I told you a story. I *don't* aim to quit . . . long as you do respectable for those little lambs. What do you think people in Hallapoosa would say if'n they march in the house right now and take a look-see?"

Leaving the kitchen again, Vestavia stomped through the house until she located exactly what she was seeking. Returning, she thumped the empty jug on the table. Then, with a more subtle gesture of disgust, she gently tossed the pair of earrings beside it.

"You and me, Mr. Hiram. We got chores ahead. I raised Holcums, two litters, one as a mama and another as a granny. Raise you and then help you raise up Mr. Bobby. Now we got more raising still to handle. But I'm too olden to do it lonesome, Mr. Hiram. I need you to tote some of it."

He stared at the photograph, reached for it, then held it with trembling hands.

"Can we do it, Vestavia?"

"God willing."

She saw him stretch out a hand to pick up one of the earrings, holding it gently in his fingers.

"Glory," he whispered.

"You ain't got a choosing to make, Mr. Hiram, because the Almighty done it for you. Yesterday, on the telephone, I hear you tell the judge man in Jacksonville how you'd carry the burden. So carry it proud."

Hiram looked at her. "We're a team of tough old mules, Vestavia, you and I."

"S'pect so. Leastwise, we try to be quality." She stared at him. "Most days."

He nodded.

"Vestavia, you are certainly one of the most *quality* people I have ever known."

"Thank you, Mr. Hiram. But right now, I don't guess it's *my* quality that matters much as yours." Vestavia looked out of the window. Turning, she faced Hiram and picked up the almost-empty liquor jug. "Reckon I'll just pitch this cussed thing out into the junk barrel."

"Please do."

She did so, returning then to the kitchen. "And best you tell Mr. Jason Yoobarr that he should peddle his jars of misery somewhere else."

"Believe or not, I have already advised him that our Saturday evening transaction is to be discontinued."

"What about—" Vestavia paused—"the other gentleman who comes to the door selling earrings?"

Hiram smiled. But then his face saddened, and Vestavia saw his jaws clenching, like he was suffering a deep wound.

"Also discontinued."

Vestavia nodded her approval. Taking his mug to the stove, she poured more coffee and returned to the table.

"Thank you," he said.

"Tomorrow," she reminded him, "will add a shining day to your life. What time do you and the constable greet the bus at Kalipsa Ferry?"

"Noon."

"I'll come sunup early tomorrow morning, to ready the two upstairs bedrooms. We'll be needing some extra bedding, but

I can poke around and locate it. I just want both rooms to be tidy and welcoming. If'n it be all right with you, Mr. Hiram, we put the young gentleman in the green room, and his baby sister in the pink-flower room across the hall."

"Fine."

"And I'll cook up something real special fancy for their first supper. Ham, collards, and sweet taters, and probable a peach pie."

Hiram looked up at her. "Wonderful. I couldn't manage without you, Vestavia." He smiled. "And here I've been imagining all these years that *I* was the Justice of the Peace."

Vestavia smiled, and gently patted his hand.

"Maybe," she said, "at the courthouse."

· _Five_ ·

"**W**hen'll we get there?"

As she asked the question, Alma Lee MacHugh was looking out the bus window, watching all of Florida pass by.

"I think about noontime," Thane answered.

"Well, I sure hope Uncle Hiram will be there to meet the bus," Alma Lee said. "But maybe we won't know who he is."

She felt her brother's arm around her shoulder, giving her a brief squeeze. "Now don't fret. Of course we'll recognize him, because he'll probable look like—like Daddy."

It must be wonderful to be twelve, Alma Lee was thinking, like Thane is. He seems to know everything . . . even about Mama and Daddy being up in Heaven with the Lord. Thane could be a teaser at times, most every day, but since the car accident, he'd been acting a lot more like a big brother.

"Is it almost noon yet?"

Before answering, Thane removed his arm from her shoulder. "I don't know, on account I don't own a watch or carry around a clock in my pocket."

"You don't have to talk so uppity."

"Well, you ask me if we're there about every minute. How should I know? Neither one of us has ever been to Hallapoosa, so I don't guess I'd recognize it even if we were smack-dab in the center of town."

"I don't like Hallapoosa."

Thane sighed. "How do you know that? You've never seen

the place. Maybe it's nicer than Jacksonville, with trees and flowers and a lot of other pretty stuff."

"If I don't like Hallapoosa, I'll just up and leave, and hitch-hike back to where we belong."

Looking at her brother, Alma Lee noticed his mouth tighten, like he was also wondering if he'd like living with Uncle Hiram in Hallapoosa. She already knew that it wouldn't be the same as home. And, she thought, I don't think I like this sticky old bus we're riding, because the seat's so hot that it makes me sweat my dress. Alma Lee yanked at the tag around her neck.

"We better like Hallapoosa," said Thane, "because it's where we have to live. Judge Tabor explained it all to me. To both of us. Remember?"

Alma Lee remembered.

"I'm scared, Thane. I'm only seven."

He held her hand for a moment. "It isn't like we have to live in some orphan home. Uncle Hiram's kin. We're going to find everything different for a while, but we can custom to it. We have to."

"I want Mama and Daddy to come back."

Thane closed his eyes. "Me too."

"I want 'em back right now. But I don't want them to fight all the time, like before."

The bus hit a road bump, forcing Alma Lee to reach for the seat in front of her, to steady herself. Up front, she thought she heard the bus driver say a bad word. Nobody else on the bus seemed to care. There were only eleven passengers. Some were sleeping, others were merely staring glassy-eyed out a window, as if they didn't give a hoot where they were going or when the bus would get there.

Silently, she repeated the bus driver's word, one which Alma Lee MacHugh knew wasn't fit to use before company. Or in church. Then aloud, she said the word to Thane.

"Alma Lee, you're not supposed to swear. Ladies don't use words like that."

"Sometimes you do. I've heard you do it aplenty."

"That's different. I'm a boy. Men are allowed to steam at things, like whenever a car won't start and the driver has to keep cranking it."

Daddy cussed that way, Alma Lee thought. And then Mama

would cover my ears so I wouldn't listen. But I got to know the swear words and practiced saying them in my room, because they'd probable come in handy someday, if I ever own a car.

Right now, she was wishing, I'd about give up ice cream just to hear Daddy cuss, and then listen to Mama telling him to mind his language. Her hands tightened into fists, wondering if the hurt could ever stop. It felt like a sharp knife, cutting her inside, as though it was trying to make her cry. Thane was lucky to be a near-grown-up boy because he didn't cry in front of the neighbors. At the funeral, he had stood up tall and strong, even when the two plain boxes had been lowered by ropes into the cemetery ground.

The hymn they sang afterward, "In the Sweet Bye and Bye," sounded so holy, and it promised that they'd meet by the beautiful shore. Thane had told her, after the funeral, the hymn meant they would all be a family again, someday, a lot of years from now.

I believe so, Alma Lee was deciding, because it's all we got to believe in. She was hoping that her parents weren't yelling at each other up in Heaven the way they usual did on earth.

"I wish we'd get to Hallapoosa," she said.

"Good going," Thane told her. "You haven't said that in close to five minutes. Now you can maybe try for ten."

"I guess I'll take my tag off. This doggone string worries my neck, and my skin is starting to itch."

Thane's hand stopped her. "Leave it be. I'm wearing mine. The tags are so we won't get lost during our trip."

"How can I get lost on a dumb old *bus*?"

"Because once you got yourself lost in Mr. Filman's grocery store, and Mama ran around screaming your name. We found you away out back in the storeroom, sitting with some kittens." He took a breath. "You could get lost in a closet."

"I wasn't lost at the grocery. All I wanted to do was *explore*, like Frank Buck, the guy you read to me about who went to Africa and captured wild animals . . . lions and leopards."

"Promise me that you won't go exploring in Hallapoosa, at least not on the first day. Uncle Hiram can't run around to chase you down."

"Why can't he?"

Thane's hand turned her chin to look at him. "In case you forgot, Uncle Hiram's got a crippled leg and walks with a cane. Daddy told me all about him one time. He couldn't play baseball or climb trees, or even trot. Uncle Hiram liked to read books instead. That's how he got to become a Justice of the Peace."

"Will he read us stories?"

"Probable so, providing you never cuss."

"Thane, are you sure that Uncle Hiram is going to look like—like Daddy? He certain don't sound like it to me."

"Yes, I'm sort of sure. He was already my age, or maybe more, when Daddy got born. So I guess Uncle Hiram's some older now."

Alma Lee sighed. Life in Hallapoosa wasn't going to be much of a picnic. Nobody to play tag with, or to bounce balls. Her thoughts were disrupted when the bus slowed to a stop and she heard the brakes hiss.

The driver yelled over his shoulder. "Kalipsa Ferry." Rising from his seat cushion, the bus driver walked up the aisle, coming their way. "Okay, you two youngsters. This is it."

"We're going to Hallapoosa," Thane said.

"No bus stops at Hallapoosa, son. This here's the closest point. But your other driver up in Tampa mentioned that somebody'd meet you here. So don't fuss at me. I'm equal hot as y'all. Get your stuff together, and please don't leave nothing above on the rack."

"Sir, are you certain the other driver said Kalipsa Ferry and not Hallapoosa?" Thane asked him.

"Sure as the good Lord made little green apples." The bus driver crossed his heart with a finger. "Now don't worry at it. Before I pull out, we'll make sure somebody's come here to meet you."

They were the last passengers off the bus. Looking around, Alma Lee MacHugh couldn't spot even one living soul who favored her father. A few Negro people, some dirty-looking white folks, and a pair of chubby old men walking their way. One of the men limped with a cane. Behind him, the other old fellow had stopped, allowing the limping man to continue toward her. His white suit looked rather messy. He kept coming.

"*He* can't be Uncle Hiram," she said.

"Easy," Thane whispered.

"But that fat old geezer certain doesn't appear to look anything at all like Daddy. Not even a speck of him."

The man stopped.

"Are you . . . perchance the MacHugh children?"

Thane nodded. "Yes, sir, we are."

"I'm—I'm your uncle."

"Excuse me, sir," Thane said, "but before we leave the bus, I'd like to know your name. Just to make sure."

"My name is Hiram MacHugh. Bobby, your father, is—was my younger brother. Your mother was Della MacHugh and you're from Jacksonville. Young man, your name is Thane Hiram MacHugh and you are twelve. Your sister is Alma Lee and she is seven."

Hooking his cane over an arm, the man held out his hand. Thane hesitated, then shook it.

"Thane MacHugh," he said firmly.

The old man looked down at her, extending his hand. "And this is Alma Lee."

"Yes, sir," she told him.

"May I shake your hand?" he asked.

She nodded.

Her uncle's hand felt big, and sweaty warm. Yet she didn't pull her own hand away until she felt his fingers loosen.

"You are very brave children to travel so far alone. If you'll allow me to say so, I am very pleased to meet you."

"Thank you, sir," Thane said.

Looking over his shoulder, Hiram MacHugh motioned for the other man to join them. As he approached, Hiram said, "This is my lifelong friend, Mr. Carney Ransom. He's our local constable in Hallapoosa, and he'll give us all a ride in his official patrol car."

"Howdy," the other man said, "and welcome. Hiram, I sure wasn't expecting to see such growed-up youngsters. To hear you tell it, they weren't more than toddlers."

"I was a bit surprised myself," Hiram said.

"Here," said Carney, "let me offer you kids a hand with your suitcases." He smiled. "Just might be the only lick of labor I do all day." Walking slowly, the four of them reached the patrol car. "This is it," said Carney. With a key, he opened the rear trunk. "Soon as we stow your stuff in the back, we'll load up and head for Hallapoosa."

"Is it very far?" Alma Lee asked. "I certain hope not, because I got a notion."

"We have to go inside the bus station," Thane said, "to the toilet. Come on, Alma Lee."

When they returned, their uncle was sitting alone in the back seat. "Perhaps," he said, "the two of you would enjoy riding up front with Constable Ransom and seeing the sights as we come to your new home."

"Yes, sir," Thane told him.

The constable started the engine without cussing, Alma Lee observed, and they left the bus station. The black patrol car, she decided, felt even hotter than the bus. She knew it had something to do with being August, and Kalipsa Ferry certain had to be the hottest place in the whole world. Maybe even too hot for Mr. Frank Buck to tolerate.

"What's it like in Hallapoosa?" she asked.

"Real nice," said Carney Ransom. "Fact is, there's good people everywhere in these United States, and I'm proud to brag that we have our honest share. Ain't that right, High?"

"Indeed so. We surely have."

"Are we almost there yet?" Alma Lee asked.

"Not yet, honey," said Carney. "But we'll be to Hallapoosa before you can spell it." He chuckled, his belly bumping the lower rim of the steering wheel. "Say, how'd you kids like to hear my siren?" Without waiting for an answer, the constable turned a crank with his left hand, producing a screaming wail. As it died, he said, "That'll let some of the tough nuts know there's a lawman around, and maybe they'll keep straight for another day."

"You're a wise man, Constable," said Hiram. "As you've often enough said, sometimes a short warning is more peaceable than a long night in the courthouse basement."

Peering over her shoulder, Alma Lee MacHugh stole frequent peeks at her uncle. Mercy, she thought, Uncle Hiram looks to be nothing like Daddy. Could it all be a lie, a story? Her father's hair was brown and curly. Uncle Hiram's was almost white, and his face wasn't tan at all. He looked like a pale pie.

"Face the front," Thane said. "You're sometimes doing that in church too, and it's not very polite."

"I like seeing who's behind me."

Feeling a mite huffy, Alma Lee turned around to face forward, resisting an urge to tell Thane to manage his own manners and she would attend to hers. Her eyelids sagged. Right about now, she thought, it would be cozy to curl up in Mama's lap, or on Daddy's, and take a nap.

Instead, she leaned against Thane, and slept.

· Six ·

"**V**estavia?"
Wearing her apron over an old house dress, Miss
Sellie opened the front screen door of the MacHughs to call
once again.

"Anybody to home?"

"Yes'm, in the kitchen."

Selma walked through the parlor to find Vestavia dicing
collards at the kitchen table, but she started to rise as Mrs.
Fulsom entered.

"Oh, sit quiet, Vestavia. It's only me. I just thought I'd scoot
over to lend you a hand, if need be."

"Would you favor some tea, Mrs. Fulsom?"

"Oh, not right away." Opening a drawer, Selma fumbled for
a second paring knife, sat down with Vestavia, and reached
for a collard stalk. The kitchen smelled of baking cookies.
"Are you as excited as I am?"

"Yes'm, reckon so. Been too busy since sunup to excite
myself too high. Got the upstairs ready, both rooms, and the
house dusted. Put a smack of polish to the silver, even if all's
holding it together is the tarnish."

Miss Sellie sighed. "To both us old biddies, I guess Hiram is
still a little boy."

"Yes'm he be. Always will."

Finding a small root sprout on one of the collards, Miss
Sellie got up from her chair and went to the sink to wash it.
Returning to the table, she chewed the root slowly, tasting

the bitterness. The munched pulp was not swallowed, but instead rested comfortably between her cheek and gum. Perhaps, she thought, a collard root would ease the arthritis pain in her fingers. Mornings, she knew, were always the most hurtful part of day. Trying again to work the paring knife, Miss Sellie told herself that the only reply to arthritis was constant motion.

"So," she said to Vestavia, "I came over to be useful. Or perhaps just to get underfoot. There's nobody quite as useless as a willing woman in a strange kitchen."

Vestavia smiled slightly.

"All right," Miss Sellie said as she feigned a huff, "so perhaps I came to be an old busybody neighbor."

"Yes'm," Vestavia said, causing both ladies to look at each other and laugh. Unknown to the town, these two women had shared many a bottle of seltzer water together, just for fun.

We are two old widows, Miss Sellie thought, from different parts of town. Coal and lard. We've known each other too long to tell new stories. Vestavia Holcum knows me too well. I was little more than a bride, years back, when she came to work for the MacHughs. How long has it been? Better than fifty years, half a century ago, and Vestavia wasn't anything but a little black bud of a girl, leaner than a finger, and those wide-open eyes looking so afraid she'd drop something and smash it.

Miss Sellie grunted, recalling that Mryna May Singletary had remarked more than once how improper it was for Selma and Vestavia to chitty across the back fence like neighbors. Well, we *are* neighbors in a sense. Vestavia Holcum's spent more of her waking hours here than in her own house in Darky Town. Spent as much time raising MacHughs as Holcums. At home here in the house like butter in a firkin.

She sighed. "Bobby's clean gone."

"Yes'm. It's sorry."

"Well," Selma said, "nobody on earth ever *enjoyed living* any sweeter than Bobby MacHugh. Made more noise than a Yankee army, but I don't guess I have to tell you that."

Vestavia nodded. "Mr. Bobby had a way of saying a mite more than his prayers."

"Hiram . . . he was the silent prayer, in a way."

"Yes'm. Still, when Mr. Hiram puts hisself talking, it comes out highborn fancy."

Miss Sellie's right thumb pressed against the sharp blade of the paring knife, almost firmly enough to hurt. "I wonder if Hiram will speak to his niece and nephew as an uncle, or as a Justice of the Peace."

"Reckon Mr. Hiram will let me say what needs to get spoke out. S'pose I ought to know a speck more about child caring than he do."

"Indeed you do."

I never had the chance, Selma Fulsom was thinking, to tend children. Lord didn't see fit to bless me. And here I sit with possible the town expert, so best I hold my old barren tongue and be wise enough to allow Vestavia to correct them. I'm presuming Hiram will do exactly that. He'll be as tongue-tied with children as he always was with young ladies.

Except for Glory Callister.

"Mercy, I near forgot." Miss Sellie almost jumped to her feet in order to open the back door and call over the fence to Charlie Moon Sky, her handyman. "Charlie, don't forget to spruce up a bit over here, too. Judge MacHugh has company coming today."

Charlie smiled and nodded.

Selma watched him fetching a rake and a large wicker basket. A good worker, she thought, yet I wonder what he thinks about. A strong buck like Charlie Moon Sky's bound to have notions on rambling off to chase excitement. But he stays close-by during daylight.

"Charlie, I'll pay you something extra."

She saw him smile, then shake his head at her, as if to say there was no cause and that he was willing to do anything she asked of him, including aiding a neighbor.

"Just do a bit on the worst of the storm trash, so the place sparkles some. That's all. I won't ask you to do it again, Charlie, just this one time."

Waving an arm to her, he edged his lean body through the gap in the fence that divided the two properties, and began to rake the fallen leaves and twigs.

"I'll cook you something good for supper."

Returning to the kitchen, she saw Vestavia at the sink, scrubbing a sweet potato.

"How can I help?" Miss Sellie asked.

"No need. But I still got to peel some peaches for a pie."

"Good. Where are they?"

"Sack's on the pantry floor."

Again the two women sat at the kitchen table and skinned peaches, helping themselves to an occasionally tempting morsel. Holding the knife, Miss Sellie blotted a drop of peach juice from her chin with the back of a hand.

"Mighty good."

"Yes'm. I hope they be special. Brung 'em here this morning, on account Tally Thurman had more'n she could eat, so she say."

"Do you have all the cinnamon you'll use? If not, I can just scoot back to my own kitchen and supply whatever spice you're vacant of."

Silently to herself, Selma recalled seeing Vestavia Holcum bringing food to the MacHugh home, time and again. Early mornings, before Hiram was even awake, Vestavia carted her gifts in secret. Well, she thought, it was part of a working Hallapoosa system. The Darky Town people wanted to keep in good with Vestavia, because she had the Judge's ear. It wasn't exactly a bribe. Just community relations. Vestavia Holcum no doubt knew she had a certain *position* among the Negroes. I doubt, Miss Sellie was concluding, that the Holcums ever went hungry.

A few weeks ago, Hiram had mentioned the fact that Tally Thurman's youngster—she couldn't recall the boy's name— had slipped himself into a spate of mischief, something to do with an after-dark bonfire over on Clemson Smather's south pasture. Hiram had, so he said, doused the trouble and let young Thurman off the hook, even though he'd been collared on the spot. Well, the kindness had been repaid.

In peaches. Selma Fulsom smiled.

Biting into another peach, she knew that was how many a matter was settled in the Hallapoosa locale. Peaches and forgiveness could quench a heated temper and allow the citizens to go about their business without furthering friction. These days, she was thinking, with the Depression and all, there wasn't too much cash money around. Yet the bartering continued, among the Negroes and whites, as though nobody in Hallapoosa ever cared a fig whether or not those Yankee banks up north were failing.

"You be a mite quiet, Mrs. Fulsom."

"Just cogitating, Vestavia. You and I certain have a right to our private thoughts, both living alone as we do."

"Yes'm, I s'pose. Sometimes even in a Sunday morning church, my mind got a notion all its ownself, to ramble some, and I catch myself paying no caution to what Reverend Micah is up there shouting against."

Miss Sellie nodded.

"Same with me. We're too old for sin and too busy to repent. Yesterday, during service, I just couldn't seem to budge my brain away from Hiram MacHugh, and Bobby, the sons I never bore. Oh, I guess I loved Bobby too. Anyone would. But I'll confess Hiram was my favorite."

"Yes'm."

"That's why I feel sorry for him. He's been so *alone* for so many years. At times, I could just grab him by the collar and shake sense into him. But who are we to price-tag our fellow humankind? You and I, Vestavia, will never really understand what it's like to be Hiram."

"That be true."

"Oh," said Selma, "I've got to quit eating your peaches or you won't have enough for a tart."

"They's plenty. I been eating too."

Tart! The word she had so casually used was still clanging inside her. How could Hiram seek the company of a Cricker woman? Julia Blount would have wed Hiram if he'd as much as snapped his fingers. She still would. Julia'd trade her eyeteeth to become Mrs. Hiram MacHugh. Well, she silently admonished herself, it certainly is no business of mine. Selma was actually hoping that Julia would land him. A good solid woman, Julia Blount.

Miss Sellie stood.

"Best I get myself home. Now, if you need any help at all, getting things ready, please give a holler and I'll rush right over." Selma laughed. "I'm aiming to be a good neighbor, but it'll be all I can do to keep home when the children arrive. To be honest about it, I'll probable be peeking through my curtains for a look-see."

Vestavia smiled. "You be welcome here, Mrs. Fulsom. You know that. Anytime at all."

Before leaving, Miss Sellie turned. "Thank you for allowing me to help. At my age, it's warming to be a neighbor."

She left out of the back door.

"You're doing good, Charlie," she called to the young Seminole. "Place is starting to look spanking. Remember now, I'll bring you an extra-good treat, later on."

Several times, Selma was remembering, she had invited Charlie Moon Sky into the house, but he'd always shaken his head. Perhaps, she concluded, he was only protecting himself from a possibility of being accused of stealing something. My stars, she admitted to herself, there's nothing in my house worth lifting.

"Abercrombie," she asked her cat, "what can I do until they get here?"

Hearing her voice, he stretched, paws spreading into fans on extended legs, his buff body momentarily rigid. He then relaxed, eyes closed, continuing his midday nap.

She heard a car motor.

Heart pounding, she recognized Carney Ransom's black Ford patrol car.

"They're here!"

Rushing to the window, not caring if anyone saw her or not, Selma saw the two children. Much larger than she'd expected. The boy looked so much like Bobby it was near to spooky. And that adorable little pigtailed girl. Wiping her hands on her apron, Miss Sellie squinted through the glass pane, resisting the urge to join them.

Vestavia appeared on the front porch, smiling teeth, a cookie in each hand.

Everyone seemed to be talking at once, but the words mattered little to Selma Fulsom. At the car, Hiram was thanking Carney for the transportation, but Selma wasn't spending more than a second watching the two men. With an arm around each child, Vestavia was marching them toward the house, hugging the breath out of both of them.

Hiram came placidly along too, on his cane. Behind him, Constable Ransom followed, carrying a pair of shabby-looking suitcases, complaining about the afternoon heat.

"Bobby," Selma whispered to her apron which now covered her eyes, "part of you came home."

· 43 ·

· *Seven* ·

Kelby Callister sniffed.

Bending over, with a fingertip pressing one nostril closed, he blew his nose on the ground. Then he cleared the other nostril, wiping his hand on his overall bib. He wore no shirt, no shoes.

"I see 'em," he said.

Staying out of sight in the evening shadows, Kelby stood among the scrub pine and low oak, behind the MacHugh place, silently watching. He was grinding the few teeth he still had, feeling the hurt of it, as though he enjoyed the discomfort. Squinting in the half-light, he could observe the children in the back yard of Hiram MacHugh's place. Two of them. One was a half-grown boy. The other was a little girl about Lotty's age.

Glory had told him they were coming.

His daughter had been moping on and off for a pair of days. Sunday and today. Judge told her not to come sugar him no more. Damn uppity people. They hold they're better than us Crickers, he was thinking. High and mighty Justice of the Peace who had to buy a woman. Closing his eyes, he pictured Judge MacHugh with Glory, both of them jaybird raw. The mental vision made his gut ache. But, he knew, the hurting would ease off, because Kelby Callister was going to get even.

He spat.

Today had been a sorry day. Mr. Spafford, at the turpentine mill, had let three men go, and Kelby had been one of them.

It was because of some Depression, up north, and the mill might shut down entire. Spafford said it could mean he'd soon be out of work too, like today's three.

"Some job," Kelby said aloud.

A man sweats from six o'clock in the morning to six at night, and for what? Eleven puny cents an hour. And late years, it was working alongside a nigger who got paid the dogblame same amount as a white man. What, he wondered, was Hallapoosa coming to be? Not even a Cricker should have to work the same as a bunch of lowdown spades. The Hallapoosa Turpentine Company had even dared to fire a white man, then twist around the next day and hire on a shine to fill his place. Do the same job as a decent white.

"Well," Kelby had said as he picked up his final pay, "I been laid off before, plenty of times, from a lot higher job than this here one."

I got to have me a drink, he thought, wanting to feel the burning trickle down inside his gullet. Maybe I could get Jason Yoobarr to trust me for a small jar. I'll pay him whenever he can catch up with me. Not even Jason would dare come to the island; leastwise, not in the darksome.

"But I need it now," he said.

A drink of corn wasn't all Kelby Callister was wanting. What he hungered for most was his own daughter. It was a father's right, he knew, and more righteous when a man's woman had died off. Then a growed-up daughter should sugar down her pa. Ease him dry. Not only that, Glory ought to sugar a few more men to trade whiskey for her father.

"She dang ought," Kelby whined.

If'n it hadn't be for that Justice of the Peace, he thought, Glory would be more dutying toward him. But the Judge put some highfilooty notions in her head, telling her to be uppity, like him.

Well, there were ways of settling a score. Good-ol'-boy down-home ways. Cricker way. Now that Hiram MacHugh's young kin had come to Hallapoosa to live, a plan was beginning to form in Kelby Callister's mind. He would have to tread lighter than careful, on account that Judge MacHugh and Constable Ransom were thick buddies. It wouldn't have shocked Kelby to learn that Judge and Carney were both sissies together. Fairy boys.

"And I don't mean Kalipsa Ferry."

Kelby snickered. He enjoyed thinking about what wasn't true, hoping that it was the truth. Closing his eyes, he relished his vision of MacHugh and Ransom together. It would take a dang giant of a bed to hold those two, bigger than a shack floor.

A child's hollering turned Kelby Callister alert. The two MacHugh whelps were throwing a ball back and forth, spouting noise, making a racket like they already owned the cussed town, even though they only arrived today. Dang brats. It would be so nice, Kelby decided, to grab the pair of them and drag them to the island in the crick . . . and, one by one, force them to perform . . . or make Hiram MacHugh watch it happen.

The trouble would be Glory.

She would, Kelby was imagining, kick up one heller of a fuss when she'd find out that her pa had captured a MacHugh, one to sell downcrick. There were places in Miami, he had heard, that would buy young children to use as entertainment. Younger the better. And the younger the whelps, the higher price they paid, in cash, and not a question asked. Kelby's downcrick kin had told him so.

Big Callister had told it all. Kelby wouldn't call Big a liar. Nobody would. One time, in a fight, Big had chewed off part of Kelby's ear. He'd bled like a pig.

Kelby wondered if Big still kept three wives. All of them were young too. The youngest was fourteen, Big boasted. "If a gal be big enough, she's old enough . . . and if'n she be old enough, she better be big enough." That was how Cousin Big had said it.

There was money to be made, Big had said. Trouble is, there was a problem of trucking the live cargo all away east and cross-state to Miami. If you got caught hauling kiddy slaves, the law would go harsh on you. Best to travel at night, Big said, using only the sand roads, keeping wide clear of any village. Big had made one haul, by his lonesome, all the way east to Miami. They had paid him handsome. But when Big got drunk, a couple friendly ladies took his poke, cut his belt that his billfold was chained to, and took off. Even robbed every thread of his clothes. Big woke up in some roadhouse room jay naked and without a dang penny. Even took the specs off his eyes so he couldn't see clear no more.

Luckily, he'd left the keys to the truck he'd borrowed under the seat, well hid. Yet on the way back to Hallapoosa, the cussed truck broke down. There stood Big Callister beside the road, naked as birth, until some renegade Seminoles came along and cane-lashed him until he was all-over raw.

Kelby had to laugh.

Standing in darkness, he wondered how Big Callister ever worked up the bowel to tell about it. Well, Big's brain was known to be as wee as his body was giant.

"Maybe," Kelby said, "I could sell Glory and Lot, as well as them two MacHughs."

He'd turn a small fortune. Yet he had to admit that such a purpose bothered him some.

Then he could parade into some fancy Miami store and outfit himself in a new white suit, like the Judge wears. And a spiffy hat to top it off. And shoes! Then, sometime soon, he might visit the turpentine mill to strut around uppity and let all those niggers and trash stare at him like he was a slick-city gentleman. So much cash in his pants that it would bulge all his pockets.

"Yep, that's what I'll do."

He'd bring a fancy lady with him, all the way back from Miami, and show her off to that crew of turpentiners until their tongues hung out. My, how they'd envy old Kelby Callister. Once he'd proved he was a mite more foxyheaded than they were.

With a lick of smart, Kelby figured he might set up a running business, and he could offer up a job to Big Callister to handle some of the Miami people. Big had all the connections, knew the right gents to pay up. But he would have to keep a watchful eye, both eyes, on Big and his double-cross ways, or else Big would skim off the lion's share of the profits. A man like Cousin Big was nothing more than downcrick trash.

"Big," he said, "you're all through. You be fired. Fact is, I just might lay off everybody, on account I'm the *boss* and I run things *my* way."

Kelby smiled.

His hand almost slapped his thigh as he considered it. What

an idea! He would buy up the Hallapoosa Turpentine Company, and make Mr. Spafford his hireling. Then it would be *Mr.* Callister.

Respect. That was the word. Inside, he sort of wanted Glory to be respected too. Maybe it wasn't too late for that. If he could have another good woman to live with, and do for him, he'd willing let Glory and Lot drift off on their own. Pretty as she is, Glory certain could find somebody to wed. Trouble is, the man she wanted was the Judge.

"MacHugh."

Saying the name was like poison in his mouth, making him want to puke at the sound.

It was probable people up north, like Hiram MacHugh, who wore white suits and *shoes* . . . they were the cause of the pesky Depression that was to close the turpentining down. Maybe for keepers. Kelby would bet it was some dang Justice of the Peace or some constable sidekick. Yankee lawyers too. Book people. The sort you'd see sitting around on a park bench or up on a hotel porch in a rocking chair, reading a newspaper, pretending to understand all that fancy writing.

Kelby grunted.

"I'd wager it's them kind of gentlemen that sport at the kiddy places in Miami."

He let out a long sigh. When he final died, Kelby was convinced, nobody would weep over his grave, or say Bible words. Not even Glory, or Lot. No respect. Neither his daughter nor grandchild held a lick of honor for him. It wasn't fair. In fact, not much was fair in this world, if you were hatched a Cricker, a Callister.

In Hallapoosa, it sure helped to be born a Singletary or a Moffet, or into some other highbreed family. Some old Moffet, years back, started the sawmill, and then raised a few head of beef cattle. Planted oranges. Why, he wondered, didn't my old Granddaddy Callister do likesome? Then we'd be on Easy Street, living high, and having niggers to handle a skittle and broom. Some young coffee-skin gal with a hot wiggle body, willing to please, and do.

Again, the voices of children shook Kelby Callister out of his dreaming.

The ball they were tossing had bounded away, heading

toward where he was hiding. The boy said something, and the little girl was coming to fetch it, right toward him.

"Now's my chance," he said.

It would be a lead-pipe cinch to step out and surprise her, clamp a hand across her mouth, then carry her back to the shack on the island. Dumb old Judge would probable think that maybe she only got herself lost, and suspect nothing. Besides, not too many town people would venture down to the crick after dark.

The child was closer now.

Kelby could almost have stretched out a hand and yanked one of her pigtails. Yet he didn't. Instead, he waited for another time, a chance to take both children. Two would bring a better price than only one, and it would worry old Judge to death.

"Callister, you ain't got the sand," he nagged himself. "Can't even muster up the salt to take what's coming to you."

He watched the little girl pick up the ball and then run back to the MacHugh place.

Hiram MacHugh appeared at his back door, calling the children inside. They went, after a bit of protesting that it was still too early to come in.

Kelby said a dirty word.

Behind him, off a bit to one side, he thought he heard a noise, a footstep. Turning away from the MacHugh house, Kelby squinted into the dark. Cocking an ear, all he heard was the chatter of evening bugs, coupled with the steady croaking of swamp frogs. Underneath his bare feet, the fallen leaves felt dry, too crisp to allow any careless step. So he froze himself quiet, listening for some telltale noise that would warn he wasn't here alone.

Holding his breath, Kelby listened, almost able to hear the beating of his heart.

He sniffed the woody air. Only the sweaty stink of his shirt seemed to enter his nose. Nothing more. The surrounding smell was dampy, like moss and wood rot blending into the black soil. It was a clean smell, not like people, or turp from the mill. Almost sweet, the way Glory sometimes smelled before she scooted off to sugar a customer.

One little whiff of Glory could drive any healthy male close to crazy.

"Even her pa," he whispered.

Years back, Kelby was recalling, when Glory began to show her swollen belly, she wasn't more than a child of fourteen fixing to birth another child. Even though he had cuffed her around, again and again, she'd never let out who'd got her in a family way. Glory just wouldn't tell him. Glory had quit going to the schoolhouse too, Kelby remembered. Stayed close to the shack on the island and waited for her time to come.

"Lotty's got a MacHugh look to him. And I knowed some money changed hands, from a MacHugh to a Callister."

It had also been the Judge's money that had hired the midwife, that old Simpson witch who died off right after Lot come aborning. That much Kelby knew for certain surer. Yet he was still doubting that Hiram MacHugh was the gent who'd troubled Glory.

"No," he said, "it weren't the Judge."

Lot's father be the one who'd sneaked back to Hallapoosa, and then left again.

Bobby.

· *Eight* ·

"Thane?"

Hearing his name, Thane MacHugh blinked his eyes in the dark of the strange bedroom and sat up in bed.

"Alma Lee?"

He saw his sister walking toward him until she reached the bedpost beyond his feet. She was carrying her rag doll, Claudine. "I can't sleep," she said. "Please let me crawl into bed alongside of you. Okay?"

"Okay." Throwing open the sheet, he hitched over to make room for her, offering her half of his pillow. "I wasn't quite asleep either," he confessed.

"It's so quiet across the hall that I could almost hear Claudine breathing."

"Dolls don't breathe." Thane gave Alma Lee a gentle nudge. "But you're right about the stillness. Sure is different from Jacksonville."

"Well," she said, "if you ask me, it certain's a lot darker in *my* room than it is here in yours. And mine's more than a mite quieter."

"How could a room be quiet with you in it? People could hear *you* in a sawmill. And they might even be able to hear Claudine."

Alma Lee punched him. "Claudine didn't really like sleeping in my room. She wanted to visit you."

"I suppose she said so."

"Yes, but Claudine only talks to me. She wouldn't say as much as *mud* to anyone else."

"Hey," he said, covering his sister with the sheet, "if you and your dolly talk to each other, it's okay by me."

Lying in bed, looking up at the ceiling, Thane MacHugh was questioning whether or not the two of them would like living in Hallapoosa. From the looks of the place, it wasn't much of a town. No big buildings. Sort of the opposite of Jacksonville. So far, he and Alma Lee had only met four people . . . Uncle Hiram, Constable Ransom, Vestavia, and the nice white-haired lady who lived next door, Mrs. Fulsom, who told them they could call her Miss Sellie because most of Hallapoosa did.

Miss Sellie had hugged both of them, as had Vestavia. And tomorrow, Miss Sellie had told them, she intended to bake brownies, so many that she would have a full pan left over, enough to throw out . . . unless, of course, she could find folks who liked eating chocolate brownies.

Thane smiled.

His mother had always said that it's best to believe there are good people everywhere, even up north among the Yankees. Well, his mother had been right on that score. Even as he left, before supper, Mr. Ransom had squatted down to hug Alma Lee.

The only person in Hallapoosa who didn't seem to hug children was their uncle.

As though reading his mind, Alma Lee asked, "Thane, do you cotton to Uncle Hiram a whole lot?"

Thane nodded. "Sure. I bet when we get to know him, he'll be warmer than a morning pillow."

"You think so?"

"I figure our chubby old uncle just isn't used to having kids around. It'll take him a spell to custom to us."

"How long will it take him?" she asked.

"Well, no matter how long, best we give Uncle Hiram a chance. Old folks are probable a bit like winter trees. They can't bend so easy to a spring wind."

Alma Lee sighed. "Thane, how did you grow up to be so doggone smart-minded? When I'm twelve, will I be as smart as you?"

In the dark, he grinned at her. "Oh, I guess in five years, you'll even be a speck smarter."

"Honest?"

Thane knew Alma Lee could feel his nodding, and accept it for an answer.

"That old Vestavia was a mite bossy," said Alma Lee, "when we were eating supper. She ordered me to sit up straight, and to put my feet under the table like President Hoover always does."

"I heard her."

"Do you reckon Vestavia knows President Hoover?"

"No," Thane said, "but perhaps she saw a picture of him in a newspaper, eating, with his feet under the table. Vestavia's real old. And old folks turn cranky sometimes."

"Miss Sellie's not cranky."

"She might be just as bossy, if the two of us were eating over at her house. Miss Sellie might also expect your feet to act like President Hoover's."

Alma Lee punched the pillow. "Well, I aim to put my feet where I doggone please, and if old Vestavia nags me too much, I'll show her some real fancy cussing."

Thane sat up and yanked her pigtail.

"Little sis, seeing as we're going to be living here in Halla-poosa for a spell, maybe we best go along by what people tell us. And try to make friends. I don't guess we'll make too many by cussing at them."

"You don't have to get ornery. If you don't watch out, you'll grow old and crotchety as Vestavia."

"Alma Lee, don't hatch trouble. So far, the only crotchety person around here is *you*. Maybe you ought to remember how Vestavia hugged us, and handed each of us a fresh-baked cookie when we got here."

"I know why you're standing up for Vestavia, and don't think I don't. It's because she likes *you* better than she does *me*."

Thane sighed. "That's not true. Vestavia probable likes us both exactly the same."

Alma Lee socked his shoulder, not very hard, yet Thane said "Ow" to make her happy. Smiling, he said, "My feet were under the table. I guess President Hoover and I are almost twins." He looked at his sister. "If you really want to get uppity about it, I s'pose you could eat your meals somewhere else, where people don't care if your feet are stuck in the mashed potatoes."

She was silent for a moment, as though considering his fooly suggestion. Finally, she spoke up.

"Thane, I wonder why Vestavia says words like *quality* and *proper* so often. But I noticed something funny. When she's saying those words, Vestavia sort of stares direct at Uncle Hiram."

"I didn't notice. Because I was too busy eating my supper. You have to admit that Vestavia is one heck of a good cook."

"It was okay."

"That peach pie," Thane said, "was certain a lot tastier than *okay*. It was great. Vestavia even asked me if I wanted a second slab and then served me one. To tell you the straight of it, I could have put away a third, but I didn't want to look too piggy in front of Uncle Hiram."

"He wasn't piggy at all. Fact is, Uncle Hiram hardly touched his food. Maybe he had gas."

"Maybe. All he did during supper," Thane said, "was watch the two of us store it away, almost like he'd never seen anyone else eat before. First he would look at you, then at me, as though we'd come to Hallapoosa from someplace like Saturn."

"Is that in Florida?"

"No. Saturn's like Earth. It's another planet but a long ways off. Miss Davidson explained all that in school last spring. Once you start school, you'll learn all that stuff. You won't be stupid forever."

Reacting at once, Alma Lee straddled his chest as though he were a horse, then bounced up and down a few times, still holding her doll.

"Quit. Get off and lie quiet, or I'll march you back across the hall to your own room."

She dismounted.

"I sure get tired," Alma Lee said, "of being ordered around by everybody. Why is it always *me*?"

"Hey," he said, touching her shoulder, "when I was seven, Mama and Daddy ordered me plenty."

I wish, Thane was thinking, they'd come alive again and still do it. I'd even wash the car, without asking for a dime. His fists tightened, knowing that now the time had arrived to be a big brother, to act grown-up, for Alma Lee. Maybe she just became seven, yet Alma Lee had been a brave soldier this past week. His sister had also been understanding whenever their parents had fought and thrown dishes at each other.

"You're okay," he told her.

"So are you."

"And soon, when September comes, you'll be attending school, too. We'll be meeting lots of other kids and making friends."

"If I go," she said, "I'm taking Claudine."

"Claudine won't be too interested in school subjects. Perhaps it might be wiser if you left her here at the house, so she can rest her mouth while you're at first grade."

"What grade will you be in?"

"Grade six."

"I want to sit beside you."

"Alma Lee, it doesn't quite work that way. First-graders sit with other first-graders. That's the rule. Our desks are a lot larger than yours, and what we have to learn is harder." He pointed a finger at her. "We can still be pals here, at night, but at school you can't follow me around like a shadow. I don't want the other guys to know that my sister sometimes sleeps in my bed, or they'll think I'm afraid of the dark."

"I bet you're not afraid of anything . . . not even Vestavia."

Thane MacHugh felt his jaws harden as he pressed his teeth together. Yes, he thought, I am afraid without Mama and Daddy. What if old Uncle Hiram dies? Then he would have to quit school, get a job, and earn to support himself and his sister. In a strange town, one in which he didn't know anyone. He was wishing that Alma Lee was across the hall, instead of here, so he could cover his face with a pillow and let loose.

It wouldn't be right to show all his feelings in front of Alma Lee. Big brothers can't do things like that. He would be soon turning thirteen on his next birthday, and people in their teens have to stand up taller than children.

Mama had said that, Thane was remembering. For a year or so, he recalled, Thane had started to think of his father as being sort of a tall child. His mother was quieter, but stronger. She was brains. But his father was temper, screaming and throwing things, kicking the car when it wouldn't start, until his mother climbed down and lifted the engine hood. Or opened the toolbox on the running board.

Uncle Hiram, he was deciding, didn't seem to be the sort of person who would swear or throw anything. Not even a tantrum.

Thane wondered what his uncle feared. Perhaps, the boy concluded, Hiram MacHugh was only frightened of being an *uncle*. Hands beneath his head, Thane was curious about how old Uncle Hiram really was. Possibly sixty.

"Thane, what are you thinking on?"

"Nothing," he lied. "I was fixing to do myself some dreaming, and maybe you ought to do some too."

"I can't sleep. These beds are too hard. They're not soft and comforty like they are back home."

Home?

The word almost punctured him. "This is our home now, Alma Lee. We have to make our best of it. Both of us have to really try. Uncle Hiram and Vestavia will try too. They're not like Mama and Daddy, not a bit, but I don't guess they're bad people. Just old. At least they don't argue or fight."

"How long do we have to live in Hallapoosa?"

"Not forever. Only until we're eighteen, Judge Tabor told us. After that, we're free to scoot anywhere we please. That's the law."

"I want to go back to Jacksonville."

Thane held her hand. "So do I. But we would be alone there, Alma Lee, with no Uncle Hiram and no Vestavia either. Besides, the bank owns the house in Jacksonville because we had a mortgage."

"A bank owns *our house*?"

Thane nodded. "I don't full understand it all, but someone else will be soon living there. That's what usual happens when people move away. Houses stay, and get a new family."

"We're not a family anymore."

It hurt to hear her little voice admitting it in the night. Almost enough to cramp his stomach. He wanted to curl up his knees and become a ball, or a little boy again, to hear his mother tiptoe to his bed and kiss his cheek. Perhaps, he was thinking, the Lord didn't build me strong enough to be a big brother right yet. But he couldn't let his sister know about that.

"Yes, we are," he said to her. "We're a family. Because we will always be together. You and me . . . and Claudine. She needs us both. So best we don't let Claudine think we're afraid."

Alma Lee moved closer to him, as though preparing to sleep. Their faces touched.

"I'm lucky you're my brother."

· Nine ·

Charlie Moon Sky stood quietly.

Through the screening fans of low-growing palmetto he watched the two white men who were fishing with heave lines at a crick pool.

One man was tall and bare-chested. His companion, much shorter and heavier, wore a gray work shirt, the sleeves of which were rolled to his elbows. As the two men talked in discontented tones, Charlie listened.

"A rotten shame," the tall man said.

"We knowed it'd soon happen, Vernon. The mill was bound to let more men go. Spafford said so. Even claimed that he would get axed too, like us."

"Maybe they could've put us all on half wages, to earn enough leastwise to put bread on the table. Mabel says she'll maybe try to take in washing."

The short man sighed. "Times are tough."

"Yeah, and fixing to harden tougher. We both gotta locate jobs, but they won't crop up easy."

Charlie Moon Sky waited for the two fishing men to move downstream. They hauled in their lines, yet Charlie still did not stir. He continued to stand in the daytime shadows, listening, but without movement. A forest, he knew, has few tongues but many ears.

The two white men passed within fifteen feet of where he stood. One of them, the taller of the two, actually glanced his way without alarm. Looking, yet not seeing.

Inside his face, Charlie smiled.

He knew he possessed the power, the gift from the Spirit to all Seminoles and to some, like himself, with half-Seminole blood. The gift was to stand, in plain sight, yet never be seen by white eyes. The power could blend a Seminole into trees and land, as though he had grown there, to see and remain unseen.

As the two fishermen walked by him, a bug was biting his neck, yet Charlie Moon Sky did not raise a hand to swat it. Or even to shoo it away. Instead, briefly closing his eyes, he allowed himself to be gratified that his blood could feed another, with so little cost. Even though the two men were gone, Charlie Moon Sky waited for the discomfort on his neck to fly away, as the bothersome bug had also flown.

Through it all, he had remained as undetected as the bug herself. I have fed you, he thought, to thank the Spirit for feeding me with the gift that blinds a white man's sight.

He now moved.

Each footfall was light, a Seminole step, as mute as a toe. His bare feet were weightless, like wings, floating over the black muck, feeling each footing prior to the step. More of a dance than a walk, an ancient dance, one that worshipped the beauty of silence as though it were unheard drums.

His feet disturbed nothing.

The legend even claimed that a Seminole warrior could stand all day on a hill of fire ants and not crush it, nor would he feel the sting of its defenders. Charlie had once attempted to do just that, yet the ants had swarmed over his feet, gnawing his flesh. And he had allowed them to do so in return for his having destroyed their home for so vain a purpose.

Slowly he moved upstream, to a place where he often had stood, to see what hastened his heart to behold.

Now he saw it again.

It was an island, a long place where the crick divided, upon which sat several gray shacks. People lived there. Yet they did not appear, to Charlie Moon Sky's eye, to be like the town people who lived on dry roads of sand. Not like Miss Sellie. Unlike her, they grew no flowers.

The Crickers were wild people like the Seminoles, but loud and untamed. Easy to smell; he seldom saw them wash. Miss Sellie had warned him to avoid the Crickers.

"Have nothing to do with those trashy people back yonder," she had advised. "Leave 'em be."

Even before seeing the island shacks, Charlie's nose had sipped the wind, and it informed him they were there, as obvious as the carcass of a dead bear. Miss Sellie, he was thinking, smelled like a small delicate flower, or sometimes like her kitchen and the good things she used to spice her cooking. Her baking rewarded a nose long before a stomach. Miss Sellie, he had sometime ago decided, was an old white rabbit, so soft and gentle, a lady who could harm no one. Charlie had vowed that no one would harm her.

He continued his walk, moving closer, on higher ground now to observe the island shacks.

"I wish to see her," he whispered. "The girl."

Many times before, Charlie Moon Sky has stood at this very place, hoping to catch sight of the pretty girl with her long sunlight hair. Often she played with a little boy and the two of them threw stones that danced upon the pond water.

Charlie waited.

All day and all night, he thought, I would stand to await seeing her for a time of only one breath. Last night, lying on the ground in the cowshed, he had not been able to sleep. Instead he worked, by moonlight, doing what Miss Sellie had asked him to do, and more.

But, he thought, I will not go inside Miss Sellie's house, even though she holds the door open for me and tells me that I would be welcome.

My Miss Sellie is a dear old grandmother to me, to her flowers, and now to the new children who have come to live next door with Judge MacHugh. I believe, Charlie Moon Sky was thinking, that Miss Sellie would be a grandmother to a chigger bug. Or, could she reach it or not, to a cloud.

Thinking about Miss Sellie, his heart smiled.

The morning sun sifted down through the live oak and palms, fragments of sunlight that sprinkled the land like broken glass. Charlie Moon Sky was hoping that the sun would not awaken Miss Sellie too soon, as he did not wish to alarm her because of his absence.

His breathing stopped as he saw her, the pretty island girl with hair of gold and silver.

"Lotty," she said, leaving a shack of gray boards, "you coming along?"

The boy appeared, a small copy of the girl. He looked lean. As he stood beside the girl, Charlie thought, they were bright and shiny as new money, a small coin and a larger one.

"I ache to touch you," Charlie Moon Sky silently whispered to them. "Both of you, because the boy seems to belong somehow to his sister, not to the old father who shares the shack with them. A cactus and two blooms."

The young woman and the small boy were now walking along the wet rocks, balancing, sometimes wading. As the boy pointed at something in the shallows, the girl looked with him. She also pointed, extended a graceful arm with fingers that almost floated with grace.

There is music in my heart, Charlie thought.

Yet he knew the girl would not run south with him to the swamp and leave the little one behind. Without thinking, Charlie knew this. The two Crickers he now watched belonged to one another, as a leaf to its twig.

"Soon," he said softly, "I will allow myself to be seen by the woman."

Would she fear him?

No, Charlie decided. He would stand to greet her, clean and smiling, with white egret feathers in his hair and flowers in his hand. Then, before she could dash away, he would sing softly to her in words foreign to her ears, and still the pounding of her heart. Yet his own heart would beat harder than a war drum.

His body would also harden, flex, to show her his strong arms and shoulders, because he was now a man capable of holding a woman, this young woman, as he would also hold flowers and egret feathers, with lightness. Then he would beckon, and she would walk to him, take the flowers, and inhale his sturdy manhood, then touch him as though he were a tree trunk freshly bathed by summer rain.

Soon, he again promised.

"Glory," the boy called.

Charlie Moon Sky nearly laughed. So that is her name. Glory, a name like her hair, light and golden as sunlight on a summer day. Or any day, even winter.

Could he take her to the swamp to show the other Seminoles

his treasure? Joe Votaw would be jealous, and his brown face would darken to see the prize that Charlie Moon Sky had won. A trophy woman. Glory was a woman that a man could almost wear around his neck like a garland of wet flowers.

"Lotty," the girl was saying to the child, "we can build ourselfs a little dam." Bending, she began to arrange twigs to choke a narrow rivulet that surged between a pair of rocks. But the water's force rushed them away. Joining her, the little boy started to pile a row of pebbles where her twigs had briefly rested. The girl assisted him. But again the water's pressure was too strong, and the dam of pebbles toppled.

The current inside Charlie Moon Sky was also strong, insistent, more urgent than he ever before had known. Years ago, his own father, John Moon Sky, had wanted a white woman who had become his mother and now lay among clouds, with the Spirit.

His father lay there too, above, beyond the sky in an unseen holy place.

He had run away. As the halfbreed son of John Moon Sky, a Seminole who had taken a white wife, he was no longer one of them. Out of place. Alone. All he knew was that his mother's name had been Eleanor Murdock and she also had run away, because of her white baby, the one who had died before Charlie was born. Yet she had never run from John Moon Sky.

"I still do not understand," Charlie admitted softly. "Nor will I ever. People are akin to the fish, birds, flowers . . . not alike. All shapes and colors, and some with names that make Seminoles laugh, a name such as Eleanor Murdock."

His father, John Moon Sky, had told him secrets, about when a man first sees a woman whom he desires. "Do not pounce at the first rustle of heart leaves, or because of your rising manhood. Wait, with patience, watching as a swamp panther silently watches, until you are sure. Until you would kill to possess her."

Seeing the girl with the sunlight hair, Glory, he believed that as sure as his name was Charlie Moon Sky, he could kill in order to mate with her. Inside his chest, the manhood drum was booming. Also in his gut, above the belt and below. Still he would wait, as his father had spoken, allowing his passion for Glory to grow as slowly and as beautifully as one of Miss Sellie's flowers, those that she tended with so much care.

He liked to learn the names of Miss Sellie's flowers, the little colorful beings that she loved as though they were her children.

Never had Miss Sellie feared him. Charlie had run away from the swamp, then could travel no more becuase he was ill with fever. He remembered feeling dizzy, as though the sun was bouncing against the sky. His world blackened. Upon awakening, he saw an old white woman, looking down at him where he lay. The woman smiled.

"My name is Selma Fulsom," she said to him in a gentle voice. Her hand felt cooling to his hot brow. "And don't you be afraid. Are you hungry?"

In his illness, the Spirit had somehow guided him to the yard behind Miss Sellie's house where, at last, he had fainted. Now, he wondered if he could ever leave the old lady who had tended him, fed him food, and then allowed him to stay and work for wages as her handyman. He had spoken to Miss Sellie hardly at all, except to tell her that his name was Charlie Moon Sky, his parents were dead, and that his mother had been a white woman, Eleanor Murdock.

Now, he thought, looking at Glory, it is Charlie Moon Sky who wants a white woman for himself, though such a hunger had rarely made his father happy. Perhaps it was wrong for a robin to mate with a sparrow, and the Spirit would frown on him as the other Seminoles had frowned at his parents and often turned away their faces.

He looked at the girl.

"Forgive me," he said softly, "but you are the only woman for me, Glory Sunshine Hair. I give you this new name now, but sometime soon I shall give you my name, and you shall be Mrs. Moon Sky. Only to me will you forever remain Glory Sunshine Hair for so is how I picture you, nights when my eyes cannot see you but my dreams bring you to where I sleep."

His body stiffened.

An old man appeared in the shack doorway, blinking, squinting in the morning sun, scratching himself.

"The ugly cactus," said Charlie, "who seems foreign to his two young blossoms."

The Cricker man was yelling something to Glory and to the little one, and his words sounded unpleasant. He was the same man who thought he had been unseen as he watched the new MacHugh children bouncing their ball. Charlie Moon Sky had seen him, as he had also seen Glory go visit the man Miss Sellie called Hiram as though this judge man was still a child.

The half-ear Cricker man was yelling now, waving his arms, complaining about no money and no food. He wanted both, telling Glory to bring these things to him.

Taking the boy's arm, Glory waded further downstream, away from the shack. Still hollering, her father picked up a pebble and hurled it at them. The two fled.

As he watched, the hand of Charlie Moon Sky rested on the handle of his belt knife.

· *Ten* ·

"Wash," said Vestavia.

She didn't have to look very hard to notice the resentful expression on Alma Lee's face, or to observe her dirty hands.

Marching her to the kitchen sink, Vestavia grabbed the brown bar of Octagon and scrubbed the child's hands. The boy, Thane, had washed without being told and already had seated himself at the kitchen table, awaiting his noon meal.

Vestavia soaped and rubbed a bit harder than necessary, feeling the small white hand struggle between hers.

"Ain't a proper way to come to a table with half the soil in Hallapoosa on your hands," she informed Alma Lee.

"There won't be anything left of my fingers if you keep scrubbing at me like I'm laundry."

Alma Lee winced as Vestavia applied a dishrag to her cheeks, removing several grimy smudges.

"A lady proper be a lady clean."

"Why do you say *proper* so much?"

Vestavia tossed her a hand towel. "On account that's how I intend you and your brother to grow up—to become a lady and a gentleman. And if you don't like it, Miss Alma Lee, I'm fixing to fill the washtub, dunk you in it, and scrub some rightful *proper* all over you."

Alma Lee wiped her hands.

"And when you git done your drying, you can hang the towel on the nail where it belong. Now go sit."

Turning away to face the stove, Vestavia Holcum allowed herself an unseen smile. Healthy children always got dirty. It was a child's due. However, dirt outside the house was one thing, inside it was another. Nobody in Hallapoosa was going to say that her little MacHughs appeared shabby. She placed two steaming plates of greens and hot bread on the table. The little girl looked at her meal, then up at Vestavia.

"Collards again?" Her nose wrinkled.

"They put a curl to your hair."

"Is that why your hair's so curly?" Alma Lee asked her.

"Reckon so. Part of it be the Lord's doing, with maybe a smack of help from all the good greens I put myself outside of." Before each child Vestavia served a generous glass of milk. "Try not to spill it for at least a minute. Best you take a quick sip so that some goes to the right place, instead of everywhere else."

She saw Alma Lee make a face at her brother.

Thane was already eating, forking it in like it would be the final meal of his life. "It's good, Vestavia. Real good."

"Thank you. I try doing my best on what Mr. Hiram can afford to put on this table. Times is hard these days. Talk going that the turpentine mill might shut down entire. Only working three day a week as it be."

"Are people here all poor?" Alma Lee asked.

"Mostly." Vestavia stood in the center of the kitchen, hands on her lean hips. "Might even become more poorly than we already is. So nobody ought to complain about having to sit to collards. Best we be grateful to the Lord that the plate ain't vacant."

Standing nearby, Vestavia watched Thane and Alma Lee finish their meal. The boy downed his milk to the very drop. But the girl only drank half of hers. Her upper lip was now a white mustache. She looked at her glass.

"How come you give us so much milk to drink?"

"It's good for you. A hot day like today tend to burn up the wet inside you, and the milk'll restore it back. And stout up your ribs."

"If I live here another week," said Alma Lee, "I'll probable turn into a cow."

Vestavia nodded. "Possible so. Leastwise, you'll be a cow that's healthy handsome."

"Moooo," said Thane, causing his sister to glare at him as she chewed.

"I can't honest say," Alma Lee announced, "that I'm fond of collards a whole lot."

"My," said Vestavia, "ain't that a caution shame." She pointed a finger at the girl's plate. "There's youngsters all over the world that ain't *never* had a collard to eat. Not a blessed solitary one, even though they don't cost hardly a penny and grow quick. So you best be thankful you be so lucky."

"It's hot in this kitchen," Alma Lee said. "I think maybe I just might skin off my shirt while I finish eating."

That child was testing her again, Vestavia sensed. Some children will usual dare one extra step, over the line, to see what's allowed. Or to find out how far they could sneak.

"I think maybe you won't," Vestavia said. "A decent young lady don't hardly parade around shirtless. Keep your shirt where it belong, unless you want me to skin you another way."

"It's not really *my* shirt. It used to be Thane's before he got so big. I have to wear almost all of his dumb old clothes, even though they're for a boy."

Vestavia carried the dirty plates to the sink, rinsed them off, and stacked them for a later washing. "That's the way of it," she said. "Ain't my fault you the youngest. Or your brother's. The older ones always hand-down to the small." Returning to the table as Alma Lee was draining the last of her milk, Vestavia bent to kiss her on top of her head.

"How come you kissed me, Vestavia?"

"It's my duty. Your uncle pays me wages to keep house, cook, and give out a once-a-day kiss to any little girl who drinks all her milk." She winked at Alma Lee. "Providing she starts coming to meals when she's called, like her brother do."

Leaving the table, Thane went back outside, saying that he might see if he could climb up Miss Sellie's big camphor tree, as Miss Sellie had told him her tree needed a climber. Alma Lee, however, stayed behind to watch Vestavia tidy the table.

"Do you really like my brother better than you like me?"

Vestavia snorted. "Stuff!"

"Well, sometimes I think you do."

"Ain't so. Do you actual believe that I couldn't like anybody who owns the name of MacHugh? They was always good white people, child. I know. I've worked in this kitchen over fifty year. Since I can clear recall. Fact is, I can't even recollect a time when I didn't come here every morning except Sunday."

Feeling a mite tired, Vestavia sat herself down in the chair Thane had vacated. The chair felt warm, boy warm, bordering on hot and healthy. Before the children had come, several days ago, Vestavia would sometimes sneak a short nap in the afternoon, on the parlor sofa. But now, with Thane and Alma Lee to tend and feed, a nap was seldom possible.

"Are you very old?"

Vestavia nodded. "Older than that old swamp back yonder, or near as old. I can recall Hallapoosa when it was nothing except mud and mules." She laughed briefly. "In a way, Hallapoosa was sort of the same then as now. Except a mite littler. I born me my babies here, and then their babies come. All growed up and off. My, I would go myself if'n I still had me the gumption."

"How come you don't go?"

"Don't reckon I could ever cut strings and leave Mr. Hiram. He's a good man, your uncle be. In my lifetime, I knowed plenty bad and plenty good. Just like everybody do. But my Mr. Hiram be about the most kindly I ever pleasured to know, or work for."

Alma Lee looked curious. "Vestavia, why do you say *my* Mr. Hiram that way?"

She smiled. "People don't own people, child. But one heart often can hold hands with another."

"He walks home with you every night."

"Always has. Near since I can recall. When he started doing it, he weren't more than a small lad. Yet, lame leg and all, he walked behind me on his little cane, all the way to the town fence. Maybe because I was still a young woman back then, and Mr. Hiram wanted to see I got home safe. Now that I'm olden, he still do it. I never ask him to. But I certain never asked him to quit doing. It become a part of sundown."

"Uncle Hiram told Thane and me that you knew our daddy, away back when he was a little boy right here in this house."

Rising slowly to her feet, Vestavia looked out of the kitchen window at Mrs. Fulsom's big old camphor tree. Thane was climbing it now. Closing her eyes, she still saw Mr. Bobby, hanging by his knees hooked over a slender branch, causing her heart to leap with alarm. Vestavia could even hear Bobby yelling like that Buffalo Bill man about whom his older brother read to him.

"Yes," she said, opening her eyes and swallowing. "I knowed your daddy real well."

Returning to the table, she sat down again, to rest her legs for a moment, and to reach over and touch Alma Lee's hand.

"And," she said, "I put this old paw of mine to the backside of Mr. Bobby MacHugh a lot more than often."

"You—you spanked my daddy?"

"Deed so. Wasted his time doing it and my energy. Figure I'll probable not have to spank *you,* on account you're to become such a proper lady."

"And wash?"

Vestavia nodded. Then she pointed to the metal tub behind the stove. "See that tub? Well, I used to wash your daddy in that thing. He'd be spilling suds all over my floor, yelping fit to murder, but I'd scrub Mr. Bobby until he'd shine like a fresh nickel."

"Honest?" Getting up, Alma Lee went to examine the tub. "Daddy wouldn't have fitted into this."

"Oh, he be a right smaller then. He stuck to dirt about as much as you. Maybe even worse."

Alma Lee's eyes widened as another thought crept into her mind. "You certain didn't put *Uncle Hiram* in this tub?"

"No. Your uncle was really good at washing up his ownself. Usual clean. Lots neater than Mr. Bobby. Even when he was a little boy, your uncle was a small gentleman. Small and olden. I guess his illness turned him solemn."

Alma Lee returned to the table. But then, jumping up quickly, she left the kitchen, reappearing in almost an instant with her doll.

"Her name's Claudine."

"So you told me near a dozen time."

"We talk a lot, just the two of us. She doesn't say anything to Thane because he's only a boy. Claudine and I are girls." Alma Lee looked up at Vestavia. "You're a girl too."

Vestavia laughed. Later tonight, she would have to tell Tally Thurman about Alma Lee and her dolly. And about still being a little girl for a moment. No matter how old a woman grows, she ought to mother a doll once a season.

"When is Uncle Hiram coming home from doing all his business down at the courthouse? If you ask me, he ought to come home a bit earlier."

"Mr. Hiram will be fetching along home, like usual, when he see fit."

He was working longer hours now, Vestavia had noticed. Up earlier in the morning, staying later, probable trying to earn money and collect more fee. Now that times turned harder in Hallapoosa, it wouldn't be easy for Mr. Hiram to keep a roof, and feed everybody. But he would find a way to manage. No use sharing trouble with the children.

"Looks to be there's loose stuffing about to spill out your dolly's chest." Alma Lee handed Claudine to her. "Child, go fetch me the sew basket. You'll locate it in the cubby closet beneath the stairs."

It didn't take long. Only a stitch here and there to repair Claudine's wound.

"Be careful with the needle," Alma Lee warned her. "Thane had to have three stitches in his leg when it got tore open one time, and it certain hurt him fearful because he yelped like a kicked dog. I don't want you to harm Claudine."

Vestavia smiled. "I'll go cautious."

"I don't mean to nag," Alma Lee said. After a pause, the child went on to say more. "People that nag at other people a lot aren't very nice."

"Even about washing before a mealtime?"

"Yes," Alma Lee said firmly.

"There now," Vestavia said as she held up the doll, "I do believe Claudine is feeling fiddle again. Fact is, I thought she cracked a smile at me."

Alma Lee smiled. "She did."

· _Eleven_ ·

Hiram locked his office door.

As he walked along the dimly lit hall of the Hallapoosa courthouse, he was hoping that August wouldn't linger and that autumn would bring a cooling of the sultry weather.

Cane in hand, he carefully stepped down the front stairs and out onto Exchange Street.

"Hiram!"

He turned, wincing, seeing Julia Blount heading in his direction. At moments such as this, Hiram thought, it surely would be a blessing to possess a pair of sound legs, to escape being cornered. Forcing a smile as she approached, he tipped his hat to her.

"Good afternoon, Julia."

"Good my foot. It's hotter than the Devil's drawers." She playfully nudged him so he wouldn't miss her humor. "My, there's a button coming loose on your suit jacket. Doesn't that poor old Vestavia take any better care of you? You'll need a _wife_ when she retires, and she must be teasing eighty."

"Julia, I do not need a wife. Now that I have Bobby's two, it's well beyond what I can afford to support. Had I one more dependent, my dear, we would all be packing up and heading for the poor farm."

Julia playfully touched his elbow.

"Tush, how you talk. But, as I was saying, there's no way on earth that you and Vestavia could ever be expected to raise two youngsters to be fine Christian children."

"If we try our best, Julia, then a host of angels can perform no better."

Julia grunted. "I seriously doubt if there's a single soul in Hallapoosa who would call *you* an angel." She stepped a few inches closer. "You should hear what people have been saying." To add emphasis, Julia covered her ears.

Hiram sighed. "Yes, I'm sure the local tongues will continue to wag as usual." Pulling out his pocket watch, he said, "Goodness, look at the time. Whenever I chat with you, my dear Julia, I sometimes forget the hour. If you'll excuse me, I shall be getting on home."

Stamping her foot, Julia Blount looked distressed. "You're always in too much of a scurry, High MacHugh. Too busy to savor the fruits of life that could be practically within your grasp."

Hiram rapped the board sidewalk, using his cane as he often employed his gavel, stifling the urge to say, "Case dismissed." How, he was wondering, does a Justice of the Peace dismiss a woman so obviously forward as Julia Blount? Yet there were many qualities in Julia that Hiram admired, one of them being that he sensed her concern was genuine.

Physically, Julia was not unattractive. Her breasts, intimated by Julia as the hinted fruits within his grasp, were more generous than average. Despite her fifty-five years—three years his senior—Julia carried herself with far more grace, plus a provocative hip wiggle, than several other local widows. Upon his passing a few years ago, Horace Blount had left Julia financially *comfortable,* which was more than Hiram could assess for his own particular monetary situation.

Julia, he imagined, would also be rather comfortable after dark.

For an unguarded second, the temptation of a convenient matrimony crossed Hiram's mind, but then was quickly negated. No roof could lid a Julia Blount and a Vestavia Holcum without confrontation, he decided. Besides, it would hardly be fair to Thane and Alma Lee.

"You're staring at me, Hiram."

"Oh," he said, "pardon me, Julia. It was merely a minor matter of my office that rudely captured my attention." He smiled. "Now I best be getting along. Sorry if I so selfishly delayed you with my errant woolgathering."

"Have a pleasant afternoon," she said with a curt nod. "Sometime soon, I shall pop around to your house to see how your brother's children are adjusting."

"Yes," he said, "please do," hoping that Julia would postpone her supervision for at least a decade.

She stalked away.

Hiram watched her departure. Then, continuing homeward, he wondered if he was being shortsighted. How would Alma Lee and Thane survive were anything terminal to befall him? Yet it wouldn't be fair to Julia to marry her, because he really couldn't care for her enough to be truly a devoted husband.

Passing beneath one of the giant live oaks that lined Exchange Street, he heard a mockingbird above him, warbling its variety of song. He looked up. There were two mockingbirds, both singing, mates. Mating with Julia, Hiram considered as he walked onward, perhaps might create more problems than such a union would solve.

"Glory," he said softly, "I do miss you."

Walking slowly, measuring every other step with a reaching of his cane, Hiram tried to purge the rapturous memories of Glory Callister from his mind. No doubt the whole town knew about the two of them. Knew, yet never attempted to understand the needing, his or hers.

Had it not been for Bobby, years ago, Hiram knew that his business with Glory never would have commenced. It had been an irreversible circumstance, forced upon Glory and then snaring Hiram with the responsibility, because Bobby never could be responsible for his own illicit paternity. He was too young. At least that is how Hiram had absolved his brother's wildness. Too immature, and too . . . Bobbyish.

As he walked, he recalled the secret conversation with his brother as though it had happened yesterday. Bobby couldn't tell Mama or Daddy. Rightfully so, because neither of them would have been sympathetic about Bobby's sneaking back to town, getting drunk, and then seducing a very young girl, a child of fourteen.

Someone had caught the two of them together.

His parents had died unknowing, thinking that Bobby had left Hallapoosa to pursue further education. But the complete truth was, he had left the second time to escape Kelby Callister.

Nobody in Hallapoosa even knew the entire story, that Bobby MacHugh was already married and a father, up north in Jacksonville. He and Della had been bickering, Della had been unfaithful, so Bobby had run home to Hallapoosa . . . and had stayed just long enough to create a problem.

Glory Callister's problem.

Hiram had given Bobby bus money. "Return to your family," Hiram had told his wayward brother. "I'll see to it, Bobby. You have my word on it."

Hiram MacHugh had kept his promise.

It had taken him months to discover all of the facts, finally learning the whereabouts and name of the young girl Bobby had carelessly impregnated. Earlier, he had known that she was a Callister, yet he did not know which one. Along the meanders of Kalipsa Crick there were several shacks of Callisters.

Carney Ransom had been helpful and, as always, had also remained a discreet friend.

"My parents must never find out," Hiram had firmly warned Carney. "Never."

But by then it was too late for abortion, Carney reported. His contact wouldn't attempt it. The Callister girl could easily have died, and the only course of action now was a midwife for the delivery. It had been costly, Hiram remembered. The purchase of silence was tacked on to the services of childbirth, but someone had to be responsible and assume the expense. The someone had been Hiram MacHugh.

Until the birth of Lot Callister, Hiram drank very little, practically not at all, despite the convivial urgings of Carney and a few other contemporaries. Somehow, at the time, it seemed appropriate to toast the arrival of a new citizen. So he toasted, and toasted, but only with Carney Ransom, feeling the burning whiskey invading his gullet and hoping it would help to combat the shame of Bobby's indiscretion.

For some naive reason, Hiram was hoping that the illegitimate birth and its payment would dot a final period to the chapter. It did not. His parents died a month apart. Then, at last when he was living alone, came the unexpected knock at his back door, late one night. Opening it, he blinked into the darkness and saw a pair of strangers.

Two children. But a mother and a child.

Glory and Lot.

Kelby, her daddy, had abused her, and what she then told Hiram had been almost too shocking to hear. The marks and bruises on her face and arms, however, more than substantiated her story. Hiram prepared both of them something to eat, watching them as they ravenously finished every bite of the bacon, eggs, and grits. The boy in ragged clothes, Lotty, was frail and frightened, sitting close to his youthful mother while staring at Hiram with his wide furtive eyes.

Glory had told him that Lot was almost two.

During the following months, they came again and again, for shelter from abuse as well as for food. Always at night.

Hiram fed them at every visit. After they left, he cleaned the kitchen thoroughly, hoping that Vestavia, when she arrived the following morning, would not detect the fact that someone had disturbed her tidy kitchen. A black Sherlock Holmes, that old woman.

In spite of recent expenses as a result of two funerals, Hiram began giving money to Glory, to help her maintain Lot, expecting nothing in return, except to ease a conscience. The small child, after all, was half MacHugh.

Hiram stopped in his walk.

Closing his eyes, he remembered when Glory had first come to his back door *alone*. Little was said. He couldn't even find the words to protest her advances, as Glory was explaining her need to repay him for his food, funds, and kindness. She was so young, so beautiful, a water lily fresh from a crick pool, alive and exciting, eager to touch him and to be touched. Never before had Hiram been with a woman. Not once. But suddenly, there he lay with her, unclad, experiencing more emotion than he had ever allowed himself to feel.

The pain of his loneliness was washed away by sweet innocent kisses, embraces, and awakened dreams.

Glory became a candle to his darkness.

So, year after year, Hiram MacHugh continued to give Glory support, and she gave him her love. It had never been a purchase. Rather it was an exchange of gifts, presented freely, the joy belonging to the one who gave to the other. The most painful aspect of their friendship was hearing how Glory's father was becoming increasingly demanding of her, wanting personal favors that no decent father could expect from a daughter.

Instead of sex, Glory gave money to Kelby, to buy her protection, and Lotty's.

Hiram did not have to ask Glory how the money was earned. Somehow he guessed that she was meeting other men, for payment, and had become a prostitute. Yet this awareness of her profession never sullied his devotion to her. To the contrary, he was awed by his respect for a young girl who could so sacrifice herself for her son.

"I want to marry her," Hiram had told himself aloud, again and again. "And I will."

Although their difference in age bothered him, many were the times when he almost asked Glory to be his wife, so that she and Lotty could move in with him. At last Glory and her child would be safe from Kelby. He had even gone so far as mentioning to Vestavia that he had become tired of living alone and was toying with the idea of a change.

To his dismay, Hiram discovered that Vestavia Holcum was just one more Hallapoosa snob.

Although she never mentioned Glory by name, Vestavia told him point-blank that she would share no house with a Cricker, and spoke of islanders like the Downings and the Callisters whom she considered to be trash. Vestavia knew! She also reminded him of his position in the community as Justice of the Peace, plus her pride in working for quality MacHugh people.

Her lecture left Hiram speechless.

So, in cowardly fashion, Hiram had fled the dream of marrying Glory and adopting Lot as his legal son. For weeks, following Vestavia's moralizing tirade, Hiram could not sleep. Nor could he eat. Instead, he soothed his lack of fortitude by patronizing the after-dark wares of the bootlegger, Jason Yoobarr.

Visions of Kelby's abusing Glory and Lot haunted him constantly. For weeks he drank often, and many a morning Vestavia arrived to find him still in bed, or else staggering to his feet, then falling.

Hiram had expected more comeuppance from Vestavia, yet no further lectures ensued. Instead, she seemed to understand his hurt, prepared him his favorite meals, and baked cakes and pies that persistently added to his bulk. With needle and thread, Vestavia let out collars and the waists of his trousers, saying nothing, yet continuing her pampering cookery.

"Uncle Hiram."

Lost in the past, Hiram MacHugh couldn't quite revive himself back to the present. Someone was speaking to him, yet the voice seemed to be hailing him from a faraway planet.

"Look. I'm up here."

The same voice was persistently yanking him from thoughts of years ago, of opportunities lost, and heartbreak. The cane slipped from his fingers. Stooping, he fetched it, then straightened to search for the young voice that had shattered his yesterdays. Looking up, his vision cleared to focus on Thane, high up in Miss Sellie's camphor tree.

"Oh," he said, "there you are."

"Have you ever climbed up this high?"

Hiram shook his head. "No, indeed. I'd surely be afraid I would fall," he said cynically, "and fracture my brittle Hallapoosa reputation."

"I'll climb down," Thane said. "Watch me."

Almost as would a jungle baboon, the twelve-year-old boy slipped from limb to limb, down from Miss Sellie Fulsom's camphor tree, and finally leaped to the ground in August dust. There he stood, a new young Tarzan of the Apes, black with tree stain, the way a boy ought to look during summer.

Hiram MacHugh blinked. In his mind, he was not seeing his nephew, but another boy who had climbed this very tree, oh, so long ago.

He saw Bobby.

· *Twelve* ·

Carney slowed the patrol car.

Tucking an exploratory finger into his shirt pocket, he felt the four tickets. It would be a shame, Carney thought, to drive all the way to Kalipsa without them.

Thane and Alma Lee deserved a big evening, after what both those kids had weathered. Hiram had lost somebody too. Well, tonight Carney would spring for a special outing, a real treat for all three. Inside, he wanted to go himself, since early this morning when he had heard all about it from Bert Swicegood. A year ago, Bert had seen Miss Heavenly Hades and admitted to Carney that she certain was worth watching, balloons and all, but okay for the kids. Not a smoker, as the guys at the firehouse called a dirty show.

As Carney neared the Darky Town border, he spotted Thane MacHugh standing at the busted fence, saying good-night to Vestavia.

So, he was thinking, the young nephew has taken over Hiram's dedication to walking Vestavia Holcum part of the way home. Constable Ransom smiled, pleased to notice good folks doing good things, concluding that High was probable a mite joyous about it.

"Hop in," he yelled to Thane, "and I'll give you a lift back to your uncle's place."

It was only about a two-street ride, but the boy seemed more than happy to arrive home in constable style. Hiram was sitting in his rocker on the front porch, his cane hooked on the chair arm, slanting to the stoop floor. With a grunt, Carney eased his bulk from behind the wheel and climbed the steps, following Thane, who cleared them in one jump.

"High," he said, "go get your hat and we're off for a big surprise. My treat."

Hiram looked startled. "Tonight?"

Carney nodded. "You, me, and the two youngsters are off to Kalipsa. Let's be going. Big doings over yonder, so shake your good leg."

On the way to Kalipsa Ferry, he was poked by questions from his three MacHugh passengers, yet Constable Ransom would only shake his head and grin.

"I don't guess I can wait to see for my ownself," Carney told them, "so y'all hold patient until we reach Kalipsa."

"Is it really a surprise?" Alma Lee asked.

"Sure be," he told his only front-seat passenger. "Your eyes'll pop and your mouth'll fall open enough to park a truck in." He gently pulled one of her pigtails, watching her smile up at him.

It felt a bit strange for Carney Ransom to be going to Kalipsa for any reason. Three years ago, the elders of Kalipsa Ferry had offered him a job as deputy constable, with a fatter paycheck than Hallapoosa paid him, or could ever afford. After some considering, Carney had turned the offer down. It made little sense to pull up stakes and leave a town where he had grown up.

Perhaps he had made a mistake staying in Hallapoosa, now that times were leaner, and the turp mill could go bust. Yet it would be difficult to say so-long to friends.

Hallapoosa's good enough, he had decided, and he'd stay put, even though Kalipsa had twice the population. Maybe even three times. But at home, he could wander along Exchange Street and wave a howdy to people he had known all his life. What's more, call them all by name.

Some of the locals, in fun, called him Handsome Ransom.

However, there certain was a spate more doings in Kalipsa Ferry. Silently he chuckled, knowing about what was in store for this evening.

Upon their arrival, they had a problem finding a place to park. It appeared to Carney as though everybody in Collier County had the same idea, to visit Kalipsa and take in the big show. With the confidence of a neighboring peace officer, Carney Ransom's brainstorm of parking behind the jailhouse paid off. He located a vacant Official Car Only slot, pulled to a stop, and cut the engine.

"Everybody out," he told the three MacHughs. "By golly, we don't want to miss the parade."

The street was lined with people, on both sides. Mostly families. "Quite a turnout," Hiram commented.

"I can't see," Alma Lee said.

"Here," Carney said, lifting her high to sit behind his burly neck on his shoulders. "Is that better, honey lamb?"

"Thank you," she chirped. "I got a better seat than anybody."

"I hear music," Thane said.

So did everyone else. Necks craned, and parents hauled their struggling youngsters back to their protection, as the music grew louder and sounded closer.

"Here they come," said Carney.

T. P. Starbright's Marching Tuba and Banjo Jazz Factory pranced into view, all spanked out in their bright pink uniforms. Near to twenty of them, Carney estimated, and every bandsman kicking along in perfect step. All colored guys, except one. Three slide trombones in the front rank, followed by cornets, tubas, clarinets, and a bass drum so large that it needed two men to carry it. Must have been more than half a dozen banjo players bringing up the rear.

"See that drum major," Carney said to the kids. "That's the leader, in front. That white gentleman is Mr. Tin Pan Starbright hisself."

Carney recognized the number the band was playing, as it happened to be one of his favorites, "Toot Toot Tootsie." Never had he ever heard anybody play it with more gumption. A fellow could live a whole lifetime, Carney thought, and hardly get to witness a sight any smarter than this. Or a merrier tune.

Against his upper chest, Alma Lee's little bare heels were thumping in time to the music. It was a good feeling, from a happy little girl who had lost both her folks.

"And that's Mr. T. P. Starbright?" Hiram asked.

"Bet your boots," Carney said. "Himself."

Thane pointed. "Who's the lady behind him?"

"Well," said Carney, "according to the poster I saw on a telephone pole over in Twilla this morning, she ought to be their star dancing performer, Miss Heavenly Hades."

Hiram chuckled. "What a name."

Carney laughed too. "Sells tickets."

Thank goodness, Carney was thinking, he had had the foresight to purchase four tickets, two adults and two junior, in Twilla, because he was guessing that the Kalipsa Opera House was going to be packed. The agent from whom he had bought the tickets swore that their reserved seats were in the first row, right up front.

All mouths hung agape as the assembly of pink uniforms pranced by. Carney stared at Miss Heavenly for all his money's worth, noticing without disappointment her scanty attire.

"High," he said, "she's some stepper."

"Indeed so. I hope she doesn't have to wear that outfit all winter."

Carney grinned. "I hear tell she won't even wear it all evening." The two men nudged each other. "Don't worry, High. Bert Swicegood said it was a family show. Nothing obscene."

"Good," said Hiram.

Alma Lee pointed at something other than Miss Heavenly Hades. "Look," she said, "here come the ponies."

Sure enough, they were coming. Four proud little ponies, with plumes on their heads and spangled tack, were pulling a small wagon upon which rode a steam organ. "Toot Toot Tootsie" had blown itself out, and the organist, a slightly plump lady with red hair to match her fancy gown, was fingering "Over the Waves" in waltz time. A showy sign festooned the side of her bright yellow wagon.

Madame Regina Ringfinger

"Wow," Carney admitted, "she sure can make that steam organ sit up and beg for supper."

Alma Lee said, "I like the ponies the best."

Carney turned to Hiram. "If you ask me, it's doggone decent of them show people to throw a parade before the performance. That way, the folks that are feeling the pinch of hard times can share in, even if'n they can't dig up the scratch for a ticket."

"I'll pay you back for our part of tonight's damage," Hiram told him.

"Forget it. You and Vestavia's piled my plate plenty of times. Call it square. Okay?"

"Okay, but thank you."

The parade, to no one's surprise, headed directly for the Kalipsa Opera House. Some of the better-dressed people followed, while others turned away, their sober faces reflecting the Depression.

As the four of them turned to go to the Opera House, Carney beamed. "No need for us to scamper. We got ourselfs the best doggone seats in the theater. Right smack in the front row."

"How," asked Hiram, "did you manage that?"

"Influence." Carney winked. "Bert Swicegood called me on the contraption before I was up, and told me all the news."

Inside the Opera House, however, it began to dawn on Constable Ransom that other patrons aplenty had influence as well. The front-row seats were solidly occupied by people who didn't appear to Carney as though they would be even slightly inclined to forfeit their positions.

Fumbling in his pocket, Carney produced his four ticket stubs, the other halves of which he had surrendered at the door. "Excuse me," he said generally, "but I think maybe four of you good folks just might be sitting in our seats."

Other people who stood nearby were also voicing a similar sentiment. More enthusiasts crowded to the front and said likewise, that some ticket agents had sold them preferred up-front seating.

People who sat were smiling. Those who still stood were not. Carney winced. "High, I think I've been took," he said, feeling his face beginning to redden.

Hiram held up a soothing hand. "No matter. We'll just ask Thane and Alma Lee to hunker down here on the floor." He turned to the front-row occupants. "Would it be agreeable to you good people if my two polite youngsters camped here at your feet?"

No one, Carney Ransom observed, seemed to mind in the least. In fact, one kindly matron said she would keep an eye on them, for safekeeping. High certain had a way with him,

Carney thought, and people had always been willing to treat Hiram MacHugh with courtesy. Maybe it was his cane.

The two men found seats, finally, in the rear of the auditorium.

"Sometime," Carney growled, "I'm fixing to catch up with that shifty gent in Twilla, and settle his hash."

"You never shall," Hiram said. "I'm presuming he's long gone, busily fleecing the hopefuls of distant communities."

"S'pose so."

He felt Hiram pat his arm. "It's the thought that counts, Carney, and we're all in your debt. So ease yourself back and enjoy the show."

Enjoy they did.

Mr. T. P. Starbright certainly knew how to entertain a crowd. His joke about the preacher and the stripteaser made Carney slap his beefy leg. The punch line had more than one meaning, without using any dirty words, and Carney Ransom hoped he could remember it until tomorrow, so's he could spring it on some of the boys back in Hallapoosa.

Three banjo players came forward and played three different songs, all at the same time, and it sounded really great. Then came a juggler, two tapdancers, and a guy who could rattle spoons as well as hambone his hands.

Tin Pan's impersonation of President Hoover near about had the audience throwing their hats in the air. T. P. Starbright was white, as were his two lady performers, a dancer and an organist. The band players were colored men, but the all-white applauding crowd didn't care. Music had a way of getting people together, Carney was deciding, and a trombone worked toward friendship as well as a sermon. Maybe even better.

"I'll bet your two youngsters are eating this show right up," Carney said.

"I pray so. God knows, losing both parents is a rough deal, and they are holding each other up rather well. I'm proud of them, Carney. Really proud."

"How's Vestavia doing?"

"Ruling our roost, as one might expect of Vestavia. As I clearly recall, she always dominated Bobby and me. With my brother, perhaps if I or Vestavia or my parents had been a bit more strict with him . . . who knows."

"Yeah, maybe so. Don't go on blaming yourself, High. You done good for Bobby. Always did. Best you let it heal and don't keep on picking a scab like it's a busted banjo."

Hiram nodded.

The lights dimmed.

The band struck up another number, a slow Oriental rhythm, one that made Constable Ransom lean a bit forward on his seat. His expectations were rewarded.

"And now," said Tin Pan Starbright, "the moment that you patient gentlemen out there have all been so politely waiting for." He paused for the crowd to hum anticipation. "Here she is . . . to perform for the very first time . . . an exotic dance routine that could revolutionize the American stage with its grace, its artistry . . . and . . . its *daring*. I'm proud to present . . . The Temptation Dance of Delilah."

"Who gits to be Samson?" a wit hollered out.

"Not you, sonny," Tin Pan quickly answered with a friendly smile. "Your mother wants you home for chores."

The audience howled.

"Now," he said, "the moment has come. So please allow me to present the star headliner of our show this evening . . . let's hear a big hand for the little lady . . . Miss! Heavenly! Hades!"

She got a big hand. Carney found himself contributing to the noise until both of his palms were smarting like they were on fire.

Nobody yelled "boo" when Miss Heavenly appeared fully attired in a long crimson robe. In fact, hardly anyone breathed. Item by item, Miss Heavenly discarded her wardrobe, layer beneath layer. Carney squinted, wishing he could dash out to the patrol car and fetch back his binoculars. Each garment she took off promised to be the last, yet there was always one more article of decency between the eyes of the audience and her most personal properties.

"Take it all off, honey," a male voice suggested.

"I would," said Miss Heavenly, "if you weren't wearing lace on your undies."

The crowd hooted.

A sudden storm of large colorful balloons fell from the stage ceiling. Heads all darted from side to side, in an effort to see what they knew was the finale, the big capper . . . and there it abruptly was, *her only garment,* tossed into the crowd of eager male hands. More balloons fell, but Miss Heavenly Hades had already exited, her virtue unobserved.

The show was over.

"Thank the goodness," Hiram sighed. "I was a bit worried about the children's seeing too much."

On the return trip to Hallapoosa, Alma Lee and Thane were sleeping soundly in the back seat, or so Carney thought. High sat beside him, in front.

"Some show," Carney said to Hiram. "I sure wish I'd sat closer to catch a hold of Miss Heavenly's final offering. I wonder who caught it."

Over his shoulder it came. It was tiny, spangled, silky pink, with a tempting perfumed aroma. In dismay, Carney stared at it.

"Here," said Thane. "It's all yours, Mr. Ransom."

"Well," said Carney, as he weighed the almost weightless article in his hand, "I guess you're Bobby's boy."

Hiram sighed.

· *Thirteen* ·

"**C**ome sit," Vestavia Holcum said.

"If'n I can waddle that far," the younger woman replied as she came to visit her friend.

The outside chair that Vestavia was sitting in was older than she was, tied together with lengths of frayed rope. One of its arms had been missing ever since Vestavia could recall. The chair creaked as she stood up to greet Tally Thurman.

"A nice evening," Vestavia said, glancing upward at a darkening sky.

"Good enough." Tally eyed the sorry chair, patted her hips, and then shook her head. "Little bird woman, you don't s'pect a milk cow like me to squeeze down on *that*. I just might collapse it and bust my beauty."

Both ladies cackled.

"Sit," Tally said. "You old enough to be my mama, and plenty more. I'll just squat here on the stoop ledge."

As they sat together silently, six or seven children ran by, whooping and chasing each other. The two smallest were naked, their little black bodies covered only by dirt.

Tally grunted. "The way some folks allow their little ones to show all they got. I certain never let none of mine prance around like that. Deed no."

"Me neither." Vestavia shook her head. "It's that Bunkum bunch who lives in that fall-down shack at road's end. They come here from up Tampa way. An old granny about useless as me, a mama, and children close to a dozen."

"Ain't no earning man?"

"No."

Tally sighed. "Hardly ever is. Our bucks ramble away and leave us to raise and care."

Vestavia was silent. All of what Tally was saying, she knew, got proved true. Her man had left, long ago, as had the menfolk who had daddied the children of her daughters. Upped and scattered.

"Only the Lord knows how youngsters would raise," Tally said, "without us mamas and grannies to do for them. So we does and does, on account they's nobody else."

Vestavia slapped a stinger bug.

Whenever the wind changed to blow from the swamp, the bugs would come along as well. Hot weather, like the kind that had been persisting lately, always brought more bugs than hands could shoo away. Had a way of breeding children too. Closing her eyes, Vestavia remembered being a young gal in the moonlight, naked as the road-end kids who had recent run by her shack. But alone with her man.

"How's your two little whites?" Tally asked.

"Prospering, thank you. I don't know yet if Mr. Hiram will prosper too. But if I know their uncle, he'll do for them in his way."

Tally looked at her. "How's that mean?"

"He will provide."

Tally snorted. "Takes a lot more'n *provide* to raise."

To herself, Vestavia was agreeing. There had always been a sadness inside Judge MacHugh, one she had failed to heal. Not just a single sad. There were many inside Mr. Hiram, some of which she knew entirely, and others about which Vestavia had always prayed she could shut her eyes.

For ten or so days, Vestavia was hoping that the coming of Thane and Alma Lee would brighten Mr. Hiram's life. Nothing of the kind had happened. True enough, he spoke to his niece and nephew, yet almost as though he greeted strangers who had stopped on a street corner to ask a direction to somewhere else.

"He don't touch," Vestavia whispered.

"What you say, woman?"

"Nothing. It was gas from supper."

"Is the Judge quit that Cricker gal?"

Vestavia frowned at Tally. "Lady, you watch your tongue. MacHughs be decent white people. So best you speak proper on Mr. Hiram. You hear?"

"I hear." Tally paused. "I hear lots."

"Plenty besides praying gits spoke in Hallapoosa and always has," Vestavia told her. "And when it do, this old granny turn herself deaf as a stump."

"Seems to me, a MacHugh could up and murder somebody, and you'd call it dancing."

"Maybe so." Vestavia pointed a thin little finger at her neighbor. "But I work my life in that house. Nobody going to foe Mr. MacHugh to me. Or soil him."

"You blind, woman."

Yes, Vestavia was quietly agreeing, so I am. And that is my choosing, to blind myself to the sorry matters so's to look at the sweet.

"He is quality. That be how I help to raise Mr. Hiram, to grow up proper. Mr. Hiram treat many a Hallapoosa soul with kind goodness, be they a Singletary or a Callister."

Tally kept silent.

Vestavia guessed that Tally Thurman was itching to ask more questions, to find out if that Cricker gal still knocked at Mr. Hiram's back door on Saturday evening. She probable wanted to know if that piece of Yoobarr trash come too, to peddle his liquids. Well, Vestavia decided, Tally would have to do learning with her hungry ear leaning close to somebody else's lips, and not hers.

"Mr. Hiram got raised a gentleman," she said.

How she was wishing she had put a harder switch to Mr. Bobby, years back. Vestavia knew. Because that old white witch flashed money before she died. MacHugh money. That old Mrs. Simpson, the midwife. She claimed it be the constable who'd handed it to her, but that witch knew where the cash money originated. From the Judge. And then Mrs. Simpson said that as the child got born, the Callister girl was crying out a name.

Bobby.

Vestavia's mouth tightened as she looked at Tally. My secrets, Vestavia silently promised, will die inside me, and go when I go. Many a young white Hallapoosa lady, in trouble, got rid of matters with Mrs. Simpson's help.

White folks, Vestavia Holcum had long ago concluded, were so different than niggers. No decent colored woman would ever dream of knifing her unborn to death, then to claim it never happened. Or leave town "to visit her aunt" as white people claimed, like to birth a baby be shameful.

Vestavia had been proud to drop her babies, each and every one, and she had raised her daughters to bear in pride. It was a joy of being Holcum.

"Maybe," she said to the evening, "our only joy."

"Old woman," said Tally Thurman, "I s'pose you suffering your gas again. Funny, how your gas bubble out in talk."

Vestavia smiled.

It made no sense to scold Tally for trying to understand. She was only being a friend, one who was guessing that her olden neighbor had more MacHugh loads to carry.

"Excuse me, Tally. You'll turn gray someday too."

"Feel old already. Leeman is too much manchild for me to stand over. Elston, he going to be another one. Hang around with the toughs and be street niggers." Tally slapped a fat thigh. "Not under my roof they doesn't."

"Gals raise easier," Vestavia said.

Tally nodded. "They certain do. Both my Bessie and Earline is settled and busy raising up their own. Left town to find work. But that Leeman, he don't sweat hardly a lick, except to whisper he got a *deal* going. Deal? If he wander in home tonight, too late, this big old hand is fixing to deal with his smart nigger backside."

"They be good boys, Tally. At church, they's always so respecting and proper. Why, a person would think they be Moffet and Singletary."

Tally smiled. "Good to hear. Lord Above knows I try to put *straight* into them. A fair measure of it." She sighed. "Too soon both Leeman and little Elston stretch up to men."

"That be the way of it. So enjoy 'em now, Tally Thurman, while you can still do for them. Ain't easy to raise quality boys. Some shine like gold, but others are mostly rust."

As she spoke, Vestavia was remembering Mr. Hiram and Mr. Bobby. Nobody could say they were two peas. Her mind shifted to Alma Lee and Thane, the fruit of Bobby MacHugh. Well, he had sired beautiful children. Alma Lee could be fresher than wet paint, then turn around one time and act sweeter than a peach. Thane might become a Mr. Bobby or a Mr. Hiram, and Vestavia could not decide which way that manchild would go. For that boy, his daddy's dying could turn out a blessing.

Again and again, Vestavia Holcum had prayed to the Lord that the dark secrets of Hallapoosa remain in the quiet shadows. Nobody need know. She had thanked God that the old white witch, Mrs. Simpson, had died off sudden. Forgive me, Vestavia was thinking, for wishing a death to some other person, even to a baby-killing witch woman. It was the woman's silence and not her death for which Vestavia Holcum was thankful.

"Truly be," Tally was saying. "But I didn't believe a word of it, and you know there ain't no hope trying to wheedle Cassie to do more than breathe fresh air."

Tally was telling more, about how she'd spoke to Cassie Bellows, a woman who sang in their church choir. The subject had something to do with their preacher, Reverend Micah Fewsmith, and last Sunday's sermon, but Vestavia Holcum was paying Tally little mind. That was a blessing of years. An old woman was always allowed to sit quiet, not expected to keep up with whatever was getting said, or what needed doing. She could shrink back to hide inside herself.

"Old women," Vestavia said softly, "be turtles."

Tally Thurman looked at her, eyebrows raising, as though confused at what Vestavia had said.

"You asleep?" she asked Vestavia.

"I'm near to. My lambs wear me out somedays. Don't have the gumption no more."

"I s'pose the Judge paying you extra."

"We in hard times, Tally. You know that."

Tally stretched out a leg as though to loosen her stiffness. "Still all, I think the Judge ought to sweeten your kitty a dollar. Maybe more. It's only right. Justice of the Peace in a white suit of clothes rakes in plenty of scratch. Your Mr. MacHugh's been housing alone, with not a chick or a child to feed and dress, so I don't guess the Judge is anyhow close to flat busted."

"Mr. Hiram is—is prospering," Vestavia lied, knowing that about every stick of furniture in the MacHugh house was as worn as a hall rug.

"All the reason he ought to spread a little your way, woman. Kick in some bonus. If you took a misery, how would you live?"

"I'd git by," Vestavia said.

Tally stood up slowly, groaning, as the boards of Vestavia's modest porch also groaned, perhaps in relief.

"Best I go."

"Thank you for coming to see me, Tally."

"I come visit you near to every night, you know that. Just to see if you keeping sound."

Vestavia nodded.

Rising from her broken chair, she walked a step or two with her large friend. Her ankles were hurting fearful, yet Vestavia would not express her discomfort to Tally Thurman. Ache was a private thing, a secret that nobody else could share, a one-mule burden.

Tally turned to face her. "I see the young MacHugh boy walking home with you recent, far as the line, the way the Judge used to do. He a fine-looking child. Appear like you cleaned him up before supper."

Vestavia Holcum smiled.

"Thank you, Tally. I want Mr. Hiram's kin to dress rightly. It wouldn't be fitting for anybody in Hallapoosa to see them looking shabby."

Tally touched her hand. "Nobody do."

Standing in her dooryard, she watched Tally's big body moving away in the darkness, heading for her own shack. Again, she smiled. Tally Thurman had a heart to go with her size.

Returning slowly to her chair, then sitting, Vestavia rubbed her swollen ankles with skinny fingers. Soon it would be Sunday again, and she could go to church wearing her white gloves, the ones that had been worn by Mr. Hiram's mother. She was hoping that Reverend Micah would select hymns she knew by heart . . . perhaps "Sweet Hour of Prayer."

Closing her eyes, Vestavia began to sing the words to herself, blessing each phrase as it also blessed her, and allowing the meaning to bathe her clean.

"I don't want to go to bed yet," she said.

Tomorrow, she knew, there would be so much to do. Yet the

thought of doing it pleased her, because a birthday for a child was always a special day. A *birth* day.

Alma Lee and Thane were hers now. All hers, because Mr. Hiram spent more time downtown at the courthouse. So they were hers to raise, to touch or to scold, and to reward with some special baking. Tomorrow, it would be a birthday cake, all milky white with icing and dotted with rainbow candy gems, aglow with candles. It felt so good to pretend that Bobby and Hiram were still small. With her pair of new responsibilities, in a way they were all youngsters again.

Folding her hands in her lap, she remembered the little ones, two generations, that she had helped to raise and form. Both colors, like Bible sheep.

"My proper lambs."

· *Fourteen* ·

"**C**limb down."

Alma Lee was standing beneath Miss Sellie's camphor tree, holding her doll and looking so straight-up high it was beginning to cramp her neck.

Her brother was already starting to think that he was the biggest onion in the patch, just because today was his birthday, and he'd turned thirteen. Well, Alma Lee was thinking, Thane MacHugh wasn't the boss around here just yet. She knew who was *boss* . . . and it wasn't the Judge.

"Vestavia says I'm to coax you down out of that tree, so you can wash up for supper." Alma took a deep breath in order to shout the important part. "Or else she's fixing to scamper up that tree and fetch you into hot water that'll fry your hide."

"Now that I'm thirteen," Thane hollered down to her, "I bet I can climb up a lot higher than here."

Alma Lee sighed.

It had not been the happiest of days. Several times, but mostly since their noon meal, Vestavia had ordered her to keep clear of the kitchen, because something right special was baking in the oven, and a lot of heavy foot-stomping might cause it to fall to busted.

When she finally turned eight, Alma Lee was considering, she doubted very much if Vestavia would fuss so much about *her* birthday. Not since the everyday battle had started. Alma Lee had already suggested to Hiram that he fix himself rid of Vestavia, and sudden quick.

"Uncle Hiram," she had said several times, "if you want my opinion, Vestavia's too olden to work so hard. Maybe if she found herself a housekeep job somewhere else, things would run a lot better around here."

"Oh really?" her uncle had asked.

"Yes," Alma Lee said. "Besides, I'm going to be eight someday, so best I start to handle the cooking myself, all by my lonesome."

"And what would you cook?"

"Well, it won't be collards," she told him.

"I see."

"And another thing. I certain won't waste so much time peeking at other people's hands and knees, to inspect if they look tidy. And I don't guess I'll parade around our kitchen saying *proper.*"

"It may surprise you, Alma Lee," her uncle replied, "but when I was your age, a long time ago, Vestavia said *proper* to me more than once."

"Seems like if we send Vestavia packing," she said, "we ought to do it soon."

"Why soon?"

"On account that my skin is fixing to disappear. Or maybe melt away because of so much scrubbing, the way Vestavia's bar of sink soap does."

"She only wants you looking clean."

"But I'm not the laundry. I don't belong to old Vestavia. I belong to you. Thane says Vestavia's okay and she cooks better than anybody in the whole world. That's because she doesn't snake *him* over to the sink."

"So you're recommending that I discharge Vestavia."

"I certain am . . . if that means she'll get fired. Then maybe I can have a minute's peace. When she's gone, I guess I'll go visit in the kitchen any time I doggone please."

"Ah, and does Claudine agree to all this?"

Alma Lee was silent for a minute, remembering how Vestavia had repaired Claudine last week, when her doll was looking and feeling a mite poorly. But then Alma Lee recalled how Vestavia had even washed Claudine and hung her, *upside down,* out on the sunshine line to dry. She told her uncle all about it.

"I bet Claudine got soap in her eye," Alma Lee stated, "the

same way it gets in mine when Vestavia dumps all that sissy suds in my hair."

"Now then," Uncle Hiram told her, "as soon as you become eight years old, and assume all of the dusting, cooking, washing, ironing, and cleaning both the upstairs and down, perhaps we'll consider sending Vestavia away. Then you shall have our kitchen all to yourself, preparing the meals and paring all of the potatoes, as well as emptying the stove ashes, doing the dishes, and walloping all the dirty pots and pans. Oh yes, and mopping the kitchen floor every day."

After that, Alma Lee had spoken less often about getting free of Vestavia. Perhaps, she had decided, she could somehow train Vestavia into keeping her proper nose where it properly belonged, and leaving the soap to rest for a breather.

Thane was still up in the camphor tree, climbing even higher. But then she saw Uncle Hiram coming home from the courthouse. He'd be able to command him down to ground.

"Thane won't come. But if you're the Judge, seems like you could order him to do it."

She watched her uncle hook the curve of his cane over his left forearm, then cuff back the floppy white hat in order to squint upward at her brother. His face seemed to freeze, as though he was wandering off somewhere, to another day, another time.

Alma Lee saw him swallow.

"If you come down, Thane," he said in an even voice, "I'll just imagine that Vestavia might have something special in your honor. And we also have somebody coming for supper, a very nice guest for your party."

"Who's coming?" Thane yelled down.

"It's a surprise. So hustle, but take caution you don't become careless and fall. You'd hate to spoil your birthday."

Saying no more, her uncle unhooked his cane and walked slowly toward the house. Alma Lee stood wishing that her Uncle Hiram would pick her up and swing her around, just one time, the way her daddy sometimes had done when he came home from work. Then she realized that Daddy had not performed this trick for a long time. And late years, not really at all. Hardly ever. Back home, there had been yelling and fighting and throwing things. Cussing too. Words that grown-up people shouldn't use "in front of the children," so they claimed.

"Claudine," she said, "you're lucky being a doll. You don't get hung upside down as much as I do."

Her thoughts were interrupted when Thane landed with a surprising thud, on both feet, close to where she was standing.

"What's it like to be thirteen?"

He smiled. "It's really great. I feel taller and stronger, and smarter, like someday I'm going to wave so-long to Hallapoosa and go fistfight the world."

Alma Lee sighed. "Well, I shouldn't be telling you this, but seeing it's your birthday and all . . . "

"Tell me what?"

"I don't want you to go away to the world. I'd miss you awful. Maybe not a whole lot, but Claudine would miss you."

Thane grinned. "Did she say so?"

"Sure did. Besides, if you went away and I got scared at night, there wouldn't be anybody across the hall to jump in bed with." Alma Lee paused. "How old are boys when they final go to the world?"

He poked her ribs. "Thirteen."

"Honest?"

Throwing back his head, Thane laughed. "I don't guess I'll be leaving tonight, because it's my birthday. But come tomorrow morning, reckon I'll be near halfway to India, or maybe South America."

Dropping her doll, Alma Lee rushed to him, wrapping both her arms around his chest, pressing her face close to his shirt. Thane always smelled like a *boy*.

"No . . . don't go away. Please don't. If you up and leave here, I'd just about die."

She felt his hands on her shoulders. "Hey," he said, "take it easy. I was only kidding you, little sister. Really. Besides, when I go away someday, I'll probable take you along too."

"You will?" she asked, releasing her hold.

"Sure. Trouble is, you'd possible miss Vestavia so much that you'd cry all the time, and then I would have to stuff you into a crate and ship you back here to Hallapoosa, to get washed." Bending down, he picked up Claudine, dusted her off, and handed the doll to his sister. "Come on. Uncle Hiram's home,

• 96 •

so let's take a trip inside and get cleaned up for supper. The old Judge expects us to mind what Vestavia tells us. Okay?"

"Okay."

In a few minutes, their surprise visitor arrived at the front door. As Alma Lee answered the knock, she was glad it was Miss Sellie from next door. In her hand was a small round present, neatly wrapped in a red bow and white tissue paper, the kind that whispered when it was crinkled.

"Happy birthday," Miss Sellie said to Thane, handing him her gift. "But you can't open it right away."

"Why not?" Alma Lee wanted to know.

"Because half the pleasure's in wondering what it is. It's a mite like when you're outdoors and you smell supper cooking through an open window. And waiting to taste it is the honey on the biscuit."

Miss Sellie kissed Thane on the top of his head, then kissed Alma Lee too. Alma Lee was surprised when Miss Sellie even kissed Uncle Hiram as well. It took courage, she thought, to kiss *him*.

Vestavia had placed fresh flowers from Miss Sellie's garden in the very center of the dining-room table, which had been set for four people. There was little use, Alma Lee knew, in asking Vestavia to sit with everybody else and make it five. Uncle Hiram had explained why, that Vestavia knew her place, and Thane and Alma Lee were not allowed to question whatever Vestavia knew was quality manners.

As she ate, Alma Lee had to admit that supper was something really special. Extra good. Brisket beef and *no collards*. In a fresh white apron, Vestavia kept on toting one delicious thing after another from the kitchen to the dining-room table, and she didn't even scowl when Alma Lee slopped a drip of brisket gravy on the white lace tablecloth. And not a single word came from Vestavia's direction concerning feet or President Hoover.

"My," said Miss Sellie, "I wish Thane turned thirteen every day, so I could stuff myself to busting like this. I best not eat another bite for a week."

Alma Lee started to get up to help porter the meat dishes back to the kitchen, but a warning hand informed her shoulder that she was to remain seated. Vestavia's hand was silent, but firm.

"I don't allow nobody in my kitchen tonight," Vestavia announced in her army voice. "What's to come is a surprise . . . for Mr. Thane."

Alma Lee stared at Vestavia, wondering if her ears were working correctly. *Mister* Thane? It had always been Mr. Hiram, and Vestavia always called Miss Sellie by Mrs. Fulsom . . . but this was a new twist. A clean napkin covering the pan of hot rolls was one thing, but a Mister for Thane was sure another.

Thane was all smiles.

"I believe," said Alma Lee, "I just might reward myself with another roll. Would you please pass me one, Mr. Thane?" Taking a hurried sip of milk, the comedy caught up with her, and Alma Lee coughed some milk on her dress front.

"Serves you right," Thane said. "Maybe if you'd *drink* your milk instead of *breathing* it, you might become a proper lady, Miss Alma Lee."

Uncle Hiram flashed him a brief look, not stern, but hardly joyous. As Alma Lee turned to look at Miss Sellie, their guest winked at her, as if to say she understood little girls who had to contend with big-onion brothers.

Still and all, Alma Lee was thinking, it really wasn't quite fair. Thane wasn't acting bad, not exactly, yet was being called *Mr.* Thane. Whenever she was either late or dirty, sometimes both, Vestavia addressed her as Miss Alma Lee MacHugh. The Miss usual stood for misstep. No, it wasn't fair at all.

Vestavia had retired to the kitchen and had not reappeared. Cocking an ear, Alma Lee thought she heard a match being struck, but wasn't quite sure. But then in marched Vestavia holding a large white cake, aglow with candles. Thirteen of them. Lettering on top of the white frosting said THANE. It was something real fancy, with tiny little sugar candies sprinkled all over.

Uncle Hiram cleared his throat.

Raising his water glass, he toasted, "To my nephew, Mr. Thane Hiram MacHugh, upon the event of his becoming thirteen."

They sang "Happy Birthday to You" . . . and even Vestavia sang along too. Thane made a wish and blew out all of his candles. The cake was special delicious, because, according to

Vestavia, it had taken almost a dozen egg whites, and Miss Sellie commented that it was lighter than a moonlight kiss in June, whatever that meant.

Thane opened Miss Sellie's present. It wasn't new. It looked to Alma Lee as being a bit used, but Thane was happier than a dance, because the baseball had a name written on it.

Somebody named Ty Cobb.

Miss Sellie said that the baseball had belonged to her departed husband, Mr. Dewey Fulsom and God rest his soul, and it had been one of his very prized possessions. And were he alive, he would have wanted it to go to Bobby MacHugh's son. The real Ty Cobb was a famous baseballer and had signed his name on the ball, up in Georgia, in person.

Everybody kissed Thane except, Alma Lee noticed, Uncle Hiram. He never kissed or hugged anybody at all, and probable never had.

After the supper was over, Miss Sellie had to depart for home, but not before Thane insisted that she carry a wedge of his birthday cake along with her, to feed Charlie Moon Sky. When he said it, Miss Sellie looked very pleased. So did Vestavia. As Miss Sellie was leaving, taking the cake on a little plate for Charlie, she turned to Thane and kissed him once more.

"It's fitting," she told Thane. "It's so blessed fitting to learn that your middle name is Hiram."

· *Fifteen* ·

"**R**un!" Glory screamed to Lot.

It was too late for her to escape, because old Kelby had her cornered in the shack, and she prayed her daddy wouldn't hurt Lotty.

"You ain't no good to me," Kelby yelled at her. "Ain't no good to me at all."

His fist crashed against her face.

"Daddy . . . please don't . . ."

Again he struck her, first with one hand and then the other, until everything in the shack was a whirling blur. During the beating and pounding, Glory thought of nothing except her child. Would he have sense enough to stay away and hide himself safe? Covering her face with both hands, Glory continued begging Kelby to stop, yet he kicked and kicked until she was nauseous with the pain.

"Damn you, girl." He kicked her harder. "I ain't got a job no more. Can't ya savvy that? Them dirty bastards at the turp let me go. Fired me." He paused to regain his breath. "You ain't brung me no money near to a week."

"No money around," Glory tried to tell him.

He slapped her across the eyes. "For a slut they's always a dollar. You gotta cut your fancy price, you hear? Unless ya bring me some cash, I'll kill ya." Kelby panted. "I'm fixing to whack you to death with my bare hands."

Glory sobbed. "Ain't no money."

Grabbing her throat, he held her close to him. Glory could smell his hot body pressing down on her.

"Don't . . . don't do it on me. Please."

"I don't want your sugar, whore gal. I got my pride. What I want is something to eat, money to trade with. And I need me a drink too. Real bad." He shook her. "If'n I find your brat kid, I'll sell the little bugger, sell'm downcrick, and you won't see Lotty no more."

"Please . . . please . . ."

"You ain't no good, Glory. Never was! You don't know nothing and you can't earn nothing no more." Kelby spat into her face. "Maybe you're too wore out for a man to want your sugar. Soon you'll look old and ugly as me. How'll ya like that?"

As his fingers were tightening on her throat, Glory fought for breath, trying to loosen his grip with her hands. She kicked at him where it would hurt most, and saw his face wincing in pain. So she kicked him again, meaner, as hard as she could.

Kelby hollered.

When she saw Lotty standing in the doorway, she screamed. "Lotty, go run. Please."

Her daddy turned to look, but the boy darted away, as Glory kept hollering to warn him not to come back.

"I'll git ya, Lotty," her daddy was saying. "I know where you hide, and I'm coming to git ya, and *sell* ya."

Kelby pushed her down again, but as she fell against the rough wood wall, Glory's hand found a hammer. Cocking it, she hit her father on the cheekbone. She hit him again, this time with more force, and thought she heard a bone shatter.

Kelby was crying, holding his bleeding face in both hands, kneeling on the shack floor.

"You . . . ," he whimpered. "You . . ."

Despite her hurting, Glory leaped to her feet, stepped over her crumbling father and made for the door. It was dark outside, with no moon, or perhaps it was because her face and eyes were swelling to a point where she could no longer see clearly.

"Lot!"

No answer.

Dropping the hammer on the rocks, Glory cupped both hands to her mouth to call louder. Because of the earlier rain, the crick was running stronger, high enough to drown Glory's calling to her son. Even had Lotty been as close as a few yards away, Glory knew, he would be unable to hear his name.

"Lot! Lot!"

Perhaps he had slipped on the wet rocks, fallen into the deep of the stream, and been washed away. The thought almost strangled her. Although covered with her own blood, Glory felt nothing, not even pain, except the need to locate her child. She wondered why the night seemed to be darkening. Try as she would, Glory could not find the hammer, yet remembered the sharp clattering sound it had made on the rocks as she dropped it.

"Lot?"

Did he go upcrick, or down?

Glory could not see. Had her son been standing directly before her, she would hardly have been able to recognize him. Cupping her hands to her mouth, she inhaled deeply, preparing to call his name again. Yet she was never allowed to do so. She heard cussing. A stone hit her head. Pitching forward, she fell into the water, knowing little except that the sucking current was cold and was knocking her against rocks.

Her fingers clutched at the shore, feeling no grip, the ferns and moss tearing loose in her hands.

As a sharp twig stabbed her face, Glory grabbed it, hung tightly, and slowly managed to feel the thicker branches of a fallen tree guiding her into shallower water. Stumbling to the shore, she crawled upward on a wet bank, tried to stand, then fainted.

Glory tasted mud.

Raising her head, she attempted to spit but could not, because her lips were too swollen. Her finger helped to remove some of the slime; then, hanging her face downward, Glory let the cricky mud ooze out of her, and fall.

It was still nearly impossible to see. Glory's one thought now was to escape her father and get away from the island, as far as she could. She kept thinking that Lotty was dead, or had run away to Kalipsa. Maybe by now he was grown up, married, with children of his own. The picture of a happy family of smiling faces beamed into her brain. Little of it made any reason. Was she in Kalipsa Ferry? Where is Halla-poosa?

And where's Lot?

Stumbling, often falling, then regaining her feet and bal-ance, Glory Callister headed away from the sound of crick water. She had to run away. Houses seemed to be sprouting all around, homes with lights, electricity. It was juice that turned things on, like at Hiram's place, and the Hallapoosa Hotel down the road on the outskirts of town, a place she had visited many times, with gentlemen. Some had not always been gentle, and Glory was wondering if this was the reason her face was so painful and puffy.

A whippoorwill sounded its call.

Glancing upward, Glory Callister squinted at the tree now spreading above her. A big old camphor tree. Something made her aware that she had seen this tree before. For one thing, a camphor tree this large was uncommon. One just like it grew between Hiram's house and the place next door. But looking straight up made her dizzy. The world spun. Glory fell again.

Lying on the cool ground, Glory was trying to remember where Lotty had gone. Had she passed out again? Rising to her knees, she covered her face with her hands, reacting instantly to the agony of her own touch. Realizing that she could not handle what was happening by herself, she wanted help from Hiram. He would be the only person in Hallapoosa who could understand, and perhaps assist her in locating her son before Kelby did.

Nearby, the houses that had once been lighted were now dark, yet she knew which house was Hiram's. As always, he would be there alone, waiting for her.

Was today Saturday?

Yes. So she best go to Hiram. Why did the houses look the same? Which home was Hiram MacHugh's? Gaining her feet, Glory stumbled forward through a stand of weeds, finally reached a rear door, and pounded on it with her fists.

In the dark, Glory waited.

Her deadened mind wondered where she was, who she was, where she could go. Was there no escape from old Kelby? Touching her body, she felt her dress caked with dirt, a tangle of bark, leaves, and damp mud.

"Lot," she said weakly.

Her body felt brittle, broken, less than alive, yet longing to live for Lotty and for a someday that now seemed to be beyond her grasp. A mirage of faces danced in her mind . . . Hiram, Lot, Kelby . . . and another face of years past, Bobby Mac-Hugh. Oh, what a beautiful young man Bobby was, standing before her, smiling, looking at her up and down, causing her to feel like she was a woman for the very first time.

"No," she said to the darkness, "it ain't Bobby no more." It's Hiram, sweet old Hiram MacHugh who cared, loved, touching her with such gentleness as no other man had ever touched.

But her daddy was fixing to sell Lotty, for money, to somebody afar off, and she would never see her child again. He'd be clean gone. Nobody would know where Lot was. If they did, they wouldn't dare tell, because of Kelby and his mean streak. No wonder they didn't want him around the turpentine mill, because her father had turned too ornery to work alongside other folks. No pay. And there weren't no spare money to bring home, to force old Kelby to promise that he wouldn't touch her child. Or touch her.

Someone opened a door.

Glory heard a voice asking, "Who are you?"

She tried to answer, yet could not. Glancing up, Glory saw a little girl holding a doll. The child's face was looking at her with wide-eyed surprise.

"I'm Alma Lee," she said. "How come you're bleeding? You best not come in the kitchen all covered with dirt, because Vestavia will scrub you raw the same way she does to me."

A boy appeared, standing close to the little girl as though to protect her. "What's wrong?" he asked. "Who is it?"

"Help me . . . please," Glory managed to say.

"I'll help her, Alma Lee. You go wake up Uncle Hiram and hurry."

Glory tried to stand, but her legs seemed too weak to support her weight. As she pitched forward, the boy caught her, guiding her into a dimly lit kitchen. It looked familiar to Glory, as though she had been here before, and she was wondering why the young boy had mentioned Hiram's name. He helped her into a chair and she leaned on the table, lowering her head to rest upon her arms.

"What's happening? Who is this person?"

The sleepy voice she recognized. Hiram's. A kind voice, one which bore no resentment of an intruder, not even in the middle of the night. His tone was only one of concern.

"Alma Lee found her," the boy said. "She came to the kitchen door and knocked. I heard it too."

"Turn a light on," Hiram said. "Without my glasses, I can't see much of anything, or anyone, in the dark."

As she raised her head, a sharp light almost blinded Glory. Her face was hurting, throbbing, as though Kelby was still beating her with his fists, and kicking her.

"Dear God," she heard Hiram say. Then she felt his hands touching her, gently exploring to learn where she had been cut and bruised. "Thane," he said, "please take your sister upstairs. Please go, both of you."

"I want to see," the little girl said.

"Please go upstairs, Alma Lee. You too, Thane, and take her with you. Right now."

Glory heard footsteps. The children were leaving, obeying Hiram's instruction, whispering to each other as their bare feet were climbing the stairs.

"Hiram," she tried to say.

He touched her again. "I'm right here. Glory . . . Glory . . . what happened to you? Were you in an accident? Did someone do this to you?"

"Hiram . . ."

"Yes, I'm here. You'll be safe now." Moving away from her, he filled a basin of water at a sink, added something to it, then returned. "Let me bathe you. I'll do it very carefully, I promise, and try not to hurt you." He paused. "We MacHughs have harmed you enough." As the damp cloth touched her face, Glory winced, feeling as if she were again being beaten. The water smelled sweetly of lilac. "Who did this?" Hiram asked.

"Kelby."

"Your own father brutalized you?" Hiram shook his head. "I believe you, but it's just too difficult to accept how a man . . . even Kelby Callister . . . could . . . could . . . " His voice cracked. Then regaining composure, Hiram said, "As soon as I clean you up, I'm tempted to telephone Carney. Nobody in this town ought to get away with this and be allowed to run around loose."

"No," she said, "Kelby'll kill Lot."

Glory heard Hiram wringing the rag into water, dipping it again, wringing again. It was on her face now, barely touching her, yet she felt Hiram's love with every soft angelic touch.

"Glory," he said. "My sweet Glory."

"It hurted so. My mouth is all puff swelled and I can't see you clear."

"There, there . . . you'll be all right soon. In the morning, I'll locate some ice if I can. Our icebox isn't working too well. The lady who lives next-door will loan ice to us."

"Lot . . . Lot."

"I'll find Lot, I promise." He glanced at his kitchen clock. "Soon it will be daybreak, and I'll go find Lotty and bring him to you."

"Hiram . . . I'm sorry . . . but I don't have nobody."

"It's all right." Gently he used a kitchen knife to cut away her clothing, bathed her, and then brought her one of his enormous nightshirts. "Here, I'll slip you into this. Careful now. Let me do it."

She felt him half carrying and partly dragging her to his downstairs bedroom. Everything felt soft, dark, with a fragrance that was fresh and clean and inviting.

Best of all, it smelled of Hiram.

· *Sixteen* ·

Selma Fulsom lay in bed.

Opening her eyes, she noticed the early dawn teasing her east window, bringing the promise of a cheery Sunday morning.

Before rising, Miss Sellie began her daily ritual. "Thank you, God, for bringing us your gift of another good day. And bless you, dear Jesus, for loving us all, even useless old crones like me."

Starting to move her hands, Selma winced from the stinging pain, disciplining herself not to think of the word *aspirin*. "I'll turn my stomach as sour as my disposition," she said with half a smile. Mornings, she knew, were always the troublesome time for anyone with arthritis. Her fingers felt more brittle than twigs in a Yankee winter, yet she made herself wiggle her hands, aware now of every knuckle crying out in alarm.

"Wake up, you old joints."

Get yourself going, she was ordering herself, and try doing something useful. Lifting her head, she spotted Abercrombie still asleep at her feet, his buff body curled into a mound of contented repose. What a dear old thing he was. Fair company. Always around when she needed someone to gossip with, and too often rubbing himself between her shoes whenever she was baking.

"Someday," she told him, "I'll probable trip over you and perish the pair of us."

Working her hands made her eyes water from the stiffness, yet Miss Sellie continued her exercising by sitting up to stroke her cat. Touching his warmth and softness always seemed to help her fingers enjoy a fresh day.

"Up," she said. "Because it's Sunday morn, and your lady friend here has to find her church clothes."

As her fingers became more awake, so did her memory. In the night, Selma had overheard some strange noises coming from Hiram's place next door. Nothing loud, and perhaps it had only been the leftovers of birthday excitement. Yet she had heard the children chattering away about something. Then all became quiet and her sleep had peacefully returned.

Getting out of bed, she moved to her north window, looked out into the mist and saw somethiing that caused her a start. Charlie Moon Sky was with somebody in the back yard, and it looked to be a small boy. The two of them were coming toward her back door and Charlie was carrying the child in his arms.

Hurriedly, she slipped into her robe, not even bothering to pin up her long white hair, and almost leaped down the stairs. She met both of them at her kitchen door. There stood Charlie, smiling at her as he always did, holding a boy who appeared to be a little older than seven, about the age of Alma Lee. The child was dirty beyond pardon. But what really captured Miss Sellie's attention was his eyes, wide and frightened, as if expecting a scolding or severe punishment.

"Who is he, Charlie?"

Her handyman pointed back toward the crick, but said absolutely nothing in the way of explanation. But then he smiled again, and offered her a brief reply.

"I find him."

"Does he have any folks?"

Miss Sellie nearly fainted away as Charlie Moon Sky looked directly at Hiram's house. "His sister go there. Glory Sunshine Hair."

As Miss Sellie glanced at the MacHugh's, she saw a light burning in Hiram's kitchen. How strange, she was thinking, recalling so many past Sundays when Hiram had wasted in bed, recovering from his problem.

"Please bring him into the kitchen." To her dismay, Charlie entered her home for the very first time, still holding the frightened child. "My name's Miss Sellie. Now then, I'd imagine you have a name too, and I want you to tell us *your* name."

No answer.

Well, she was thinking, it was sorry enough to have one boy, Charlie, who would hardly say "boo," and now she found herself with two. Three, counting Abercrombie, who had just strolled casually into the kitchen, his tail high. Bending, she picked up her cat, holding it as Charlie held the boy.

"See," Miss Sellie said, "I have a little one too, and his name is Abercrombie. He's a pleasant gentleman, and I'm sure he wouldn't mind if you petted his head."

As she stepped closer to the child in Charlie's arms, the boy reacted by clinging to Charlie, shrinking away, as though afraid.

So, she was thinking, Hiram MacHugh wasn't mending his ways. The suspicion nagged at her conscience. How, she asked herself, can I call myself a good Christian and a Methodist if I suspect evil of my neighbors, on a Sunday morning to boot? Silently she chastised herself.

Another peculiar thought pestered her.

Why did Charlie refer to the Callister girl as this boy's sister? Perhaps she was. Then again, perhaps she wasn't, as this soiled little boy could be the girl's child. The impact of a sorry notion almost caused Miss Sellie to drop Abercrombie. There was certainly a MacHugh look on that scruffy little boy's face. She knew that look as well as she knew her own kitchen.

Miss Sellie swallowed.

"Charlie, please give me a minute to catch my breath." She paused. "I think you had best run over to next door, and tell Judge MacHugh that we have an unexpected visitor." She thought for a moment. "No, never mind. I'll do it myself." Miss Sellie told him to clean up the boy as best he could, while she was boiling oatmeal for the two of them. She sprinkled a generous spoonful of brown sugar on both bowls, fixing nothing for herself.

"I can't eat," she muttered.

While Charlie fed the boy, and himself, Selma Fulsom dashed upstairs to change into her church dress. Her hands still smarted as she eased each button into a buttonhole.

"Lord, please guide me this day," she said, "because I'm

about to stick my nose where it doesn't belong. I inherited a problem, and perhaps Hiram can help."

Ten minutes later, she knocked on Hiram's kitchen door and called out his name. To her surprise, he was up and dressed, yet looked positively dreadful, eyes appearing quite bloodshot and his balance less than stable.

"Pardon me, Hiram, but I don't guess I know exactly what to do."

She expected him to say something, to push open the screen door and invite her to come inside. Instead, he merely stared at her, appearing to be also confused. Perhaps he wanted further explanation for her early morning visit, so Selma offered it.

"Charlie found a little boy. Down by the crick. He was filthy, so Charlie polished him some, and the pair of them are now in my kitchen, eating oatmeal."

"Thank God," Hiram almost whispered.

"Charlie said something rather odd. He pointed over here and implied that the child's sister was with you people." Miss Sellie took a deep breath. "And for Lord's sake, Hiram, open the door!"

"Oh, I'm sorry. Do come in."

She entered.

Standing close to Hiram, she took his hand in both of hers. "I'm only a mixed-up old woman, just trying to do right. So possibly I might help you if I took Thane and Alma Lee to church with me. Whether or not they're Methodist, at this point I don't really give a hoot or a holler. Just tell me what to do, anything to help, and I shall do it." Her mouth tightened. "And no questions asked."

He almost smiled. "Dear lady, you are the truest meaning of the word *neighbor* that anyone could ever treasure."

"I'm the lucky one," she said. "Forgive me, Hiram, but to me you'll always be one of those two little adorable boys next door."

"I know," he said softly. "With you on my one flank, and Vestavia at the other, how did Bobby and I turn out to be so . . . *so improper*?"

Looking up into his eyes, Selma said, "Nonsense." She sighed. "What am I to do with that new person in my kitchen?"

Hiram looked to one side, beyond the parlor. "Someone is here. She came in the night, horribly beaten, wondering where her child was. As you arrived, I was fixing to search for him. Incidentally, if he's who I'm guessing he is, his name is Lot."

"Lot Callister?"

"Yes. I don't quite understand how Charlie Moon Sky knows so much. Believe me, I'm more confused than you are. Right now, I am thankful and grateful that Charlie found the child and brought him to you."

"What are you going to do, Hiram?"

He shook his head. "I don't know just yet. An hour ago, I telephoned Carney Ransom."

"Good."

"Hold on." Hiram held up a hand. "Early on a Sunday morning, Carney is doing well if he can answer the contraption. From his voice, I realized that last evening was Saturday night, and he might have been out rather late, celebrating with the boys. So I hung up prior to explaining fully."

Trying to reason, Miss Sellie paced to and fro across Hiram's kitchen. "Well, it might ease matters if I took your youngsters to church. Only if you approve."

"Please do. Vestavia's not here today, but I'll go upstairs and tell Thane and Alma Lee that they're to groom themselves presentable."

"Have you eaten any breakfast?" she asked.

"No. Food isn't what's on my mind. To be honest about it, Glory Callister is asleep in my bedroom. She isn't seriously wounded, but her face and body are hideously bruised. The children know she's here. There was no other place for her to go, and I'm glad Glory came to me. Now if Hallapoosa doesn't like it . . . too bad."

"It's none of Hallapoosa's business," Miss Sellie said. "Nor is it any of mine. Excuse me for charging over here, but somehow I was figuring that you'd want to learn about the boy."

"Bless you for coming."

"Shall I keep Lot at my house?"

Hiram thought for a moment. "No, that won't be necessary, but thanks anyway. I'll come over to your place and bring him back here. A mother and child deserve to be together."

Mother and child, she thought. Well, stranger things than this have happened in Hallapoosa. Best to look ahead at what begged for doing, rather than over a shoulder at whatever took place yesterday, or years ago.

"You should have seen that child eat," she told Hiram, "as though he hadn't spooned in nourishment for a week. And rail skinny."

Hiram's face winced.

"I have shirked my responsibility," he said. "In a sense, it was up to me to help support him. But, since the arrival of Alma Lee and Thane, more proximate duties have narrowed my caring." He leaned heavily on his cane.

"Don't blame yourself. You can't spread one butter pat on the entire loaf."

He touched her shoulder. "So I'm discovering. There are vestiges of the past that you don't know. Secrets better left unshared. For years now, I have tried to sweep them under the rug, to hold up my head, but I was faking it like a player on a stage. Yet trying to keep a shine on the name of Mac-Hugh, perhaps for the sake of my parents and their memory. Maybe for myself." He looked at her. "Pardon my self-pity. I haven't been through nearly as much as Glory and Lot here have suffered. Believe me, I truly know far more than I'm admitting to you. I've told you more than a respectable lady ought to hear."

Miss Sellie was about to leave. But then she turned back to face Hiram. "Somehow," she said, "I feel as though someone other than you ought to be responsible. Somebody who left town."

Hiram stared at her. "You know?"

Miss Sellie nodded. "Old women have a way of becoming old witches, my boy. I have lived for close to eighty years in Hallapoosa. All my life. An old widow woman knows more than she up and tells. Far more. We oldfolks understand why a certain Moffet's face bears Singletary features. We know. Because that old Mrs. Simpson wasn't Hallapoosa's only witch."

"Yet you haven't spoken of it. At least, never to me. How did you know? You amaze me," he said. "How?"

"Seeing that boy," she said, "I saw your brother."

· *Seventeen* ·

Hiram left by his back door.

Lotty and Glory were both asleep, side by side, in his double bed on the first floor. According to plan, Selma Fulsom had taken Thane and Alma Lee to church, and Charlie Moon Sky would stand guard to watch both houses.

Now, he thought, is my chance.

Leaving his property in an upcrick direction, carefully walking so he would not fall, Hiram tested almost every step with his cane. It had been perhaps twenty years, possibly even thirty, since he had hiked to the crick. Now there was no choice. It would not be manly, he had decided, to allow Carney Ransom to handle the situation. This wasn't really Hallapoosa's official mess. It was of MacHugh concern.

"Mine," he said aloud. "Carney won't be doing my dirty work."

Earlier, he had considered telephoning Carney a second time, hoping that the constable would be more alert, then had stopped himself as he lifted the receiver off its hook. Carney Ransom deserved a Sunday morning's respite equal to other citizens. No reason why a constable had to be on duty seven days a week.

"It's up to me," Hiram said.

Remembering how battered and swollen Glory's face had still appeared in this morning's early dawn, Hiram shuddered.

Well, a time had come for Kelby Callister to be warned, and

lectured so severely that he would forever be afraid to touch his daughter or his grandson again. Or even to threaten them. As he moved slowly down the sloping land, Hiram steadied himself by touching the trunks of the small scrub oaks with his left hand. Gradually he began to smell the dampness, just ahead, and the frogs seemed to croak louder.

Had he been foolhardy, he wondered, not at least to inform Carney whom he was resolved to pay an unexpected call, and what he intended to do there? Hiram knew that he was acting impulsively, perhaps in error, attempting to make it all the way to where the shacks squatted on the island.

"Can I do it?" he asked himself.

Indeed, he silently answered, because there is no one else to handle the task. An unpleasant chore to be sure, yet something that demanded his doing. At best, a spur of conscience; at worst, a hot-blooded raging of revenge. As he walked closer to the water, Hiram was well aware of how rarely he had ever acted in temper. Ironic, he mused, that it is I and not my brother who finally braves a quest to even the score for Glory Callister.

Leaning against a shaggy oak trunk, he paused for breath, almost smiling at these rushes of imagination promoting Hiram MacHugh as a knight errant and, more absurdly, tempting him to believe that he was physically able to hold his own.

"Why?" Hiram sighed. "Why in the name of Hell is it always up to me?"

Instead of being the star athlete and baseball-team captain as Bobby had been, he had been only the sideliner, a disease-crippled brother whose fervent cheering was swallowed by a crowd's roar. God, he thought, how fortunate he was never to have hated Bobby, or even resented him. Perhaps a wisp of envy. But certainly no greater measure than the natural jealousy of many another boy in Hallapoosa.

However, as his years limped by, Hiram had slowly arrived at the realization that *he* was the strong brother, not Bobby. No man's worth was to be tallied by home runs, or touchdowns, or giggles of adoring cheerleaders. His gradual awareness of Bobby's weaknesses and frailties had almost crippled Hiram more brutally than had the polio. His hero was no longer an envied champion. Instead, his younger brother had become someone to excuse, to defend, an object of pity. He could limp farther in the world than Bobby would ever run on his two muscular legs. More than that, Hiram and his cane could support Bobby the way that an older brother ought.

Closing his eyes, still leaning on the tree trunk, Hiram so clearly remembered that moment when Bobby had asked him, "Why can't I be strong like you?"

He had been so touched by the question.

Recalling it suddenly dampened the curve of his cane, and his fingers felt moist, almost too frail to maintain their grip.

"Bobby," he whispered to the Sunday morning, "I was the only person who ever really knew your inside. I began to understand, after you graduated from high school and the cheering crowds had stilled, how alone you were in the echo. How unsteadily you stood."

The persistent prattle of frogs and crick water eventually brought Hiram MacHugh back to the here and now. Moving carefully, he continued his downgrade advance until he arrived at the crick bank. Then he followed the water, walking upstream until the shacks on the island came into view. One shack stood alone. This one, Hiram knew, was Kelby Callister's place, as Glory had described it to him on several occasions. Reaching it, however, posed a slight problem.

Luckily, the crick was wider at this point, the water lower, revealing a series of stepping stones. Searching until he located a six-foot pole that lay among the other debris at the shoreline, Hiram began his laborious but resolute crossing.

"Well," he told himself, "here goes."

With his cane in one hand, grasping the longer pole with the other, he managed to gain the first stone. Fortunately, most of the stones were flat and dry, belted by a darker and wetter area below. Once, when his foot slipped, his entire body became wet with the perspiration of panic. Why had he been so foolish to come alone? At least he could have informed Carney where he was going, or left a note on his kitchen table. Yet he persevered, using the wooden stick as a vault, landing unsteadily, but progressing until he finally gained the solid ground of the crick island. Leaning the pole against a small scrub willow, Hiram walked toward the shack. He did not enter its one door, remaining at the open doorway to call out a name.

"Kelby Callister."

He waited, saying the man's name again, until he heard movement inside the dark interior. A man's voice said a dirty word.

"Whatcha want?"

"I wish a word with you, Mr. Callister."

The man slowly appeared, clad only in a filthy suit of long gray underwear, unshaven, unwashed, blinking, and rubbing his battered face. He didn't come to the door. As his vision cleared, Kelby's eyes widened in alarm.

"MacHugh?"

"Yes, my name is Hiram MacHugh."

Stepping over the stoop board, he entered the shack to stand within six feet of its only occupant. "I have come to warn you, Mr. Callister, that if you ever again molest Glory or your grandson, I will, as Justice of the Peace, have you arrested and prefer charges of battery against you, and you'll no doubt be convicted to serve time in prison."

"Where's my daughter? You got 'er?"

"Glory and Lot are safe in my custody." As the sunlight sifted through a crack between boards, Hiram noticed that Callister's ear was mutilated. He saw Kelby's body bending into a slight crouch, a position of hostility. "You have beaten your daughter and intimidated your grandchild for the last time, and I have half a mind, right now, to give you the thrashing you deserve."

Kelby Callister almost smiled. "You?" He grunted in disbelief. "You ain't nothing but a fat old cripple sissy boy."

Hiram's vision was gradually becoming used to the shack's half-light, and he could see that Kelby Callister was reaching for something on the table, an object that looked like a hammer. Before he could quite decide what to do, the hammer was gripped, raised, and intended for his head.

"I'll learn you," Kelby hissed.

Reacting quickly, Hiram lurched to one side to avoid the man's charge, swung his cane, and landed a solid blow with its heavy knob between Callister's neck and shoulder. Kelby cried out in pain. Hiram whacked him again and again, until the hammer fell from Kelby's hand, landing with a helpless thud upon the dirty floor. Kelby swore, trying to retrieve his fallen weapon, but Hiram's attack now was relentless. Even though blood was spurting from Callister's face and head, Hiram MacHugh persisted, striking blow after blow. His cane was heavy, stout, and his right arm had strengthened for many years with its dependent use, so his bludgeoning was more damaging than Hiram realized.

Callister slumped to the dirt.

"I ought . . . " Hiram said, short of breath, "to kill you, Callister. Here and now."

The whimpering man lay helpless. Even so, Hiram Mac-Hugh raised his cane for one more blow, to put an end to Glory's tormentor. The blow was never delivered. Somehow, he forced himself slowly to lower his cane until he could rest on it.

"I wish I'd ended your life," he said to the man at his feet. "And if you ever again harm Glory or Lot, I will."

A pine support post stood in the shack's center, erect, from roof to floor. Hiram leaned against it, panting, studying his bloodied adversary. He had never intended to take the fight this far, wanting only to warn Callister. Perhaps, Hiram was now imagining, *I'll* be the person who goes to jail. For murder. For killing such an unworthy as Kelby Callister.

Leaving the shack, he hobbled to the crick's edge, where he stooped to wet his bandanna, and then returned. Bending, he bathed the man's face and arms, revealing the brutal welts that were still shining with oozing blood.

Callister moaned.

"Please," Hiram begged, "don't die."

As he spoke, he was considering the plight of Thane and Alma Lee, plus the fact that Glory and Lot now complicated the situation. How could he have acted with such intensity? He had become no more than a brawling Cricker, lashing out with ire and revenge. No court of law would view it as self-defense, because he had come to this shack and the intent to do Callister harm could surely be implied. Perhaps proved by the prosecution, when all of the facts about his affair with Glory had been made public.

"I'm a fool," he muttered.

Looking down at the blood-soaked bandanna, Hiram began to tremble, shuddering with guilt, in shame, as he pondered his next step. His first urge was to leave Callister's shack as soon as possible, before some of the other Crickers came along to discover him here. Were that to occur, Hiram knew, there would be no court of law involved, but rather a swift accounting, followed by his immediate death. As the Justice of the Peace, he knew from years of experience that Callisters and Downings never brought grievances to the courthouse. They settled their troubles, usually with violence, in their own secret ways.

"Fool," he said again, realizing that the Crickers might vent their revenge against Thane or Alma Lee, perhaps even on Vestavia.

Rising, almost stumbling to the door, he peeked outside at the other shacks, detecting no activity. He was fortunate that this was a Sunday morning.

Leaving the shack, Hiram moved carefully but quickly to where he had left the long pole. Employing it, he crossed the crick to the mainland, avoiding falling. He splashed water on his trousers and sleeves to disperse the blood spatters. Both of his shoes were soaked, and each shoe sloshed uncomfortably with every step. His clothes were damp from perspiration. Glancing downward, Hiram noticed that the shaft of his cane was discolored with Callister's blood. Reaching into his pocket, he was startled to discover that his bandanna was missing. Then he remembered.

Stupidly, he had left it in the shack.

Could he go back for it? Yes, he must. But then he noticed some children over on the island, upstream from Kelby's place, throwing stones into the water. Were he to return, surely they would spot him, and possibly the children had already seen him leave the island. A fat man wearing a white suit would hardly be a common sight among Crickers, especially one who walked oddly.

Slowly leaving the crick, moving upslope, trying to remain as undetected as possible, Hiram MacHugh headed for his home, stopping only once and for a very definite purpose.

Using leaves, he wiped blood from his cane.

· *Eighteen* ·

Carney swore at his toaster.

Gray wisps of smoke were feathering from the top of the nearest bread slot. For years he had tried to adjust it, but the doggone thing didn't even toast. All it did was blacken his breakfast.

"My head's killing me," he complained to his faulty appliance, "and you gotta act up ornery."

Last night, as they had on many a Saturday evening, he and Brantley Swope and Coot Cooter had really tied one on. Here it was, Sunday noon, and he was still wearing last night's clothes. His good suit pants.

Early this morning, the contraption had been ringing and he'd mumbled "Hello" into first the receiver, then finally at its mouthpiece. That much Carney could remember. But why was High MacHugh telephoning? Something about somebody getting beat up, he dimly recalled. But in Hallapoosa on a Saturday night, a fistfight could hardly be called an irregularity. Just normal sport.

"Maybe I'm the guy that took a licking," he said, scraping the black from his toast into the kitchen sink. "I sure feel it."

Eating an overripe banana, Constable Ransom waited for his coffee to perk. As he buttered the toast, the charred slice snapped in his hand, and Carney cussed at it, licking the butter from his chubby fingers.

His hand was shaking as he poured the coffee at a mug instead of into it, depositing a brown puddle on the worn checkerboard oilcloth of his table. As he had filled the mug too full, Carney lowered his head to lap the first sip. It burned his tongue, yet he sipped again, slurping the life-giving liquid into his mouth, which previously had tasted a bit furry.

"Never again," Carney Ransom grumbled.

He was wondering if Brantley and Coot made it home. Both of them, he knew, were married, and their wives no doubt had kicked up quite a fuss. Odella Cooter might have taken it all in stride, but Thelma Swope had an adder's tongue, in a gator's mouth. As he envisioned Brantley's homecoming, Carney felt fortunate that he was a confirmed bachelor and had been spared the . . . what was the term Hiram used about Thelma? . . . her *sanguine tirade.*

The coffee cooled enough to permit a heartier gulp. Its bitter taste reminded Carney that he had forgotten to wash his percolator. The flavor could have been drained from a crankcase. Or used to poison rats.

Carney winced.

A small bottle of Bayer aspirin sat on his table, beside the salt and pepper, so Carney popped two tablets into his mouth, washing them down with coffee. With his headache, he was silently concluding, he could have taken the entire bottle.

The telephone rang.

"Hello."

"Constable, you awake?" a male voice asked.

"Just about. Who is it? We sort of have a bad connection on my end."

"It's me, Brantley."

"Oh, I figured you'd be in bed all day."

"I was. But then Harold Adkin came to the door wearing his rubber fishing waders."

"Well," said Carney, "it's Sunday. Lots of people go fishing. Nothing unusual about that."

"He was downcrick. Said he thought he saw a body float by, mostly under the water, but he wasn't altogether certain."

"A human body?"

"That's what Harold claims. Had a snarl in his reel at the moment, so he didn't take a full look-see, as it was over so quicksome. Thought you might cotton to know, that's all."

"Yeah, Brantley. Thanks for the call."

"Don't mention it. So long."

"See ya."

Hanging up the telephone, Carney felt his headache coming back, throbbing worse than before. Why, he wondered, do people have to spot bodies on Sunday? It could possible have waited until Monday morning. Pouring more coffee, Carney drank it standing up, considering the chore of changing into his uniform for official business. Harold Adkin couldn't see squat if he'd stepped in it, and probable when out fishing he wasn't wearing his glasses, the lenses of which were thicker than the bottoms of two beer bottles and caused his eyes to look like plums.

Carney sighed.

"Okay," he groaned, "I'll go check."

Somehow, his patrol car seemed to realize that today was Sunday, and refused to start. As he kept the key turned, listening to the steady but unanswered grinding of the starter, Alfred Hammin came along and bent to look in the driver's window.

"You're flooding it," he said.

"I suppose you're an expert."

"Enough of an expert," Alf said, "to know that in order to train one of these vehicles, you first have to be smarter than the car." Alf chuckled. "Leastwise as smart."

"Is that so."

"According to my second cousin Walt, who's a auto mechanic over to Fort Myers, the trick is to balance your pull-out between your spark and throttle. It'll somehow sweeten your mixture, and she'll start like a fire horse."

Carney rested his key. "And I don't guess your cousin Walt could be wrong, seeing he's an electrical engineer."

"Well, I'm not exactly claiming that Walter knows it all. Just telling you what he told me. As a kid, Walt was usual tinkering out in the barn. Strange sort of a fella. Fell down a lot."

Carney slowly smiled. "I bet."

"Here," said Alfred, "better get out and let *me* give her a try behind the wheel. All us Hammins are sort of mechanical-minded."

Simpleminded, Carney was thinking. Nevertheless, he climbed out of the patrol car, to allow Alf to take a turn. To his surprise, Alf raised the hood, folded it back, and leaned in toward the engine. "This here is Henry Ford talking," he said to the motor, "so you'd better start up." Then he snaked in behind the wheel, turned the key, and the motor started as if by magic. Alf grinned up at Carney. "Gotta talk to a car, same as a mule, to let 'em know who's boss."

Carney sighed, thanked Alf Hammin, and drove away to where he could park close to the crick.

How, he was wondering, would he be able to find a body under all that water, providing that Harold had been correct and there really was one? His headache didn't seem to want to go away, and the midday sun forced him to squint. Sunday-morning eyes. Maybe all this was a wild goose chase. Carney had better things to do with his day off than stumbling around crick banks in search of a corpse that probable didn't exist in the first place.

Just one more fish story.

He searched for over two hours. As he was about to give up, he spotted a floating object in an eddy on the far side of the crick. Sighing, he splashed through the shallow water and was finally rewarded. Sure enough, Harold had seen a body and here it was, face down. Carney felt the wet wrist. Colder than a bass. No pulse. Whoever the guy was, all he had on his back was long underwear, and dirtier than a barn floor.

Turning the body over to face upward, Carney could not recognize the man.

There was no sign of blood, yet the dead man's face and neck were a mass of welts. At first, Carney believed them to be knife cuts. He had been slashed to death. Or had he? Whipped perhaps, then bled to death. Hit with something? The victim's face was hideous. Something, fish or turtle, had gnawed out the man's eyes.

Carney gagged.

Whoever the man was, Carney concluded, he was probable a Cricker, a Callister or a Downing, and sooner or later would be reported missing at work. Or not reported at all. The man's earlobe was missing. Carney shook his head. Somewhere, he knew, he'd seen an ear like this, yet he couldn't place exactly where.

"Doggone," Carney said. "I know you, mister."

It was possible that the dead man merely fell into the crick and this was purely a drowning. This would explain the welts, because the body had been battered by the sharp edges of limestone rock. Crick coral, as some of the Hallapoosa residents called it. Much of it was tough stuff and could mutilate human flesh rather easily.

His head was throbbing again. Nobody, he thought, should try to think with a Sunday brain.

Pulling the body from the water, Carney walked upstream close to where the crick was divided by a slender island. In the distance he saw the first shack. But then a movement to his right caught his attention, and as he turned, Carney saw an old woman. She was wearing a sack dress, and sat on a rock, quietly fishing.

Her back was to him.

"Excuse me," he said to her.

She turned to stare at him, her eyes widening when she noticed his constable uniform and his badge.

"Please don't be alarmed," he said. "I'm Constable Ransom, from town. I just found a dead person a ways downcrick, and I was hoping to find someone who could help me identify him." Carney touched his own ear. "Part of his ear is missing."

The old woman grunted, then her eyes rolled and she pointed to a shack. "He be Kelby," she said. "Kelby Callister."

"Thank you. I would like to learn your name, please, just for my records, you understand. Don't be afraid, old mama. I don't mean you any harm. Honest."

"Elizabeth," she said. "Elizabeth Downing, but I don't look for no trouble with the law, or anybody else, so don't tell nobody."

Carney shot her a grin. "I won't."

"Kelby ain't dead. Can't be."

"Well, I don't yet know for sure. Where exactly does Mr. Callister live?"

Again she pointed a skinny arm. "Over yonder. He got kin. Young ones. Pair of 'em, a boy and a gal."

"Thanks."

"He ain't dead. Kelby too mean for dying. That's how people say about him. Too ornery to live and too ornery to die off. Ain't worth a grunt to nobody. Used to tend a job at the turp, but somebody say he got through there. No job at all."

"Okay." Carney paused. "How's the fishing?"

"Nary a bite. Too much ruckus around here. Too many folks

throwing people into the crick water, and it scares away the bass. Catfish too. Ain't hooked me a keeper in a long spell."

This was interesting information for Carney Ransom to consider. Apparently old Elizabeth Downing had seen someone push somebody into the crick. Perhaps the man's death had been a drowning. Maybe not. As Carney felt himself beginning to perspire, he hoped it had all merely been Sunday sporting.

"Thanks again, Elizabeth. You've been a big help to me. If there's any favor I can ever do for you, just ask. Okay? My office is in the courthouse, right near Judge MacHugh's."

"I seen him too," the woman said. "Today, and nearby."

Carney held his breath. It was almost a quarter of a minute before he could speak. "Are you sure?" he asked.

Elizabeth Downing nodded, and then pointed for a third time. "I see lots that people don't know I see. Folks call me crazy-headed. But I know what I know." For emphasis, she slapped the crick water with her pole. "I see plenty on this day. But old Elizabeth don't tell all she see." Her finger tapped her temple. "I just squirrel it all away, up here, in my pate."

No more was spoken. Carney left her, continuing to follow the crick bank upstream, heading more or less toward the first shack. Crossing on the stones, he got his feet wet, and swore. At the shack door, he knocked, waited, then entered and allowed his eyes slowly to adjust to the gloom. The shack seemed to be empty. Standing there, Carney Ransom was wishing that he had brought a flashlight, even though it was afternoon on a sunny Sunday.

His foot casually kicked against a hammer.

He was fixing to leave when another object on the shack's dirt floor captured his attention. Stooping over with a grunt, Carney touched it, picked it up to examine, seeing that it was a soiled bandanna and caked with dried blood. Was it Hiram's? Without further speculation, he stuffed the bandanna into a back pocket. A sudden rustling noise made him forget the bandanna. The sound came from the darkest corner of the shack. Using his flashlight, he beamed light on a pile of rags and blankets. A blanket moved.

"Who's there?" he asked. "Come on out. I got a revolver on my hip, so don't try me no trouble. Hear?"

A man's face appeared in the light. A stranger. His head

was totally bald and his face was dirty. Not the face of a Callister. Yet the peculiar person who blinked at his flashlight had a face that, in a way, looked oddly familiar. No sense taking any chances.

Quickly, the constable drew his weapon.

"You're under arrest," he said.

· *Nineteen* ·

"**M**yrna, more tea?"
　　　"Please."
Julia Blount sat in her parlor with her Sunday-afternoon guest and poured tea into Myrna May Singletary's cup.

"On a humid afternoon," Julia said, making casual conversation, "some people drink nothing but coolers. But speaking for myself, I do prefer a cup or two of warm tea."

"I declare, so do I," Myrna agreed. "Seems like our summers here in Hallapoosa have become stickier and stickier."

"It's getting so a lady can't stroll outdoors in the sun without *glowing*." Julia was careful not to use a term such as *sweat,* or even *perspire.* Not in front of Myrna Singletary and her arsenal of professed sensitivities.

"How nice of you to invite me over," Myrna said. Looking around Julia's parlor, her eyes seemed to be appraising the monetary value of each and every item, as though for an upcoming auction.

What Myrna did not know was that Julia had rushed home after church to make sure her house was orderly. And if she missed a speck of dust, Julia was concluding, Myrna Singletary would spot it. Or, when her back was turned, test a tabletop with her white glove.

"I hear the turpentine mill might go under," Julia said. "Have you heard any rumors?"

"Only what you have heard, my dear. Seems like arduous times might affect us all." Myrna leaned slightly forward from her chair. "If you ask me, it's the fault of all those Yankee bankers, up north, people with little or no family backgrounds themselves. They doubtless don't give a tinker about our way of life . . . having no gentility themselves."

"You are surely right about that," Julia said, "sure as we're born."

Although often outspoken herself, Julia Blount was cautioning herself to agree with everything Myrna said, or might say. Myrna May was well known in Hallapoosa to have definitive opinions on every subject. Socially speaking, it would be unwise to contradict Myrna May Singletary, in public or private.

The Singletarys were old money. Bank money. Even so far back as Confederate currency, which Amos Singletary had somehow managed to convert into Union dollars before General Lee's noble surrender at Appomattox, at a time when Amos had somehow determined the sorry outcome. Miraculously, the Singletarys, unlike many a Southern family, had escaped from the war relatively unscathed. A cousin, some down-and-out tertiary relation, had died at Bull Run, a fact of which Myrna constantly reminded everyone in Collier County.

"Quality people," Myrna was saying, "always manage to survive against the odds. And it's breeding, that's all it is, my dear. Horses, dogs, and families. Breeding will eventually toss its proud head and carry on, regardless."

Julia was itching to probe Myrna May about a certain mortgage at the Hallapoosa Bank, yet she kept herself in rein about it. The Singletarys were always nosing into other people's business, but *their* affairs were considered to be absolutely private and not to be questioned.

"What precious china you have," Myrna remarked, lifting her cup high enough to study its bottom.

"Thank you."

"Mine, of course, are all English bone. Many of them belonged to my grandmother, who was a Jackson. The general's family. She was on my mother's side."

"Yes, I recall you mentioned it."

Myrna would be in Heaven's front row, Julia suspected, if she could have spotted a Sears Roebuck imprint on someone else's saucer.

Somehow, Julia would have to steer the conversation around to the subject of a mortgage on Hiram MacHugh's property. She wasn't getting any younger. Neither was Hiram. But there were several ways to skin a cat, as the proverb goes, and Julia was becoming more determined with each passing day to marry Hiram and then to diet him down to half-bed size. A momentary flash warmed her, a brief fantasy of being alone with Hiram on their wedding night . . . not at his forlorn little residence, but upstairs, in her very own bedchamber.

Julia nearly spilled her tea. "My," she said to Myrna, "how circumstances do change hereabouts."

Myrna raised an eyebrow. "Whose?"

"Well," Julia went on, "here's our honorable Justice of the Peace with two fresh youngsters to raise and tend to."

"Yes, I have observed them," Myrna said. "In fact, you'll never *guess* where I saw both of those whelps on this very morning."

"Where?" Julia dutifully inquired.

"In church, of all places. And there they were, bolder than brass and sitting with Selma Fulsom as if they were charter members. Neither one of those children look Methodist to me. Next thing we know, they'll be passing the collection or aspiring to sing in the choir."

"My goodness," Julia said quickly. But then she again diverted the course of the conversation to their uncle. "It certainly promises to be a burden on Hiram. He must already have debts to the rafters. I'd heard that his house was still mortgaged."

Myrna stared. "Are you asking, Julia, or telling?"

"Neither one. I wasn't at all getting curious. Only concerned. We who are blessed with privilege ought not to overlook those among us who are less fortunate."

Myrna was smiling slightly. She wasn't buying a word of it, Julia guessed, and the thought was causing her hands to dampen. Hurriedly she sought her napkin.

"Another wafer?" she asked Myrna, touching the edge of her majolica cookie dish.

"Yes, I believe I shall. Only one. The Bible warns us not to overindulge . . . whether it be with a baking trifle or with a Justice of the Peace."

Julia almost ceased to breathe. Had she been so obvious?

Possibly so, and all she had accomplished was a spilling of her own beans, extracting nothing from Myrna May Singletary except one of her vitriolic epithets.

"I presume," she said to Myrna, "that Hiram was not with the children at your service this morning."

Myrna snorted graciously. "Of course not. I sincerely doubt that the Judge has held down a pew in a score of years. Besides, he isn't a Methodist, a fact for which many of us who consider ourselves to be may eternally be grateful."

"Still and all," Julia said, "one certainly must give Hiram some credit, volunteering to mother-hen his brother's children. I sometimes wonder, considering the age and condition of Vestavia, how Hiram can carry on."

Myrna May smirked.

"It's rather well known," she said, "that Hiram MacHugh has *carried on* for a number of years. Some say it runs in the family. His younger brother, God rest his soul, earned quite a reputation for himself, prior to leaving Hallapoosa." Myrna paused for a sip of tea. "However, far be it for me to dabble in gossip. Whatever our Justice of the Peace does socially is precious little concern of mine."

"Nor of mine," Julia added.

"At least," Myrna May lowered her voice, "Hiram never fathered an illegitimate Cricker, which is more than can be stated in favor of some." She placed her cup and saucer lightly on the table. "Yet it's best never to demean the departed. So I'll just let the dead remain dead."

"Quite a tragedy," Julia said. "It must be so straining on children when they lose both parents in an accident."

Myrna May helped herself to a delicate bite of a cookie, chewed pensively, then swallowed.

"Accidents," she finally said, "seem to coonhound certain families. Perhaps there's a dark shadow hovering over all those MacHughs. Mercy, I surely wouldn't want to become too cozy with a single one of them, because a person never knows when the fates will again come calling. And if this sounds like a warning, Julia, mark my words. Take it so."

"A warning?"

Myrna nodded. "There are few secrets here in Hallapoosa. Little happens around our community that doesn't eventually whisper into Singletary ears." Myrna touched a linen napkin to her mouth. "People tell me secrets that are nigh to shocking. I blush to hear them. Yet I do listen, more out of my civic duty for the betterment of Hallapoosa than merely to harken to rumor. We have a certain position, socially and economically, and such station obliges me to gather information in order to make judgments."

"Pardon me," Julia wanted to say, "but I was under the impression that Judgment is not ours to make, but rather God's." Yet she refrained from saying it. Had she been so blunt, Myrna May Singletary would have stiffened in her chair, and their quasi-cordial conversation abruptly abated. Myrna May could retreat inside her stone-faced fortress.

It made little sense to offend Myrna. She and her brother, Finley, ran Hallapoosa and reined the Town Council with a firm resolution. Finley Singletary was the banker and also First Selectman. Yet it was his sister, Myrna May, who usually told him what to do, where to announce it, and how to button up his trousers.

Hiram's job depended on the Hallapoosa Town Council. Once they turned down their thumbs on Hiram, he no longer would be retained as their Justice of the Peace. The only road to Hiram, Julia had decided, was a tricky one . . . one of economics as opposed to a flower-lined lane of love. Courtship wasn't all candlelight and gypsy violins.

Julia might, with some stealth, convince Hiram that she had Myrna May Singletary's ear, which should be enough to force *his* hand, to ask for *hers* in matrimony. Hiram wasn't emotional, yet he had always been practical. He was Bobby's opposite. Hiram had brains, a dry wit, plus a certain Southern-gentleman charm that Julia Blount had found enticing even when her husband, Horace, was still alive. Horace, she mused, had never been really *alive*. He walked, talked, ate, gargled, and snored . . . but that had been the total of his activity. On the other hand, Julia imagined that Hiram MacHugh was capable of offering more in the night than snoring.

"My," said Myrna, "you've been still as a mouse."

Julia steadied her cup which was about to rattle in its saucer. "Yes, just remembering those good old days when you and I were girls together. You never married, and I did worse, with Horace."

"God rest his soul," said Myrna, as though preventing Julia from complaining about her departed husband.

Julia was about to say something about Hiram MacHugh, and how the town of Hallapoosa might consider replacing him with a more up-to-date Justice of the Peace, but a genuine loyalty for Hiram held her back. Were he out of a job, Julia might land him. Yet such an overt action would surely be little better than kicking Hiram below the belt, and that Julia Blount would not do.

"I did not marry," Myrna May was saying, "because I chose not to, and nary for a lack of suitors. In fact, there was a time when I might have married Horace Blount."

Julia almost laughed.

"Oh, how I wish you had."

Myrna stiffened. "I declare, your remarks about your dear Horace are almost improper."

Julia smiled, knowing that her evaluation of her husband was probably the only unproper thing about Horace Blount. He certainly had been proper enough. Proper, dull, and the only thing stiff about him had been the starch in his shirt.

Somehow, Julia slowly realized, she had merely wasted a beautiful Sunday afternoon, intending to entrap Hiram, yet knowing she could not admire herself if her actions led to his professional defeat. She and Myrna had danced a ring around the subject as though it were some untouchable Maypole, and to embrace it would soil Sunday dresses and Sunday souls.

"I often ponder," Julia was tempted to say, "which fate is the sadder. To be an old maid like you, or a desperate widow like me." But she held her tongue. No sense in hurting Myrna's feelings. There had been adequate pain in Hallapoosa, and there might easily be more aborning. One thought amused her. Were she to marry Hiram MacHugh, surely Myrna May Singletary would find ways to snub her. But one genuine kiss from Hiram would more than balance all of the Singletary snobbery.

Myrna May stood.

"Well," she said, "I must be toddling along. Thank you for the delicious treats."

"And thank you for coming," Julia said, going with Myrna as far as her front porch.

As she watched Myrna walking away, Julia Blount felt

grateful that she hadn't pressed for any action concerning Hiram MacHugh. If she won him, Julia thought, it would be fair and square.

Sighing, and even dreaming, Julia picked up the tea tray and carried it to her kitchen.

· _Twenty_ ·

Charlie Moon Sky sat quietly.

Many things have happened on this day, he thought. First, he had found Glory's little brother, who was now at the MacHugh house. Miss Sellie had taken Thane and Alma Lee to church, during which time Judge MacHugh had left his home.

Miss Sellie had returned from church with the two children, and now all of them were talking at once. Yet no one was doing what Charlie had decided that he alone must do.

Charlie reached for his knife.

He did so without having to glance down at his right hip, where his belt snaked through the two flat straps on the inside of the sheath. When he was standing, or working, the knife always rode his thigh as part of his body, an extension of his leg bone.

At night when Charlie Moon Sky was asleep, his knife was never in its scabbard. It slept in his right hand.

Long ago, John Moon Sky, his father, had made the knife for Charlie when he turned twelve. Overall, the knife was ten inches long: four inches of handle, six inches of blade. The handle was oak, very hard, but earlier when it was green and pulpy, John Moon Sky had imbedded small fragments of colored stones and then coated the entire handle with resin.

"A knife is like a coral snake," John told his son. "Beautiful and deadly."

With his father's instruction, it had taken Charlie almost a year to learn how a man draws his knife. The handle is never snatched. Instead, in one smooth motion, the hand merely *wipes* the knife from its sheath. The thumb is forward, pointing downward, as the fingers guide the handle upward, and the blade is low, and raw, ready to strike with its fang of death.

The sheath of a Seminole knife is nearly twice as long as the knife itself, so the knife's handle will be where a man's hand loosely hangs from his shoulder. The tip of the sheath is tied to the thigh by a leather thong. John Moon Sky had been, of sorts, the tribe's blacksmith. He always had been very particular about the height of his anvil, Charlie remembered, so that when a hammer rested horizontally in his hand, the arm was hanging straight down and unbending.

So it was with a knife. Low, like an anvil, comfortable for the hand of a man who worked with a knife. Or fought with one.

Charlie Moon Sky moved quietly away from Miss Sellie's cowshed where he slept.

Alone, Charlie had wanted to go next door, to see if everyone was all right, because the look of sadness on Miss Sellie's face was worrying him. Yet he did not go. Something bad had happened. This much he understood because of the little boy's mutterings as well as Miss Sellie's. Someone was hurt. Inside, Charlie seemed to sense that the person who had been harmed was Glory.

Thinking so enraged him.

For weeks he had witnessed the bullying. Several times he had seen the old man who lived in the shack slap the young girl. Also the little boy. Charlie Moon Sky had also silently watched the old man with half an ear spying on the two MacHugh children. He remembered the piece of birthday cake that Thane MacHugh had Miss Sellie bring to him on the night she had gone there to eat. She had also shown him the baseball, one with a name on it, which she had given to Thane as a gift. Miss Sellie loved the children as she loved her flowers.

"No one," Charlie Moon Sky said, "will hurt anything or anyone that my Miss Sellie befriends."

Now he walked slowly in the direction of the crick, hearing

the rush of water. After this day, Charlie decided, the old man would not hurt anybody again. Someone should die.

"The old man," he said.

Yes, the Cricker man must die for the safety of four people . . . the two islanders, Thane, and his little sister who was called Alma Lee. Sooner or later, Charlie felt, the mean half-eared shack person might hurt one of them, or all, therefore it was his duty to prevent its happening.

Silently he moved through the low palmetto, avoiding the curving prickers on the long stems of the fanpalms. Lying on his belly, Charlie crawled over the black earth through a stand of ferns. Their leaves, delicate as lace, allowed him to see the island shacks without being seen. People were there. Only three. An old woman with a fishing pole was talking to two other women, both much younger, and pointing at the shack where Glory Sunshine Hair lived with the little boy and the heated old man who shouted so often and threw stones at his young ones.

No person seemed to be going to the shack. Instead, they only talked together and pointed.

"I will go," Charlie said.

He saw how his passage to the shack could be made. Near the shack's door, several rocks lay in the water, their heads rising here and there above the casual current. On the nearest shore, rushes grew thick and green, and offered him a thatch of shielding.

He removed all of his clothes. His knife was now clenched in his teeth.

Easing his body into the crick, Charlie filled his lungs and then submerged entirely, pulling himself along the crick bottom by holding a rock or a fallen tree, fighting the slow yet persistent pull of the crick's flow. The crick was wide here, wider than usual, and Charlie thought his lungs would almost burst before gaining the rocks on the island side. Though starving for air, he would not surface until he was certain of his concealment.

Crawling again, he made his way through the green rushes and mud to a spot nearest the door.

Much to his surprise, two men came out of the shack. Neither one of them was the man Charlie Moon Sky intended to kill. One of them was very fat. He was the constable, in a uniform, who sometimes came to visit the MacHugh people. The other man was much thinner, far younger, and had no hair. His face looked afraid. Lying in water, motionless as the stones around him, Charlie thought he had seen the face of the baldheaded man before, or a face like his. He wondered where.

The Seminoles sometimes said, in laughter, that all white faces are one face.

This, Charlie now knew, was not true because he could easily distinguish one white person from another, and no woman alive could ever appear as beautiful as Glory Sunshine Hair. As Charlie watched, with only his eyes and nose above the surface of the water, the fat constable clamped silver bracelets on the wrists of the bald man. The cuffs connected the man's hands behind his back. The shackled man said nothing while the constable talked.

"I'm taking you to jail," the constable said, "and if you got anything to say about whatever it was you've been up to, best you come clean and tell me the straight of it. Hear?"

As the constable led him away, crossing the crick on the stepping stones, the bald man was silent. The two of them splashed to shore and disappeared in the direction of town.

Charlie waited.

Was the old man still inside the shack? Charlie knew that he would not have to enter the house to learn the answer. Sliding out of the water, he crawled silently to a place beneath the shack, and there used his nose. Crickers had a strong smell, a dirty white smell, nothing like the pleasant smell Miss Sellie had. Hearing no breathing, he decided no one was inside. With the knife still in his teeth, he retraced his lowly route to the water and eased his naked body into the crick. Again he crossed the crick underwater and unseen, pulling himself to the mainland by using rocks and submerged logs.

He stood in the sunlight to allow his body to shed the drops of crick water.

Slowly he dressed. He had only worn two garments, a shirt and trousers. At least they were dry. He retied the lower thong of his knife's sheath to his leg, and then jammed his knife into its home, with disappointment. Charlie Moon Sky had accomplished nothing on this day. The problem still faced him, haunting him, a problem of how he would secretly end the life of Glory's father.

Silently he stood, watching and listening to the three women who were within the throw of a stone, still over on the island where the crick divided. Their chatter, Charlie was concluding, would tell him little, or less.

Perhaps the Cricker man had gone fishing.

Moving quietly through the dense cover of willows, palmetto and fanpalm, Charlie walked downstream, more or less to the place in the crick that was closest to where he now lived with Miss Sellie. He moved slowly, at only the rate of one step for every breath. A Seminole way. His father had always moved this way as a hunter.

"Study the panther," John had told his son, "and how she glides in shadow, making less sound than a floating canoe. She is unhurried, patient, receiving more information than she allows herself to give to those around her who might hear. Her ears and nose are more useful to her than her paws."

Charlie would know when to strike. As a panther knows. And as a rattlesnake realizes when to straighten his spine, widen his mouth, and expose his curving fangs. For the time being, Charlie thought, his knife would remain inert, sleeping steel in its blanket of leather.

"I will find him," Charlie whispered. "And when I do, the old islander will hurt no more children."

He stood motionless. Closing his eyes, he could still see the face of the baldheaded stranger, a face with no name. Yet he was not all stranger. Nor was he a friend.

Why, he wondered, would a man so young have no hair on his head?

Opening his eyes, Charlie Moon Sky continued to walk downstream. The crick narrowed in one place, narrow enough for a fallen pine to span the water and form a bridge. Looking upstream, and then down, he saw that he was alone and crossed the crick quickly by balancing on the fallen tree. Then he melted himself into the shrubs and trees, again to be unseen. He should, he told himself, be using his eyes instead of his feet.

His eyes were rewarded by a pair of crows. They were pecking at something.

There on the crick bank lay a man wearing underwear who

did not move. Was he asleep? Moving closer, Charlie slowly decided that the man in the underwear suit was neither asleep nor awake. The crows flew to a limb, complaining loudly. Stretching out a hand, he touched the man and knew instantly that he was dead. There was no color to the man's skin. Bloodless. Yet striped with odd-looking cuts and gashes.

Ants, as well as crows, had found him.

The dead person's face was very unpleasing to look at, as it was fish eaten. No eyeballs. A very sad face even for a man so dead. Leaning closer, Charlie noticed the man's ear. Half an ear! Charlie's knife had been too late to serve the friends of Miss Sellie.

He muttered silently in Seminole.

Raising his head to the sky, Charlie Moon Sky spoke a prayer to the Spirit, because the scene of so lonely a death was too full of sorrow, and all dead people warrant a praying.

At the close of his prayer, Charlie wondered whether or not he should tell Glory Sunshine Hair about her father's dying. Surely she would wish to know. Miss Sellie and the next-door Judge should know too. Mr. MacHugh would, no doubt, inform his friend who was the constable in the uniform, a person he had recently seen with the baldhead, the stranger who now wore the constable's shiny bracelets connecting his wrists.

The dead person was lying beneath a stand of scrub oak, short trees, few of which would grow much taller than ten or twelve feet. This place, Charlie was thinking, was not where a body should remain, lying in the summer heat and being eaten by ants. Soon, he knew, the white maggots would come too, at a much slower pace than the ants. Not even an evil person should lie here undefended, rotting in shame.

"I will dignify his death," Charlie said, "even though his life carried so little dignity."

Grabbing the cold hands, Charlie Moon Sky dragged the body to a spot beneath some dead trees. Scrub oaks. Slowly, his hands dug a grave in the soft sandy muck. He made a pit rather deep to afford the dead person his privacy. Tumbling the body into the hole, Charlie then covered it with sand and dirt, tossing handfuls of extra soil into the bushes so there would be no telltale mound, one which might capture the attention of a curious eye.

Then, on all sides, he shook the dead trees, causing a

torrent of brown oak leaves to fall and mask the ground. No mound and no grave were apparent now, as if nothing except nature herself had passed this way.

Charlie nodded.

"So you end, old man. I am sorry that, in life, you were unable to smile at the two beautiful children who were given to you by the Spirit."

The mean one-ear only threw curses, Charlie thought.

And stones.

· *Twenty-One* ·

Big Callister was sweating.
Cooking a run of whiskey was hot work at any time
of the year, and hotter on an August afternoon. The two young
women who were helping him were also wet with perspiration.
One of them grumbled about the heat and having to work on
Sunday.

"Dallie, shut your mouth," Big told her, "and stick some
more dry wood under the furnace."

The girl scowled at him. "Me and Marleen ought to git paid
for helping out," she said.

Big snorted and spat. "You'll git paid."

"When?"

"Soon's I sell my run. Soon as Jason collects and forks over
my share. That's when. So forgit your greedy ways and keep
that cooker hot. Only whiskey that'll sell a fat price gits
drawed from Hell's boiler." Big pointed at the spirals of copper
tubing beneath the sluice. "And a cool worm."

"We're hot," Marleen said. Her face pouted. "We want to go
jump in the crick."

"Later," said Big. "Dang it, I got me a run fixing. Fan away
that smoke like I told you to do, or somebody'll see it and
come curious."

Dallie was bending over gathering kindle, her little backside humping out her skimpy dress like a pair of ripe melons.
Big licked his lips as he watched her do. Marleen was breaking
up the smoke with a fanpalm frond, yet continued her griping.

Big sighed. The only worker worth squat around a still was a deaf-mute. If a man could locate hisself a woman, he thought, who couldn't talk, one who'd keep his cooker hot all day and his bed warm all night, that'd be near perfect. Marleen and Dallie were both fourteen. Young enough to train for work and old enough for sporting.

He stood barechested, his huge upper body a mass of burn scars that he'd collected over the years from the hot copper. Marks of a stiller man.

Big Callister didn't enjoy whiskey stilling. But times had turned tight in the Hallapoosa area, so a man had to do necessary in order to eat. And equally important, to purchase a few pretty trinkets to keep young gals from leaving him.

He thumped the copper barrel with a mallet that he'd padded with rags which would deaden the sound. Big thumped again to loosen the mash inside and to prevent it from crusting. Atop the cooker, the cap was working loose from the inside steam pressure, and Big burned his hand trying to tighten it down.

"Dang it to Hell," he said, shaking his fingers. He hurried to a bucket of spring water to soak his hand.

Dallie saw it and laughed.

Her enjoyment of his pain didn't please Big Callister. Perhaps, he considered, he could get rid of both Dallie and Marleen, because neither one of them had the brains of a chigger bug. Big had to tell both of them what to do next about every breath. Marleen was a Downing and Dallie was a Flagg. What he wanted was a Callister gal and Big knew the exact one.

Kelby's daughter.

Trouble was, old Kelby talked too much. He had ample more mouth than muscle, and Big wouldn't trust Kelby Callister as far as he could throw a mule. Big smiled. He was recalling how he'd won the attentions of both Dallie and Marleen, sometime this past spring, away downcrick, when he'd showed off for a whole flock of young gals by squatting under a mule. Then he lifted the dumb animal clean off the ground. He'd stood straight up, turning around a few spins, with that mule across his back and shoulders, kicking to be set free.

Afterward, he had flexed his muscles for Marleen and Dallie

and showed them the pretty-colored tattoo on his bicep, a naked dancing lady, flexing again and again to make her look like she was dancing a jig.

Big chuckled. "Gits a girl every time."

That was when Dallie Flagg had told him her name, and that she could dance a lotsome better than the tattoo lady on his arm. Marleen had claimed she could dance too. As it turned out, these little gals eventual could do aplenty more and both at the same time. Still and all, Big had himself a notion for that golden-haired Glory. But she had a kid, a little boy. Maybe if he could truck the lad to Miami, without her ever finding out about it, Glory might be a woman worth having around. Big shook his head. He had heard it told that Glory Callister did it for money. More than one person had telled it like so. Mixing with a woman like that was a quicksure way of picking up a misery.

His yearnings for Glory were shattered by a dispute between his helpers. Dallie had got sick of tending the fire and was trying to yank the fanpalm away from Marleen. Before he could stop it, both of the gals were rolling on the ground, clawing, spitting, scratching at each other's eyes.

Big had to kick them quiet.

"Hush your noise," he said, "or we'll git company here. If we do, I'll take the two of you down to the crick and hold you under to bubble until sundown."

He handed the fan to Dallie. "Work it," he ordered her. "Marleen, you wiggle your fanny around and hustle me some burning wood. I don't want nothing green. Hear? It'll raise too much smoke. Find the dry stuff. Neither one of you two little ladies'll git a penny of pay unless you honest earn it."

"We earned it last night," Dallie said. "You hardly don't never pay us for nothing. Maybe you don't got the money you claim."

Big slapped her. Not hard, yet with enough zip to knock her down. Without another word, Dallie fetched the fan and attacked the column of smoke, swatting at it like she was aiming to do damage.

The run was ready.

Opening the sluice gate, Big watched the spring water cascading down to cool the worm, to condense the draw. He rinsed his burned hand under the water. Standing there, Big was hoping that old Jason Yoobarr wouldn't show up on the scene too early. Jason didn't abide waiting. Maybe he'd bring cash and maybe no. A man didn't dare trust nobody in this business, and Big Callister didn't even once trust Jason Yoobarr.

Yet, he had to admit, Jason was a gent who could keep his mouth shut. Folks claimed they had seen Jason smile and say a howdy to Constable Carney Ransom and then tell Carney that Jason's woman was buying all that sugar for a church-baking.

"That," Big admitted, "was ample nerve."

Big doubted that Carney Ransom swallowed a word of it as truly, yet the constable had a reputation of leaving matters be. Carney and his pals were even customers, so people told. In fact, Jason had delivered plenty of jugs to the Justice of the Peace, so Kelby Callister had said. High MacHugh wouldn't stir up trouble, so the rumor went in Hallapoosa. The old Judge hadn't earned his nickname by standing too tall in the doorframe of purity.

With a rag, Big loosened the spigot on the cooker cap, allowing the vapor to enter the worm. The cold spring water would condense it to product. Presently, he saw the dripping start at the catcher tub. Big dipped a finger to sample it, several times, enough to swallow a drop or two and feel it burn his throat.

"Hot and raw," he said.

The whiskey was colorless, like water.

"Put a clean white rag over the funnel," he told Dallie. "I expect you and Marleen to strain it proper before it fills a jug. And you rinse every jug in the crick. No dirt inside. I don't want nobody to puke on my stilling. Ain't good for steady business."

Trade wasn't good, Big knew.

Since the turpentine mill had let so many workers go, there was less money around the Hallapoosa area. Jason Yoobarr had also complained, saying that even people with steady jobs, like old Judge High, had quit buying his wares. The spirit business had turned as sour as the mash, and a few tempers had soured too. Well, Big knew, that was usual the way of it . . . when money took short, tempers grew shorter. Several buyers had cussed out Jason because he didn't cut his prices, claiming instead that somebody was cutting the whiskey.

It wasn't Big Callister. Oh, maybe he might add a spoon of water here and there, but that was generally expected, and accepted. In fact, such a practice would serve also to dilute a hangover, so a bit of sly watering here and there could serve the public's welfare. For a moment or two, Big Callister was actual thinking of himself as being community-minded.

"Hold it steady, birdhead."

The gals were bickering again, fussing at each other over which one would hold the funnel, the easier of the two jobs. Some of the whiskey spilled and was lost among the leaves.

Big swore.

"You two bitches are only good for one thing, and it certain ain't ever likely to be working or thinking."

Burning his hand on the cap again, Big kicked at the barrel, and then danced around on one foot, wondering if he had been stupid enough to have busted a toe. It was stinging like all fury. Dallie threw the funnel at Marleen, an incident which did little to improve Big Callister's disposition. As he kicked at both of them, Marleen and Dallie scooted out of reach. Picking up the mallet, Big threw it at them and missed.

The sluice water wasn't splashing on the worm as it ought, so Big had to straighten the chute.

"Living," he mumbled, "is just one dang nuisance after another."

Big wanted to kick the cooker again, as well as cuff a mite of reason into Marleen and Dallie, or just plain kick at the world. As soon as times got better, he was promising himself, he'd maybe borrow a car and take another trip to Miami. It sure beat sporting around a down-and-out dump like Hallapoosa. It would do him good to get away from these two little wenches for a spell. Possible for keepers. One thing certain, Big Callister wasn't going to take either Dallie or Marleen even as far as Kalipsa Ferry. First off, they would be teasing to buy every geegaw in town and yanking him into every doggone emporium they could locate, until every cent he owned would git spended dry.

Some fellow, Big couldn't quite recall who, had claimed that a man could keep a cow, a mule, a barn cat, and a coondog . . . cheaper than attempting to even half-keep a lady friend.

"Howdy."

Big whipped around to look.

Jason Yoobarr parted the bushes and walked toward the still. "I seen your smoke," he said. "Figured maybe you might be fixing a run of mash. Ready to do some trading?"

"Not yet. It'll be a while."

"Where'd you git them gals?"

"None of your business," Big growled.

"Mind if I sit awhile and wait?"

"If'n you hold quiet and let me finish up."

Jason hunkered down, his back leaning against the trunk of a pine. Reaching into his pocket, he pulled out a rumpled packet of Red Man, unrolled it, and stuffed a wad of loose chew into his mouth.

Big waited for Jason to offer him some and he final did.

"I heared about your cousin," Jason said.

"Who?"

"They say Kelby died today."

Big stopped chewing. "Who said?"

"Island people, away up the crick. Somebody throwed him into the water to drown. Constable located him and then found somebody else in Kelby's shack. A stranger with a bald head. Funny thing, though. Constable Ransom come back to carry the body away, but it be gone. Clean gone."

"You sure?"

Jason Yoobarr nodded.

"I'm sure what I heared 'em tell me. And that's all I'm telling you. Didn't see anything of it with my own eyes, but other people did. Crickers might tell a wrong story, now and again, but not about one of their own dying so strange."

Big felt his blood rushing hotter than the day itself, hot as a cooker inside him. No, he didn't cotton to Kelby much, never had, even before he'd bit Kelby's ear off. Yet nobody was going to end a Callister and go free. His fists clenched.

"Who done it to Kelby?"

Jason shook his head. "You won't believe me when I say his name."

"Tell me."

"You know old Elizabeth, that crazy old Downing granny who sometimes sets and fishes, with no hook on her line?"

"*She* done it?"

"Nope."

"Then who be it, Jason?"

"Elizabeth said it was the Judge hisself."

"MacHugh?"

Big spat a stream of tobacco juice. Suddenly the Red Man in his mouth was tasting sour and was meaning his stomach.

"So the old woman say," Jason told him.

Big was thinking, remembering all he had heard over the years, about a MacHugh and a Callister and a child. Glory's whelp. Today wasn't the first time a MacHugh had come to the island to have-at with a Cricker. Seven or eight years ago, somebody should have settled a score, yet nobody had. No one had died, only born. Now matters had took a sorry turn, Big was thinking, and if Kelby couldn't be found alive or dead, the Callisters ought to get even.

Big said, "The Judge is due for judging."

· *Twenty-Two* ·

Thane MacHugh was not asleep.

Wow, he thought, what a Sunday. Punching his pillow, he closed his eyes and reviewed all that had taken place.

Glory had come, beaten up. Charlie Moon Sky had found Lot, and just when everything was turning exciting, Miss Sellie had taken him and Alma Lee to church. But when they returned home, Uncle Hiram had been somewhere for sure, because Thane noticed the dried mud on the heel of one of the Judge's shoes.

Miss Sellie had insisted, and the Judge had mentioned Vestavia and finally agreed, that Glory and her little brother would sleep at her house.

But that wasn't all.

Constable Ransom had also stopped by, quite late, and he and Uncle Hiram had talked for some time, almost in whispers. Neither man seemed to be too excited, but from his bedroom window, Thane had seen the constable take off his hat, several times, and scratch his head as if he was toting around one heck of a problem. Straining to hear their conversation, Thane had picked up only a word or two.

He had heard "shack" and "corpse" and then something about a disappearing body and "evidence," and that he'd buried a bandanna.

Before leaving in his patrol car, Constable Ransom had rested his hand on the Judge's shoulder, which looked to Thane as being some sort of gesture of friendship.

"Something," Thane whispered in the dark, "sure is turning Hallapoosa upside down."

Carney Ransom had also mentioned the names of several citizens, which Thane didn't recognize. Brantley Swope and Coot somebody, Harold Adkin, and some old woman, Elizabeth. From all Thane could hear, the constable had also hustled himself a busy Sunday.

One more name had been spoken.

Kelby.

Thane rolled over again, wondering what was going on, and regretting the fact that he hadn't asked Uncle Hiram about the dirt on his shoe. It didn't look at all like the dry dirt around the house, out in the yard.

"Thane?"

Opening his eyes, he sat up slowly, seeing Alma Lee standing in her nightgown and holding her doll.

"I know," he said. "It's dark across the hall and you and Claudine want to sleep in here with me, like you do almost every night."

"If it's okay," she said.

Thane sighed. "Okay, providing you and Claudine really go to sleep and don't jibber-jabber the whole night."

"We won't."

She jumped into bed with him. To his surprise, Alma Lee was actual quiet for a minute, and maybe even two. Yet her silence was too good to last.

"Thane . . . "

He groaned. "Yes?"

"Today wasn't quite like last Sunday. Seems to me like a whole lot of stuff was going on, all around us. In church, sitting beside Miss Sellie, I near to drifted asleep a couple of times, because of so much doings last night. Honest, when I opened the kitchen door and saw that Glory lady all blood covered, I near about closed it. But I don't guess that would be polite, and Glory might have told on me to Uncle Hiram."

Perhaps, Thane was considering, he could divert his sister's attention and aim it at her everyday adversary.

"Glory," he said, "might have told Vestavia, but she wasn't here to hear it."

Alma Lee sighed. "That's the main reason I'm partial to

• 148 •

Sunday, because that's the one day Vestavia's not here to boss me."

"I thought you and Vestavia were getting on better, and Uncle Hiram had suggested a truce."

"Is that what people wear on a rupture?"

Thane giggled. "No, that's a truss. A *truce* is when two enemies, like you and Vestavia, final get together, make peace, and sort of agree that they really ought to like each other, instead of spat."

"Oh." Alma Lee was quiet for a breath or two. "Then I guess a truce is what Mama and Daddy didn't have."

True enough, Thane was thinking. If any mother and father needed a truce, it had been Mama and Daddy. He had noticed for years. What saddened him was the fact that his little sister had seen and heard many of their later battles. Some kid in Jacksonville had even told Thane, "Your father has been in jail."

Thane turned to Alma Lee.

"Somehow," he said, "living here with the old Judge is a lot smoother. Vestavia and Uncle Hiram like each other."

"How do you know?" she asked.

"I just feel it. They respect each other."

"Like a truce."

"Sort of. I also think that Uncle Hiram would be pleased if you and Vestavia learn to get along. So please try."

Alma Lee was silent. Perhaps, he thought, she's considering her next tactic against Vestavia. His sister hadn't yet realized how nice Vestavia was. She was a really good person, like Miss Sellie. Vestavia wasn't at war with Alma Lee. Only against dirt and bad manners. Well, there was plenty he could do to ease a truce into practice.

"Boy," he said, "that birthday cake that Vestavia baked for us sure was a beauty."

"She didn't bake it for *us*. Vestavia baked it for her great big important Mr. Thane. When my birthday rolls around, if it ever comes, I bet she won't do such for *me*."

Thane smiled, knowing that Vestavia gladly would. He'd bet all the money in the world on it and even add his Ty Cobb baseball to sweeten the wager. In the dark, Thane's grin was stretching wider, as he thought of what to say to Alma Lee.

"Tell you what I'll do," he said. "If old Vestavia doesn't bake you a fancy cake, with your name on it, I'll give you my baseball."

Alma Lee sat up. "Honest?"

"Cross my heart and hope to burp in church."

"Thane, does Ty Cobb live in Hallapoosa?"

"No, he's up north in Georgia, like Miss Sellie told us last evening. That's where Mr. Fulsom saw the baseball game, back when he was alive."

"I'm sorry Miss Sellie lost him. It's so doggone sad when people die and go away to Heaven." She turned to Thane. "Is Heaven up in Georgia too?"

"Heaven is sort of everywhere. Up north in Georgia, here in Florida, all over the United States and other countries. When people we love die, we have to know that's where they are, in Heaven. They have to rest someplace that's all peaceful and good."

"I like how you say things, Thane."

"Thanks."

"Back when Mama was alive, she told me that she was hoping you'd grow up to be a preacher."

Thane looked at her. "Mama said that?"

Alma Lee nodded.

"Well, I suppose I could grow myself up to be a lot worse."

"Promise me something," she said. "I want you to promise that you *won't ever* grow up and be a Justice of the Peace."

Thane pretended to punch her. "Hey, you're forgetting Uncle Hiram's one. What's wrong with being a Justice of the Peace?"

Raising up, leaning her head on her hand, Alma Lee said, "They don't have a whole lot of fun. That's what's wrong with it. Uncle Hiram looks to me like he never had any fun in his whole life."

"Perhaps he never did. And maybe that's why you and I are here living with him, to show him what fun looks like, and sounds like, and smells."

"Fun doesn't smell," she said.

"Sure it does. If you're Miss Sellie, fun is baking brownies, and for Vestavia it was smelling my cake in her oven. It's fun to unwrap a fresh hunk of bubble gum. A pink smell, all happy and sweet as sugar. When you get through chewing the gum and spit it out, you're glad you saved the wrapper, to smell later on."

"You sure know a lot. How come? Is it because you think so much up in Miss Sellie's camphor tree?"

Thane nodded in the dark.

"You have to think to climb high. It's possible that you don't understand all that now, but someday you will. In a way, Alma Lee, we both have to climb in Hallapoosa. We have to *grow* in lots of ways, the way Miss Sellie's tree grew. Slowly, so slow that nobody'll ever notice, but we'll do it. Both of us will grow closer to our uncle." He pulled his sister's pigtail. "And even close to Vestavia."

Alma Lee grunted. "I don't guess I'm fixing to grow too close to that old lady. If I do, I'll probable turn into soap."

"Maybe, when you get olden, you'll be somebody like Miss Sellie and keep a cat."

"I wouldn't mind that too much," she said.

Thane was wondering if Miss Sellie was sleeping, over in her house. Or was she looking in on Glory and Lot? They could also be awake.

"I hear somebody downstairs, Thane."

"Go to sleep. It's only Uncle Hiram. He told me that when he can't sleep, he gets up in the middle of the night and mixes himself half a glass of baking soda. Whenever he does it, I can hear the spoon clinking inside the glass. Anyhow, it isn't any of our business if he prowls some at night. So get yourself to sleep. Tomorrow, you can play with Lotty."

"He doesn't know how to play yet."

"Well, teach him. That's how you make friends. Lot is really the only kid we know, so far."

"Okay," she said. "But he better not pick his nose so much. I told him he might lose his finger."

"He's only a little boy. Go to sleep."

Thane wasn't thinking about Lot. Instead, it was Glory. She was sort of a child too. Small and delicate, not much larger than her brother. Strangely enough, Lot and Glory didn't actual favor each other in looks. She was light and Lotty was dark. Hard to believe that they were brother and sister, as claimed.

"Thane . . . "

"Now what?"

"I kissed Glory good-night, but I sure didn't want to kiss Lot. He's a boy."

"Okay, go to sleep."

Thane couldn't help wondering what it would be like to kiss Glory. She was so pretty that he had tried for most of the afternoon not to stare at her, yet he had, constantly. Even though her face was still swollen, Thane suspected that beneath her injuries lay a very splendid girl. And her hair! Never had he known anyone with hair like Glory's, so shining. By accident, she had bent down close to him to retrieve Alma Lee's doll, and her blonde hair had lightly touched his face. The feeling had tingled all the way down to his toes.

Yes, he wanted to kiss Glory.

Very much.

Thane MacHugh rolled over, knowing that he was now thirteen years and one day old, and never had he come close to kissing a girl. Mothers didn't count. Nor did Alma Lee, who was usually too earth stained to receive such a tribute.

"I want to kiss you, Glory," he whispered in the darkness. "I'll kiss you very gently, because your face is still hurting, so as not to add to your pain. I would like to kiss your hair."

He knew that Lotty was close in age to Alma Lee. But how old was Glory? Was she in her teens, as he was? His heart leaped. Was it possible that the two of them were both thirteen? The folly of his hope slowly dawned on Thane. No, she wasn't thirteen. But stretching upward an inch on tiptoe, he might be taller than Glory. Or almost as tall.

Glory, he decided, might be the first girl he would kiss. As soon as her swelling went down and the bruises melted to a normal color.

She might be his girl. His steady.

Looking at Glory this afternoon, at her arms, neck, legs, was quite different than staring up from the front row at Miss Heavenly Hades the other evening in the Kalipsa Opera House. Someone would have to pay him to kiss *her*.

With his back to Alma Lee, who was possible already sleeping, with Claudine in her arms, Thane MacHugh formed the word *prune* with his lips. That was the word, he had heard last year at school, that people silently say as their two mouths meet.

Prune, prune, prune.

Silently he repeated the word to Glory's lips. Once he had seen what he had believed for years to be the most beautiful being alive. A palomino horse. With her silky voice and her gold and silver hair—that was Glory, a palomino.

A beautiful blonde palomino filly.

His own personal Heaven did not include Miss Heavenly Hades, but having his own horse. And his very own girl. Never could he ask to possess more. Every day he would have a carrot for his horse; and for Glory every moment, a prune. His lips to hers.

"Prune," he said aloud.

Alma Lee nudged him. "Thane, you're talking in your sleep again. What are you dreaming about?"

"Ty Cobb," he said.

· *Twenty-Three* ·

Hiram walked slowly.

It was a Monday morning, following a hectic Sunday, and he wanted to go anywhere except where he was heading, toward his courthouse office.

Julia Blount waved to him.

Somehow, as he tipped his hat to her, Hiram felt good about seeing Julia. They had known each other all their lives, and she was as much a part of Hallapoosa as he was. And like Vestavia Holcum was, and Miss Sellie.

On this day, Hiram MacHugh ached for stability. The weekend had been nightmarish and now, on a sunny Monday morning, he would have been tempted to exchange his soul for just one burning swallow of whiskey. Yet he knew that he must fight the urge. Two weeks ago, Selma Fulsom had frankly said it on her own front veranda, on the evening that he had shared the deathly news with her . . . he didn't actually *need* a drink. He only wanted one.

"Lord," he said, "how I want one now."

But no longer could he indulge himself into being High MacHugh, whether or not the good citizens of Hallapoosa doubted his resolve for reform.

Entering his office, Hiram lifted the worn windowshade to greet the sunlight, opened the window, hung his hat and cane on a coat tree, removed his white suit jacket, and rolled open the top of his desk. A tidy scattering of papers awaited him. Deeds, complaints, and a will or two, the petty documents that had occupied his working life for so many years but kept Hallapoosa in reasonable order. Sitting at his desk, he heard the springs of his chair filing one more complaint. Rolling up his sleeves, then pausing to polish away the vapor from the lenses of his glasses, he tried to work. Mostly he was forcing himself not to think about yesterday's foolhardy action, and Kelby Callister.

"Oh," he muttered, "what have I done?"

Yet, he mused, it was about time somebody did something, and there had been no one else to warn Kelby to leave Glory and Lot alone. Had he asked Carney Ransom do to it, Carney would no doubt have handled the job, as he had always been a willing and helpful associate. But this wasn't Carney's mess.

It was MacHugh business.

Now, as well as years ago, and seeing as he was the only MacHugh in town except for Alma Lee and Thane, the albatross was perched upon his shoulders. Staring at his papers, not seeing them, Hiram was again wondering if there could ever be an end to it, closing the book on the MacHugh-Callister problem once and for all. On a hot August morning, he felt an ironic chill, as though some voodoo swamp curse had somehow infected him, and worse, its contagion might extend to Thane and Alma Lee. He fought an absurd desire to hurry home and gather both of them into his arms. The vision of their being in some orphanage made Hiram shudder.

His office seemed stuffy, airless, more somber than usual. Hiram was feeling airless too. For over an hour, the Justice of the Peace worked at his desk, sorting and signing and filing away the details of Hallapoosa, learning who was delinquent with regard to taxes, examining unpaid fees, making notes as to what could be done to cool the ire between argumentative neighbors. The latter was how Hiram MacHugh had always assessed his duty. Peace, not Justice. To most people, the word *justice* merely meant *law,* and he fervently believed that the law was intended to serve people, not the other way around.

People didn't want so much law, or so many lawyers, and Hiram would quietly see to it that local grievances were settled with little argument and with less expense. Had he prompted more court action, his income would doubtlessly have increased. Perhaps even doubled.

Most of Hallapoosa was poor. Now, because of the Depression, even destitute. Hiram's judicial restraint had saved many a dollar for many a resident for many a year. Such lenient practice of his office, he knew, had never endeared him to the hearts or wallets of the two Hallapoosa attorneys, and neither would leap to defend him.

He heard footsteps.

Someone was walking along the hallway that led to his office. Hiram guessed who was coming and was proved correct.

"Good morning, Judge."

Hiram looked up to see the constable, as usual, in his tan uniform of law enforcement.

"Carney, good morning to you."

"Got a minute?"

"Of course. Come sit down."

Carney Ransom shook his head. "What I want can't be performed in your office. If you don't mind, I'd like to have you come downstairs and take a gander at this geezer I got in a cell. Maybe the guy's a deaf-mute."

"The fellow you arrested yesterday?"

Carney nodded. "I just brung the son-of-a-gun a decent breakfast, from the diner, but this cluck wouldn't touch it. Skinny as a dryspell bean. Looks to me like he hasn't eaten in weeks."

The constable handed Hiram his cane.

He followed Carney along the hallway, down the dark stairs, and to one of the eight cells, which was illuminated by one lightbulb that hung from the ceiling. The place smelled of stale urine.

There were only two prisoners. Each in his own cell.

"Mister," Carney said, "this here gentleman is Judge Mac-Hugh. He's our Justice of the Peace here in Hallapoosa. Seeing as you won't say squat to me, maybe you'll tell *him* your story."

Carney unlocked the cell door and slid it open. The metallic noise made a threatening echo in the near-empty basement jail. Squinting through his glasses in an effort to see in the gray gloom, Hiram entered the cell. The prisoner sat on a bunk, elbows on his knees, his face hidden in his hands. His head, as Carney had previously described, was totally bald, yet oddly exhibited a stubble of hair.

"I'll be right outside the cell," Carney warned, "in case this redneck gets any violent notions."

"Thanks," said Hiram. "We'll be fine."

Carney left to tend the other prisoner.

"Well, now," Hiram said softly, "our good constable tells me you're in a slight bit of trouble." He sat on the opposite bunk, facing the inmate. "First of all, son, perhaps you would be so kind as to tell me your name."

Slowly, very slowly, the bald man removed his hands from his face and looked directly at his interrogator.

"Bobby MacHugh," he said.

Hiram's mouth fell open. Staring, trying to breathe, he looked at the hairless stranger in scruffy clothes. Yes, it was his brother! Faces may change. Voices never do. It was Bobby's voice that had spoken. Clutching his heart, Hiram feared it was about to stop, despite its pumping in his chest.

"Bobby?"

His brother nodded.

"My God. Oh, my God, it really is you. But . . . but you're dead. You were killed by a train. You are dead."

"I wish I was."

An iron post stretched vertically from the corner of the bunk. Hiram clutched it for support, dropping his cane. It clattered to the damp cement floor, lying deathly still.

"You . . . you're alive."

Bobby nodded. "Barely."

"What happened, Bobby? How did all this happen? I have to know."

"First off, how's the kids?"

"They are well. Nice children, both of them. You and Della, . . . oh, my God . . . is *she* alive too?"

Bobby shook his head. "Ain't no way. It's a long story, High. I just wasn't any good for Della, and she was worse for me."

"All right. Tell me everything."

"We fought a whole lot. I was even in jail for most a week one time. Never seemed to keep a job. If we hadn't spawned Thane and Alma Lee, we would've split up . . . gone our separate ways. Some nights I'd never come home. You knew we'd had trouble, because I told you when I hitched back about eight or nine years ago. I should have stayed here and never returned to Della. You made me, Hiram."

"Yes, I made you go. At the time, you had Della and Thane. It seemed the proper thing to do."

Bobby's mouth almost smiled. "Proper? You sounded like old Vestavia right then."

"I know, but never mind her. Finish your story."

Bobby leaned back against the cell wall, then bent one knee to rest a foot on the bunk's edge. His shoes, Hiram noticed, were little more than shreds of leather. He wore no socks at all, and his ankles looked thin and dirty.

"About a year ago, my darling Della got herself a job. And a lover. Some travel man, a salesman she'd met someplace. Believe me, I'm no saint. But I just couldn't take knowing that Della was sparking with this guy."

"I don't understand."

"Hang on, and you will." Getting up, Bobby MacHugh walked away from the cell door and stared blankly out of the barred ground-level window. "Della would take our car, some evenings, to go tryst her lover boy. A couple of guys told me they'd seen 'em out together, at a dance hall. Also at a cheap hotel away out of town."

"Go on."

"So, one night about a couple of weeks ago, I can't remember exact, I borrowed Raymond Gibson's truck and followed. Sure enough, Della picks up this fancy gent of hers in our car, and off they go. I followed in the truck. It was dark. A train was coming, and it sudden looked to me like they were trying to outrun this train at a grade crossing. If they did, they'd lose me certain, so I mashed down on the pedal to keep up. Train was coming at a fast clip, a freighter. But then Della slams on the brakes. Lost her nerve. I hit my brake pedal too, but Ray's old truck brakes wouldn't grab."

"Is that when it happened?"

Bobby nodded.

"My truck plowed into our car, pushed it on the tracks, and the train did the damage. It was an accident, High. Honest it was. I never really intended to do nobody harm like that, and couldn't believe what I saw. All I could do was sit in the cab and hold tight to the wheel. The train kept going. I got out, went to the car and saw that Della and her boyfriend had got their necks busted. Crushed into pulp. No sheriff would have believed what honest happened, my being a jailbird out of

· **158** ·

work, and all. So I switched wallets with the boyfriend and tossed a match to our car. Then I took off and kept going. Ditched the truck and shaved off my hair. Two days later, I bought a Jacksonville paper and read about the accident, about my death, and Della's."

"Good grief, Bobby. What you did is . . . it's . . . "

"Not very proper." Bobby wasn't laughing. "But it was my only way out, Hiram. Can't you see? Besides, it's that old unwritten law."

"What law?" Hiram asked him.

"If a man catches his wife with another guy, you know, he's got a right to finish 'em both."

"No, that's not true. It's illegal."

"It was my only way to escape. Earlier, I'd took out an insurance policy, bought and paid, for a thousand dollars. Thane and Alma Lee get it. Della wasn't even in for a penny of benefit. Not a red cent. So she got what she deserved."

"How long have you been here in Hallapoosa?"

"Since early Saturday. It was Thane's birthday. I had me a hanker to see my children, just one more time. I saw y'all. It was through the window, and you people were eating birthday cake. Miss Sellie too. I just stood outside in the shrubbery and wept."

Reaching for his fallen cane, Hiram recovered it, then managed to stand with difficulty. He moved a step or two to Bobby, held out his arms, and embraced his brother. "It's all right, Bobby, I'm here now. Somehow, we'll find a way out of this."

The body in his arms felt frail, weak, the former athlete was now little more than a skeleton, a trembling memory of a crowd's cheering, and a home run. Small wonder why Carney had not recognized him.

"I'm here, Bobby. I'll take care of you. Soon as I can clear all this up, I'll bring you home."

He felt his brother shake his head.

"Bless you, Hiram. Thanks, but it's too late. At least I final did something for *you*, High. Something important. I owed you, brother. So many times you covered for me. Cleaned up my messes, all my dang fool mistakes. But at last I done something for you."

Hiram looked at him. "Kelby?"

• 159 •

Bobby nodded. "You killed him, Hiram. I saw it all, yesterday morning, when I was hiding down near the island, hoping to catch a glimpse of Glory. Not to speak to her, but only to see her from a distance. And maybe to see her kid. My kid. That's when I saw you cross the crick with your cane and pole. I was a mite drunk, but I followed close, in case you might need some help. Then I heard you beating on Kelby, and you beat him to death."

"No."

"Yes. After you left, I cleaned up after you, drunk as I was. I throwed his body in the crick and watched the current carrying him away. Then I went back inside the shack to sleep, hoping I'd see Glory. I was shirttail drunk, Hiram. But I swept up your mess."

"But I didn't kill Kelby. Did I?"

Bobby nodded. "He was dead when I found him. Deader than yesterday's chicken dinner. So I dumped the body."

Hiram had to sit down.

"So you see," Bobby was now telling him, "there *is* a killer in this cell, big brother. But it isn't me."

"God," said Hiram, in fervent prayer.

"Don't worry," Bobby said. "I'll take the rap for you, Hiram, because I'm sick of running, sick of hiding, and sort of just plain tired of living. I owe you. You'll raise Thane and Alma Lee in a way that I never could. You and trusty old Vestavia."

"No, I can't let you do it. You're their father. I'm not. But how in the name of Heaven will you be able to tell them you're alive? This could damage them."

Bobby came to him, to sit down on the bunk beside him. "Thane and Alma Lee are not to be told, High. I'm dead, remember? As far as they are concerned, they ought never know the truth about their old man. Perhaps the *Hallapoosa Weekly* will run a front-page story on how a drifter was blamed for ending old Kelby Callister. And please, don't tell Glory."

Hiram couldn't speak. He had heard too much and received too jolting a shock. Bobby alive, and Kelby Callister beaten to death by the cane of a cripple. It had been self-defense, yet the town knew about his years with Glory. His motive. No jury would believe anything except murder.

Hiram felt Bobby pulling his head to rest on his lean shoulder. "It's okay, Hiram. You'll forever be my brother and don't forget it. You will always be the kind of man I couldn't ever become, try as I might. I wanted to be like you. Strong and proper, the way Vestavia raised us."

The two MacHughs were clinging to each other in the dim light of a basement prison cell, holding on, as though afraid to lose a special someone forever.

It took a while before Hiram could speak.

"Forgive me, Bobby."

·*Twenty-Four*·

Carney Ransom sat in Hiram's office.

"Good grief," he said to Hiram, "what a story. My gut feels like somebody deflated me like an old innertube."

"He's alive," Hiram said softly.

Carney nodded. "You know, if you'd told me the doggone Easter Bunny had come to Hallapoosa, I'd have believed it quicker than all this." He shook his head. "It's Bobby Mac-Hugh, all right. High, I don't guess I know how your heart took it."

How, the constable was wondering, would Hiram keep the news from reaching Thane and Alma Lee?

"It's all over town, High. I don't mean about Bobby's being downstairs in a cell. I mean the news about Kelby Callister. Dang it! I made one giant of a mistake by finding that body, and then announcing it was a guy with half an ear." Carney slapped his chubby thigh. "Then, on top of that, the corpse disappears. Who in the name of Sam Hill would've carted off Callister? I'm going nuts."

He saw Hiram's fingers drum on the desktop, as though the Justice of the Peace was in deep thought.

"I can't let Bobby die in the electric chair for what I did."

"You said it was self-defense."

"It was, Carney. I swear to you it was. Kelby came at me with a hammer. But there's a point of law here, one which any district attorney worth his salt would base his argument on. In rage, I became the attacker, and I didn't just repel him. I beat the devil to death."

"I see what you mean. What makes it worse, pardon my saying, is that a lot of Hallapoosa folks knew about you and Glory. Some might be whispering that you're the father of Glory's son."

"I'm not, and you know so."

"Yeah, I know. But your old pal Carney won't be sitting in the jury box. What we got here is pig simple. Callister got beaten to death, and downstairs we got a suspect who maybe didn't kill Kelby, but he sure as heck knocked up Kelby's daughter." As Carney saw Hiram's face tighten, he regretted his blunt phrasing of the paternity angle. "Plus the fact that Bobby admitted to you that he had a hand in body disposal. On top of that, there's the matter of a certain Jacksonville train accident. To sum it all up, Judge, it seems like Bobby MacHugh has been a rather busy guy."

"Perhaps," Hiram said, "I shouldn't have told you so much. But you're my friend. You are the best friend I've ever had, Carney. I couldn't hold it all inside me. It's too explosive."

"I understand. You're *my* best friend too. I don't guess either one of us ever bothered to tell each other."

Hiram looked at him. "We never had to."

Both men were quiet for a moment as Carney sat wondering what to do. In the past, Hiram MacHugh had often guided him in doing a constable's duty. But this was a different story. Carney was silently reasoning how much of it was true. For certain, the death of Kelby Callister was no loss to Hallapoosa, and surely little loss in the slightest to Glory and her young boy. Hiram had told him about the condition of Glory's face, swollen and bruised. Personally, he wasn't too unhappy that old Kelby was out of the picture.

"But where the heck is the body?" Carney asked aloud. "It certain didn't get up and stroll away by itself, and according to your brother's confession, *he* only dumped Kelby into the Kalipsa Crick."

Hiram leaned slight forward, squeaking the springs of his desk chair. "If you don't mind a suggestion of a suspect," he said, "I have a theory."

"Shoot."

"The Crickers have always buried their own. It is possible

• 163 •

that Kelby's body was found by another Callister who claimed it. There's little point in asking *them,* because none of them would tell either you or me the straight of it."

Carney agreed. "Yeah, they'd clam up."

"My guess is, Kelby's body will never be found. But your problem is . . . you have already found Kelby's murderer, and here I sit."

The constable bit his lower lip. "I'm no lawyer, High. Neither are you. But the brace of us have been wading around in legal matters for near to half our lives. I even browsed through a few books on criminology." Carney took a breath. "A crime is a combination of two elements, as the law sees it. The *act,* plus the criminal's *intent* to do it."

He saw Hiram nod his head. "Correct."

"So," Carney continued, "this is how I look at it. You had no intention of doing physical harm to Callister, even though you were a dang fool to go there. Trouble is, you were seen. I'm the law in Hallapoosa, but if I just shrug my shoulders and look the other way on this, the citizens aren't going to buy it, because the whole cussed town knows that you and I are close pals. Like it or not, Hiram, I'm in this up to my fat ass, and I know how to handle it about as much as Jake's mule."

Carney stood up. He still felt lousy from yesterday and from Saturday night's binge, but he couldn't camp in Hiram's office all morning.

He pointed at the floor. "Downstairs," he said, "I got myself a prisoner. Nobody knows he's there except you and me, plus that brawler in the other cell. He's a turpentiner. His name's Jim Colly. I locked him up early this morning to sober up and cool down. Sooner or later, he's going to spot Bobby down there, and possible recognize him. Which brings up another key question. What in the name of sanity am I going to do with your brother?"

"You can't hold him, Carney. First off, you might consider ignoring what he did in Jacksonville, because it's out of your jurisdiction."

Carney nodded. "It certain is. As far as I'm concerned, that train-crash business up north is a closed case." He let out a sigh. "Until . . . somebody establishes the fact that your brother is still alive but pretending to be dead. People don't behave thataway unless they're hiding something. So, here's where all this leaves me, Hiram. How much of this can I write up officially, and, on the other side of the ledger, how much can I whitewash?"

Hiram's fist thumped his desktop. "Best you don't whitewash any of it. I don't want you to stick your neck out on my account. Or on Bobby's."

Carney's body slumped against the doorframe of Hiram's office.

"I have to do *something* on your behalf. We been friends too long. I've known you and your brother too many blessed years to go high and mighty, just to keep my own shirt clean." Carney jerked a thumb toward his own chest. "Unless our memories have failed us, I'm in all this mess too, since the time Glory was pregnant and you had me handle a few financial transactions."

He saw Hiram MacHugh slowly get to his feet, holding the corner of his desk to steady himself.

"It's a nightmare," Hiram said.

"Sure is. I certain can't hold your brother downstairs in that cell for something he didn't do. When you told me it was Bobby, I near to fell over. Yet soon as I heard his voice, then I knew."

"His voice is still the same," Hiram said, "and it appears to be the one thing about my brother to remain as it once was. Everything else is so different, as if he's a stranger." Hiram sighed. "But he's my brother, my little kid brother who wanted to be King Arthur and General U. S. Grant all in one package."

Carney took a step closer to his friend, searching for words to say that would ease Hiram's mind as well as easing his own.

"Gosh, I don't know what to say or do. Maybe we just ought to wait until night and then turn Bobby loose, if he'll promise to leave town."

Hiram looked at him solemnly. "Hallapoosa is Bobby's home, Carney, as well as being ours. His Jacksonville life is over now. Thane and Alma Lee are here, I'm here, and so is Vestavia. Some of the kids he attended school with are still around. Hallapoosa is all Bobby has left. It will always draw him back like a magnet."

"Yeah, for sure. If'n either you or I had been Bobby Mac-Hugh, I don't guess we'd done any different. Hallapoosa is home."

"I can't work today. It's impossible for me to sit up here in my office knowing that my brother is downstairs in a cell. I'm going down there to comfort him, if that's agreeable to you, Constable. After all, he's your prisoner instead of mine."

"Sure, go ahead. I figure the two of you have matters to talk about."

"Indeed so. But nothing behind your back, Carney, I promise you."

"Shucks, I know that."

Carney escorted Hiram along the courthouse hallway that led to the basement cells. Never before had he noticed how old Hiram MacHugh had become, how slouched over, how rumpled. Standing at the top of the stairs, he heard the tap of Hiram's cane, step beyond step, then followed him down. Unlocking the cell, he allowed MacHugh to enter, then closed it with an echoing metallic click that seemed to endure a long time before dying into silence.

"Sorry," he said, "but I gotta lock the two of you inside. Just a formality. Okay?"

He turned the thick key.

"Okay," said Hiram. "Bobby and I will be all right. Give us an hour or so, and perhaps we can settle a few things."

Carney left the two brothers in the cell, lugged himself upstairs, and hung the heavy keyring on its customary hook. Sitting behind his desk, he kicked up one leg and then the other, crossing his boots in order to rest his aching feet on a desk corner. Beneath him, his chair groaned as he tested its springs by pushing his weight backward. Mindlessly, he reached for a yellow pencil, chewed its eraser, then twiddled it as a drumstick on the wooden chair arm. Unbending a paperclip, Carney dislodged a pesky speck of breakfast bacon from between two of his lower teeth.

Then he said a dirty word.

With a careless toss, he flipped the paperclip into a wastebasket that needed to be emptied.

"Holy crow," he finally said softly, "if this situation ain't one dandy bucket of sick worms, I don't know what is."

Closing his eyes, he tried to think about the last time that he and his pa had gone hunting. Maybe a good ten years ago, when his folks were still alive. Now they were gone. Yet he remembered the last outing with his father as though it was only yesterday, and he could hear their two hounds bugle. No sound like it. A real nighttime-in-the-forest noise that has to be heard, and felt, and never forgotten. Together, he and his daddy had brought down a possum.

Even though Carney was a growed-up man at the time, as he was raising his gun at the treed possum his pa said, "Don't lose sight of your target, boy."

A needless warning, Carney recalled.

Yet it was sort of the last good advice he could remember his daddy's telling him. Don't lose sight of the target. And right now, the target seemed simple enough to Constable Carney Ransom . . . that nobody else in Hallapoosa gets hurt.

"Simple," said Carney.

Most of life's problems are, he had long ago concluded. Trouble is, humans try to complicate matters too much.

Pulling open the drawer of his desk, he produced a fresh sheet of paper. Making a list, he figured, would help to clear the situation. Carney liked lists. It was a sure way to get things done. He had learned this from Hiram MacHugh during their many years together in the courthouse.

He printed the names in a column:

> Thane
> Alma Lee
> Hiram
> Bobby
> Glory
> Lot

Only six names. This, in Carney's mind, seemed to sum it all up in a nutshell, listing the six people most likely to be damaged by current circumstances. His pencil drew a circle around the names, enclosing them within one perimeter. The area of protection would logically be Hiram's house. Five were there now. It would be an easy matter to suggest to Hiram that he take Bobby home and keep him in custody there. All the breakable eggs in one basket, safe from any Callister revenge.

• **167** •

Ah, but for how long?

School would soon be starting. His pencil drew two arrows from Thane's name and Alma Lee's, their shafts extending beyond the circle's circumference. Plus the fact that Glory and Lot would be returning to their island shack, now that Kelby was dead and could no longer threaten their safety. He drew two more arrows across the ring. Bobby hadn't moved home yet . . . a fifth arrow. And Hiram came down here to the courthouse every day except Sunday. Another arrow, beyond the circle's fortress wall.

Disgusted, Carney crumpled up his piece of paper and lofted it toward his overflowing waste can, wondering how he could protect all his targets. It was, Carney was thinking, almost a certainty that the Crickers would stir up trouble.

All six on his list were too easily hit. Mentally, he added a seventh name as a possible target.

His own.

· *Twenty-Five* ·

"**T**hank you so much," Glory said.
Standing on the back porch of Miss Sellie Fulsom's, she and Lotty thanked her once again, but the gray-haired lady wouldn't accept any gratitude.

"Little enough," she kept insisting. "I just wonder if you and the little boy ought to return home to the island so soon." As she spoke, her hands were wiping themselves on a dishtowel, over and over, Glory noticed.

"My papa's dead," Glory said. "He's clean gone, and I certain pray the good Lord'll forgive me for feeling so thankful that it be final. Lord rest his poorly soul."

"God is good," Miss Sellie told her. "You'll best remember that, Glory, and share all your blessings with Lotty here. Plenty more kindly people in this world that there is ornery."

Kneeling down, Miss Sellie touched Lot's cheek, brushing his hair with her hand. Nearby, watching it all, stood Charlie Moon Sky. A number of times, Glory Callister had noticed how he stared at her, always smiling; yet, whenever she returned the attention, he would turn his head shyly away. But his smile would widen. Charlie sure was a handsome devil, even if he was a halfbreed Seminole. In spite of his coppery skin, his features seemed to be more like white people, and no woman in her right mind, Glory thought, would consider Charlie Moon Sky anything except a good-looking man.

"Charlie will be walking along with you and your lad," Miss

Sellie told her, "until you reach the crick. Just to make certain y'all arrive safe and sound." The old woman waved from her back porch as the three of them started to leave. "Come back now, Glory, and don't ever consider yourself a stranger. You too, Lotty."

After waving good-bye to Mrs. Fulsom, Lot ran on ahead, but not very far. Close enough for Glory to keep an eye on him.

Charlie, she noticed, did not walk beside her. Instead, he silently followed, several respectful steps to the rear. As she walked down the gentle slope, Glory Callister felt his eyes, as though his hands were touching her hair. Turning her head, Glory looked back over her shoulder to see Charlie smiling, and then he stopped, as if again preparing to avert his glance.

"I s'pose," she told him, "you could walk beside me, if'n you're of a mind."

At first Charlie hesitated, as though weighing whether or not to join her. Up until this point, he had said absolutely nothing to her, and very little to Lot, and Glory was wondering if Charlie ever spoke at all.

"Do you speak?" she asked.

After a breath, he nodded. "Yes."

"Good, because that be how people sort of meet, get acquainted, and know one another. I already told you a thank-you for finding Lot, but I don't guess you'd mind it much if'n I said it again." Glory's hand rose thoughtfully to touch her chin. "How you knowed where to bring him, I'll never understand."

Charlie took a step closer to her. "Because . . . he is yours."

"How did you know that?"

"Sometimes I watch you, and the boy." He laced the fingers of his hands together. "The two of you belong."

Glory liked what she was seeing. "Yes," she said, "we do belong. Lotty's my brother." The lie bothered her. It seemed to hang in the air, hovering around her face like some little pesky bug that Glory wanted to shoo away with a wave of her hand.

He stood closer to her. "We will walk." Noticing the knife at his hip, Glory asked him if he always wore it. Charlie nodded. "Always. At night, it sleeps in my hand. My father made it for me."

To Glory's ear, Charlie seemed to speak proudly. A boy ought to have a father. Lately, she had caught herself thinking of Bobby MacHugh, his rascal face, those sparkling eyes that had danced so with deviltry, and recalling their times together. Somebody had once told her, although Glory had forgotten exactly who it was, that a girl always remembers her first love. Even if she lives to grow olden. Glory would ever recall Bobby and their first time. Glory sighed. There was something special about MacHugh men. Ahead, she could hear Lotty shaking a tree, and being a boy on a summer morning. I hope, she said to herself, that Lot don't get some girl in trouble, the way Bobby done to me.

"Good boy," Charlie told her, almost as though he had been reading her private thoughts.

"Yes, he certain be, most times."

"Maybe," said Charlie, "I will make a knife for your little brother." He smiled. "Then he will become *my* little brother too."

My, Glory reacted, what a friendly thing to say. To thank Charlie, she reached out very briefly to touch the faded gray sleeve of his work shirt. The cotton felt very soft, as a result of so many frequent washings by Miss Sellie, she imagined . . . but inside the shirt sleeve, Charlie's arm felt firm and hard. Quite manly.

Bobby MacHugh was dead. And dead men don't make knives for their sons. Even if Bobby was still living, Glory doubted that he would have taken the time or the bother. She had learned, in the past seven years, not to expect more from people than they are able or willing to give. Expect little or nothing and a person who is limiting the expecting won't ever get disappointed. Indeed, she had learned that lesson, many a time, and from many a male.

Charlie Moon Sky would probable turn out to act just like all the other males she had known. All, except for Hiram. He was some different. But then, when she knowed that Thane and Alma Lee were coming to live with him, Glory Callister had quit expecting from Hiram MacHugh as well. The only *expect* a woman could allow herself, she had concluded, was expecting a baby.

After the baby, a good-bye.

Together, they walked slowly through a stand of scrub oak.

Trash wood, some people liked calling it, on account it wasn't fit to build with or burn for cooking.

For some reason, one which she couldn't quite explain to herself, Glory Callister carried the urge to tell Charlie Moon Sky that Lot wasn't her brother, but in truth her child. However, such a confession might open the door to a flock of questions from Charlie, and maybe from Miss Sellie. And yet Glory had an inkling that Miss Sellie Fulsom already knew about Lot. No proof, only a hunch, because she could see sparkles of silent wisdom in the old woman's eyes. They were bright, alive, and understanding flew across her face like fireflies. Miss Sellie knew plenty more than she put to words.

They arrived at the crick.

Lotty was already there, busying himself by searching in the shallows for skipper stones to throw. He threw one, but it didn't skip at all, and merely sunk with one little *plunk*. Bending his legs, Charlie Moon Sky said nothing to the boy as he located a small stone, round and flat. He threw it, and the stone danced several tiny steps on the open pond water before sinking.

Lot looked at him with respect.

Taking another stone, Charlie showed Lot how to rim the edge with one curved finger, cock his arm, and then with a smooth and effortless shoulder rotation, launch it. Again a stone tripped along the crust of water. Lot tried it, and won. A victorious smile rearranged his freckles so they danced too, as countless little tan stones. To see Lotty and Charlie smiling at each other made Glory smile too.

"Could you show *me* how?" she asked Charlie.

He nodded. Then he did.

The three of them halfway crossed the crick, reaching the island that parted the water. As she expected, their shack was empty, with no old Kelby there to swear and complain. The dark door appeared darker, almost ghostly in the daylight, yet this shack was all Glory Callister had ever known to call *home*. Inside, she knew, there would be no food. Luckily, she had a few dollars put aside, safe hidden in a tabacco tin, more than enough to buy a few groceries and fresh milk for Lotty.

"I'd invite you to come inside," she said to Charlie Moon Sky, "but things ain't looking proper right now. My pa's gone.

My ma was a good woman and he beated on her too, well as on me and Lot, so maybe I'm better off."

Charlie looked at her. His hands still held a little fawn-colored pebble, which he repeatedly poured from hand to hand as though his mind and the pebble couldn't quite decide whether to stay or go.

He looked around the little island. "I like it here," he said. "You have land, water, and sky." Pointing to Lot, he said, "And you have the little one."

"You," she said, "have your Miss Sellie."

Charlie nodded. "My good lady."

"I hope you come to see us, Charlie," she said. "I don't have any friends, and neither does Lot."

"I will come. Tonight, I will come, after the boy has gone to sleep, and bring you a surprise."

Turning, he danced across the stones to the shore, his bare feet skipping as though they were twin pebbles. As he waved to her, Glory waved too.

"Tonight," she said softly.

· *Twenty-Six* ·

"**A** re you up there, Thane?"

Looking up into the giant camphor tree always made Alma Lee's neck ache. Her brother was up yonder, that she knew, but he wouldn't as much as hoot an answer.

"I think you ought to come down right now," she yelled up at the leaves, "and Vestavia thinks so too."

For some reason, to Alma Lee's way of thinking, adding Vestavia's opinion to agree with her own usual strengthened their side of the argument. Actually, she knew, Vestavia didn't probable know that her brother had climbed so high, because the old colored lady was asleep, inside the house, taking a little nap on the parlor sofa.

"I don't have anybody to play with, Thane."

No reply.

"If you don't hasten yourself down here, I won't ever come sleep with you at night." Alma Lee took in a fresh breath. "And neither will Claudine!"

Still no answer.

Well, as far as Alma Lee MacHugh was concerned, Mr. Thane could stay up in Miss Sellie's big tree forever. Glancing next door, she had a notion to visit Miss Sellie, but things were quiet there too. Just as Vestavia did, Miss Sellie sometimes curled down for an afternoon nap, along with Abercrombie.

Alma Lee sighed.

"Claudine, there's nobody around who wants either one of us for a playmate. Not a single precious solitary soul."

Carrying her doll by one leg, upside down, Alma Lee walked slowly toward the house, kicking the dusty sand with her bare feet. Her toes were filthy. So were her knees and shins, and she had half a mind to parade right into the house to confront Vestavia. And maybe even stand for a scrubbing.

Sitting on the back porch, Alma Lee leaned forward and rested her chin on one grimy knee, then on the other. Now her face would be dirty too, but she didn't much give a red rat's rump, as Thane would sometimes say. It sure was turning out to be a sorry Monday. For a while, there was excitement aplenty, because yesterday had been close to a circus. It was fun having Glory and Lot around, here and next-door at Miss Sellie's. But now they were gone.

"Maybe," she said, "I'll go see if I can find Charlie Moon Sky, even though he doesn't talk as much as Claudine."

She liked Charlie. Two or three days ago, Claudine's arm had worked itself loose and wouldn't hang to her shoulder right. It made her arm look too long to match the other one. In the kitchen, Vestavia had been busy at the pantry board and her hands white with flour, so she couldn't drop everything to mend her dolly's arm. So, instead, she'd ducked through the fence to Miss Sellie's and showed her doll's problem to Charlie.

In a jiffy, Charlie's knife had sliced off a length of black rubber from an old innertube and fixed up Claudine's arm like new. And he did it all without saying as much as "You're welcome," when Alma Lee had thanked him.

All he did was smile.

Raising her chin from her knee, Alma Lee considered the possibility of taking a walk all the way down to the courthouse, to see Uncle Hiram and Constable Ransom. According to what Thane claimed, underneath the courthouse was a jail. Maybe there would be prisoners inside, behind the bars, and they might be escaping.

Opening the screen door, Alma Lee tiptoed inside and through the kitchen until she could spot Vestavia, still asleep, her mouth as open as a yawn. But seeing her reminded Alma Lee of Vestavia's warning that *nobody,* meaning herself and

• 175 •

her brother, was allowed to go visit the courthouse unless the Judge said it was okay.

She decided not to go.

Returning to the back porch, she sat on the steps again and contemplated the soil between her toes, which, if rubbed with a finger, smelled like vinegar. It might surprise Vestavia if she took a bath, all by herself. But the washtub was too heavy, and it would probable fall and make a clang on the kitchen floor, wake up Vestavia, and then the scolding would come to a bubble for sure.

Leaving the porch, she searched for Miss Sellie's garden hose. It wasn't hooked up to the house at either of the two outdoor spigots. Nor was it in Miss Sellie's shed.

"My," she said, "it certain is hot."

Running through the spray and mist of Miss Sellie's hose, something which she and Lotty had done yesterday afternoon, sure was fun. But today there didn't seem to be any way to do it. Looking up in the camphor tree, Alma Lee began to wonder if Thane was still away up among the branches. Perhaps he'd climbed down and scamped off.

"If old Uncle Hiram comes home early from the courthouse, he'll throw the ball with me," she yelled up into the leaves.

Alma Lee shook her head.

"No," she said, "he probable wouldn't."

Uncle Hiram wasn't fun like Miss Sellie and Thane and Glory and Lot. The Judge didn't laugh or do anything or play with any living soul. That old Justice of the Peace wouldn't know *play* if'n it hopped up and bit his serious old nose.

"And," she said, kicking a barrel with her heel, "I don't guess I can rinse myself off to cooling until I locate Miss Sellie's garden hose."

It would be nice, Alma Lee thought as she leaned against the trunk of a willow tree, if I lived down by the crick, the way Lot does. Lot Callister had all the water he wanted. A whole doggone crick full. Water and fishing and a whole mess of croaking frogs, plus crawdads to catch and boil for supper. Yes, she thought, it sure would be fun to live down on the island with Lot and Glory and be a Cricker.

Lotty had said that people who weren't Crickers were Townies.

"Well," she said, "I guess a person has to become one or the other. Claudine, maybe that's what we ought to do." She jumped up and down in the pleasuring of her sudden idea. "Hey! We'll just toddle ourselfs down to the water and be Crickers!"

It seemed to be a farther walk than Alma Lee had originally planned.

As she stumbled around in the woods, the trees started to look all alike, and it wasn't at all like walking along Exchange Street on the way to church with Miss Sellie. It wasn't like Hallapoosa.

"Claudine," she said after a long while, "I'm sort of starting to wonder where they put that dumb old crick. I s'pect it's possible hid."

Things were different here, Alma Lee noticed. Ferns seemed to be near to everywhere, and the ground was softer, the soil much blacker. It wasn't dry old dusty sand. Instead, she was standing on black muck, moist and dark and velvety rich. Soft to touch. And damp to smell. Walking on, carrying her doll, she thought she heard something. Pressing on, she came to a place where the land almost fell away and there Alma Lee finally spotted that which she sought.

Water.

"Here it is, Claudine." She pointed. "This here is the crick. But I don't see any houses or anything. They're here though. You heard Lot tell us all about living on the island." She sighed. "Well, if we're going to be Crickers, best we get going and find the other people."

Being hot and tired, Alma Lee went in, clothes and all. The water felt cool and it was fun to be wet, and to get Claudine wet too. Soaked, in fact. Vestavia would be pleased if she could see. As her foot stepped on a sharp pebble, she lost balance, and grabbed for an outcropping branch, losing Claudine in the process. The doll floated away to just beyond reaching.

"Claudine!"

The current was slow.

Yet, beneath her bare feet, the pebbles and limestone rocks were rough, and slipping, which made overtaking the doll seem momentarily impossible. And, to make things worse, it wasn't fun anymore. Claudine kept bobbing along, out of reach, unhurried, yet always floating downstream behind her grasp.

"Claudine, please come back."

Grabbing a fallen branch, Alma Lee tried to rake her dolly to shore, without success. The lazy current seemed just strong enough to carry the doll effortlessly along, moving only by inches, but always moving. A steady pull, inch after casual inch, until the inches became feet, and yards, and far more.

Again and again, Alma Lee MacHugh screamed the name of her doll, as the water on her face became more than crick water. It was now fright, resulting from being able to see Claudine floating calmly away, yet never being quite able to touch her by hand, or with the leafless branch. Each time the branch would strike the water like a witch's claw, its jagged fingers extending, never reaching.

Alma Lee wouldn't give up.

As the crick wormed away from Hallapoosa, so did the doll, and the child. Each bend in the crick seemed to promise an easing of the current, yet the flow persisted, slowly, relentlessly, always carrying the doll downstream. Within sight, never within arm's length.

Why, Alma Lee was wondering, is the light fading? It's afternoon, she was thinking, totally unaware of how much of the day had passed. How far she had waded, screaming for her dolly, following and following, the child had no idea.

"Claudine," she cried. "I won't let you go. I love you, Claudine. You're mine. You're all I own. I own you and you own me."

The darkness came.

Her feet were hurting so much. So many pebbles. And such sharp unyielding edges. The dress she was wearing had been torn, several times, by the broken stubs of shoreline bushes, and by the jagged branches of fallen trees. Yet she wasn't going to give up. She couldn't lose Claudine. It wouldn't be right to just stand there and watch her dolly float away forever.

"Claudine! Claudine! Claudine!"

Even though her voice was now hoarse and raw, Alma kept screaming the name, hoping that the doll's dress would snag on a twig, and then Claudine could be rescued.

It was dark. No moon.

She was squinting now, her face wet, her feet nearing agony, trying to keep the floating doll in sight. But then Alma

Lee fell, and a sharp bramble scratched her face, stinging her with pain. As she tried to regain her footing, she looked up to see the biggest man she had ever seen. He wore no shirt, only bib overalls, and his chest was the hairy chest of some giant bear, except for the scars on his flesh. His hands were paws too, and they grabbed her shoulders. Trying to scream, she could make no sound at all. The man's breath was foul, sour, and mean.

"Hey! Who be you, baby gal?"

She swallowed. "Alma Lee MacHugh. I live back yonder in Hallapoosa with my Uncle Hiram." She stared unblinking and openmouthed at the man who had captured her. "What's your name?" she asked.

The man spat. "Big Callister."

· *Twenty-Seven* ·

"Vestavia?"

    In her dream, Vestavia Holcum was once again a young girl in a creamy white dress.

"Vestavia, please wake up."

As she heard her name being called, she was dreaming about sitting in church, beside her mama, where all the ladies were wearing white dresses with lace. Everyone seemed to be smiling and singing. But someone's hand was shaking her shoulder and she could hear Mr. Hiram's voice. Opening her eyes, Vestavia realized that she had slept some longer than she'd intended. Slowly she tried to sit up.

"Mr. Hiram, please forgive me for dozing off like I done. I wore myself so . . ."

She saw the Judge rap the floor with his cane. "Where is Alma Lee? She's gone. I sent Thane over to Mrs. Fulsom's but she's not there either. Nowhere to be found."

Standing up slowly, Vestavia rubbed her eyes and gradually became aware of the situation. Alma Lee gone? Gone! Concern suddenly surged through her.

"Oh, Mr. Hiram, what we going to do?"

Thane appeared in the doorway. "I ran up and down the street, like you said to do," he told his uncle, "but I didn't hear any answer when I hollered out her name. So I guess she's run off."

Hurrying to the kitchen, Vestavia called out of the back door, through the screen. "Alma Lee. Alma Lee MacHugh, you hearing me? Well, you best tote yourself home, and smart quick." Vestavia heard her words die to stillness in the summer heat. It hurt her to speak so sharply to a runaway child.

Next door, Miss Sellie was also calling out Alma Lee's name in her high twittery voice. But the only person who came hustling was her yard man, Charlie Moon Sky. Vestavia saw the two of them talking to each other, with Miss Sellie pointing one way, then another.

Thane was yelling louder than anyone else. "Alma Lee! I'm sorry I hid up yonder in the camphor tree. Please come home. Please!" He returned to the parlor to face his uncle.

Scowling some at his nephew, the Judge asked, "Is that why your sister took herself off?"

The boy nodded. "Yes, sir."

"That wasn't very nice, Thane."

"No, I don't guess it was. Maybe, soon as Alma Lee turns up, I ought to get a licking for it."

Mr. Hiram shook his head. "No, there's little need for that. Punishing you won't locate your sister." Quickly he limped to the telephone and spoke a number to the operator.

Vestavia stood by, her body near to doubling over under the weight of her guilt. If anything sorry happened to her little girl, she was thinking, there'd be no forgiving herself. Not ever.

"Dang it, Carney," Mr. Hiram snapped at the black mouth-piece, "answer your machine." His voice lowered a pitch or two. "Please," he said, "please be home." Hiram's finger jiggled the receiver hook, clacking it up and down until the operator came back on the line. "Myrtle," he said calmly, "please locate Constable Ransom, if you possibly can, and ask him to come here right away. Try the hardware store and the fire station as well as ringing his office and his home. Thank you."

Miss Sellie appeared at the front door and, without knocking, came charging inside the house.

"Is she found?" she asked.

Hiram shook his head. "We don't even know where to search."

Vestavia looked at Mr. Hiram and then at Mrs. Fulsom, back and forth, wanting to say how sorry she was feeling, and what a no-account old woman she'd become. "I'm just a worthless old ragabone," she mumbled. "No good to nobody no more."

Reaching around her, Miss Sellie's hands grasped both of her shoulders. "Now, dear Vestavia, don't you fret. We'll find Alma Lee." She looked at the Judge as she patted Vestavia gently. "We'll locate her jolly quick, won't we, Hiram?"

"Yes," he said. "We have to."

"I sent Charlie to look all along the hedgerows, out back, to poke inside every clump where a little child could hide," Miss Sellie said. "If she's out back yonder, Charlie will smoke her out and bring her home." She smiled. "He's right good at finding children."

"It's my fault," Thane said.

"Now, now," Hiram said quickly, pacing back and forth in the parlor, leaning heavily on his cane, "we won't accomplish anything if we all blame ourselves."

Vestavia wanted to cry, to wail out good and loud, yet she knew that Mr. Hiram wouldn't approve. In all the years she had known him, never once had she ever seen Hiram Mac-Hugh cry. There were no tears in him. No grieving. Only those deep sorrows that lay buried in his memory. Mr. Bobby had never been hers in the same sense that Mr. Hiram had been. Oh, how she longed to see Hiram once again as a child, as her brave boy, walking home with her and using his pitiful little cane.

Hiram's father, Mr.Clarence, offered to walk home with her only once, at a time when Hiram was sick with a fever. Yet it had been Hiram who got out of bed, dressed, and performed his nightly ritual, in his pajamas and robe.

Vestavia heard a siren.

"I believe it be the constable," she said.

Out front, tires skidded to a stop in the sandy gravel, and the Ford's patrol siren softened lower and lower, its pale scream dying just as Carney's weight shook the front porch.

Hiram rushed to open the door.

"What's up?" the lawman asked.

"Alma Lee's missing," Thane said.

"No."

Hiram nodded. "She just somehow got bored and decided to wander off. Lord knows where. Charlie Moon Sky's out back, stirring around in some of the hedges and thickets." He turned to his nephew. "Thane, try and remember. Did your sister mention anything, or have any particular toy or article in hand, something that could offer a hint as to what her interest was at the time?"

"This could be important, Thane," the constable told him, leaning forward to look directly at the boy's eyes.

The lad's chin lifted an inch or so, his face brightening. "I don't know if this'll help," he said, "but around the middle of the afternoon, Alma Lee was saying that catch-ball with Lot Callister was more fun than playing with me. And she wanted a playmate her own age."

Vestavia's heart seemed about to stop. But before she could leap to any conclusion, Thane had a mite more to say.

"Another thing," he said. "Alma Lee told me that maybe she was fixing to become a Cricker, like Lot."

Mr. Hiram and Constable Ransom looked instantly at each other.

"I'll bet that's it," Hiram finally said. "Nothing attracts a child more than water."

Carney Ransom nodded, with a brief stiffening of his lips, pressing them together. "The crick," he said with a snap of his fingers. "By golly, High, you've hit it smack right."

"We best organize a search party," Hiram said.

"For sure."

"I'll tell Charlie," Miss Sellie said, and then left without another word. Only a gesture, when she patted Vestavia's hand.

"I want to help look," Thane said.

"Me too," Vestavia added.

"We'll *all* do our parts," Hiram said. "I'm sure that Constable Ransom here will welcome any kind of assistance."

"Thane," the constable said, pointing a chubby finger at the boy's chest, "I want you to telephone some people for me." He pulled out a pocket pad and pencil and began to scribble a list of names, along with their telephone numbers, all of which Mr. Carney seemed to know by heart. "Tell 'em that you are calling for me, and to meet me down by the crick directly behind Hiram MacHugh's place. Got it?"

"Yes, I can do it. Easy."

"Thane," said Constable Ransom, "I want you and Vestavia to stay here, right by the telephone, because this will be our

C. P., our command post. After thirty minutes have gone by, tell the first guy who calls to look upstream. Then, tell the next man to search downcrick. That way we'll spread our search."

"That makes sense," said Hiram, "because if Alma Lee finally found the crick, she wouldn't know whether to go upstream or down."

Carney grunted. "I'd guess down."

"Why?"

"Just a hunch. Kids usual throw stuff into water, or maybe construct some little boat. So, if the current takes it, the child's natural inclination is to follow along, which means downstream."

Hiram nodded. "Yes, I'd have to agree to that." He looked at the constable. "I'm coming with you, Carney, if you'll give me a lift as far as the fire station. Then we'll possibly meet you along the crick."

"Okay. Let's go."

Vestavia followed the two men as far as the front steps, fighting the twisty feeling in her stomach. Oh, if she'd only had the sense to warn Alma Lee not to stray off. But no, and one of her sheep had strayed away from the fold. Behind her, she could hear young Mr. Thane already working the telephone, giving a number to the operator lady. Alone, she saw the patrol car driving away, in haste, its wheels spitting gravel.

"Please, " Vestavia whispered, "find my lamb."

· *Twenty-Eight* ·

Carney Ransom pressed the accelerator.

As the patrol car responded, its engine roaring, the constable headed toward the fire station. But then his right boot instinctively sought the brake, and he slowed, stopped, and turned into his customary parking slot at the courthouse. Leaving the patrol car, Carney entered his courthouse office, removed the large ring of keys, then clumped down the stairs to the basement jail. Funny, he thought, how a lost child might solve a problem.

"Okay, you two birds, this is maybe the luckiest day of your lives." He forced a smile as he was unlocking Jim Colly's cell. The barred door slid open. "Come on, Jimbo, you're a free man. No fine, no questions asked."

"How come?" the prisoner wanted to know.

"Let's just say that tonight's your opportunity to be a good citizen." He guided Jim Colly out of the cell. "Seems like we got a lost child, and plenty of folks will be helping out. So, do you want to be part of the search?"

Colly's hand rubbed his unshaven face. "Sure do. And thanks, Carney."

"Okay, go on upstairs and wait for me out back, inside my car."

As Jim Colly climbed the stairs, Carney turned to unlock the other occupied cell, the one that held Bobby MacHugh. "Okay, stranger . . . this'll be a break for you too." The steel door opened. "Like I told the other prisoner, give us a hand looking for a lost little girl, and you both'll go scot free."

Bobby stared at him, unmoving, as though he had no intention of leaving his cell. "Maybe I don't want to get turned loose. After all, I'm a suspect for the Kelby Callister killing, or so you claim."

"Ease off, Bobby. You didn't do it. Both of us know how it happened, but let's agree not to go around spreading the word."

"Whose kid is lost?"

Fists on his hips, the constable looked directly at his prisoner. "It just so happens to be Alma Lee." He saw Bobby's face become blank at the news.

"I'll help."

"Good. You certain wouldn't be much of a father if you didn't care enough to pitch in."

Bobby's hands flew from his sides in a gesture of desperatioin. "But . . . but what if *I'm* the one who finds her?"

Carney rested a hand on Bobby's shoulder. "In a way, I sort of hope you do. Yeah, I know. You're hiding from yourself. But that's not so important right now as locating your daughter. So I figured you'd jump at the chance to lend us all a hand."

Bobby nodded. "Okay."

Together, they started up the stairs, Bobby going ahead of the constable. But then he turned to look down at Carney.

"Do you mind my asking if my brother knows that you're turning me loose?"

"Ask all you like. But as a matter of fact, *no,* he doesn't. Hiram's not thinking about *you* right at the moment. He's probable only worrying about his niece. You got one heck of a nifty little girl, Bobby, and your son is every bit as decent. So let's all forget the past, kiddo, and do what demands doing, which is finding Alma Lee."

"I guess you're right."

"Right or wrong," Carney huffed up the remaining stairs following Bobby, "that's how I see it. And if the town of Hallapoosa doesn't like the way I handle my job, they can pin this rusty star on somebody else's shirt."

"I don't want anybody to know who I am."

Not overly gently, Carney Ransom shoved him toward the Ford. "I'm keeping out of it," he said, "for now. And if anybody figures it out and guesses your identity, or recognizes your face or your voice, tough titty." Grabbing the collar of Bobby's shirt, Carney fought the urge to spit in the younger man's face, and almost snarled as he spoke, so close that their chins were nearly touching. "Why in hell don't you forget whining about *yourself* and help us find that little girl?"

"Okay. Don't get rough."

Carney shook him. "I can get lots rougher than this, sonny boy. If you don't believe it, turn tail and run from helping, and when I nab you again, you'll wish you'd been born Joe Blow from Windy City."

"Easy. I said I'd help look."

Jim Colly was already sitting in the patrol car, in the back seat. He stared curiously at both of them, Carney noticed, as they approached. "What's the name of the kid who's missing?" he asked.

Carney nudged Bobby. "Tell him."

"Alma Lee," he responded. "Alma Lee MacHugh."

Hearing the emptiness in Bobby's wavering voice, Carney had all he could handle to keep from weeping. As he fumbled for the car keys, his hand was trembling, so he left it deep inside his pocket until the feeling passed. No sense in informing two prisoners that he was out of control. No, that wouldn't do at all. Biting his lower lip, he felt slightly ashamed that the opinions of two jailbirds might haunt him. To heck with both of them. And, by dang, they had better contribute to the search for Alma Lee in good faith or he would take pleasure in returning them both to the courthouse basement, to continue being guests of Hallapoosa's official hospitality.

Carney started his engine. Grinding the gears as he underclutched, he backed out of his parking space, shifted into low, and pulled away from the courthouse. Looking in the overhead rearview mirror, Carney studied the heads of his two recently freed charges. Jim Colly sat looking blankly out of the window, while Bobby's hands covered most of his face. Knees up, his body was curling into a ball, almost returning to a prenatal pose, as though withdrawing from a world he no longer could face, and children he no longer could claim.

Carney Ransom swallowed.

A fellow couldn't be a topnotch peace officer, he was thinking, without having a few sensitive feelings, especially about a subject as basic as a broken-up family. It wasn't normal for a man to live apart from his children. No, it wasn't right at all. How, he wondered, would Bobby MacHugh ever be able to walk along the street and hold his head up in a proud and respectful manner? Well, he just couldn't, and it might be best for Bobby to leave Hallapoosa and never come back.

Turning the corner, Carney headed the Ford down the dirt road that led to the crick. It was getting dark. Not surprisingly, his stomach growled, reminding him that he had done without lunch. He was trying to shave a few pounds. But now it was well after suppertime and his empty insides were complaining, making demands to be fed.

"Quiet," he said.

In the backseat, Jim Colly said something to Bobby Mac-Hugh, inquiring as to his name and where he was from.

Bobby didn't answer.

"You sure are a silent one," Jim muttered.

"Well, you can talk to me," Carney said quickly. "I'm Carney Ransom from Hallapoosa, Florida, in case you really got a itch to know." He grinned into the mirror at Jim who shot a grin back. Perhaps, the constable was hoping, this bit of fluffy chatter might serve to prevent Jim Colly's continuing to probe away at his seatmate. The less people knew, the better. At this stage of events, nobody could begin to predict how such a sorrowful situation would pan out.

The car suddenly hit a rut in the road.

"You always drive so fast?" Jim asked.

"Sorry," Carney explained, "but I'm in a heck of a hurry, and both you guys know why. We don't have much daylight left, so we best make decent use of it."

"So that little kid who's lost," Jim Colly said, "her name is MacHugh?"

"Yeah, that's right," Carney said.

"She a kin to the Judge?"

"His niece." Carney Ransom winked at the mirror. "Now maybe you two gents can understand that it might improve your chances for a pardon if you help the searching."

Jim's face sobered. "Hey, you already done that, Constable. So you said when ya cracked open my cell door."

Carney nodded. "So I did. But it wouldn't hurt to add a blessing from our Justice of the Peace, would it?"

"No," said Jim, "don't guess it would."

"Me and Judge MacHugh, we sort of allow one hand to help wash the other, and maybe scratch the other fellow's back."

"Makes sense."

"Besides," said Carney, "I happen to know the missing girl. She's only seven. But you couldn't ask for a nicer child than Alma Lee MacHugh."

As he spoke, Carney eyed Bobby's face in the rearview mirror. Bobby MacHugh was chewing on his lower lip, his body twisting slightly one way and then the other, as though forces within him were about to rip his body in two.

"So," Carney said, "we've got to find her."

Carney Ransom was not, by habit, a man who engaged in frequent or fervent prayer. Yet, as his car hit another bump in the sandy road, and drew closer to where the crick ran, he was praying now. Bringing the Ford to a stop at the picnic grounds near the crick, he turned off the key.

"Okay, gents," he informed his passengers, "this is it. Everybody out. Jim, why don't you start looking over yonder in those reeds. Give a yell if you find anything."

"Right." Jim left.

Turning to Bobby, the constable took a step up close. "If'n I was you," he said, "soon as Hiram's niece gets located, I'd take off . . . and not come visiting Hallapoosa no more. All it'll do is mess up two decent kids. Can you do it?"

Bobby nodded. "I have to."

"Excuse my saying it, Bobby, but I'd wager you'll eventual figure it's best if you disappear for good. For keeps." He rested a friendly hand on a lean shoulder that had once been so athletic. Reaching into his pocket, he pulled out his money clip, peeling off a twenty-dollar bill. It was more than he could afford, Carney knew, but what the heck . . . it was for High and the kids. And even for Vestavia in a way. "Here," he said. "Take it. It ain't much, but it'll get you started."

Bobby hesitated, then took it. "Thanks."

"Forget it. Just give me your word you'll melt yourself out of the picture and leave it all up to Hiram. Do I have your promise?"

Bobby bit his lip, and nodded.

"You have it."

· *Twenty-Nine* ·

Her little feet were easy to follow.

Crouching low, Charlie Moon Sky extended a brown hand, his fingers measuring the child's footprint, which appeared to be slighty more that the length of a finger, less than half of his hand.

He nodded once, deciding that the footprint had been made by the little girl next door who might be lost, Alma Lee.

"Please find her, Charlie, and bring her home safe and sound," Miss Sellie had said, and now he would do just that, willing to perform any task this elderly lady required. Nothing for her was work. All was joy, because to know a person like Miss Sellie was itself a pleasure.

Charlie smiled. More than that, a *gift*.

Quickly he followed the small human footprints, which were heading toward the crick. Rarely in a straight line, as Charlie could see that here, again there, Alma Lee had paused to listen, look, or touch some wild thing that had attracted her. Gradually, as the ground changed from sand and dry leaves to a heavier black muck where the land sloped to feed the crick, her tracks became deeper, darker, more distinct.

Ahead grew one low fanpalm, the handles of its fans bristling with curly-horn rows of thorns. One thorn waved him a welcome salutation, a silent greeting, as snagged on its sharp tip a single hair now waved. Touching it, examining its texture and childlike color, Charlie could see the entire head and face of the little lost child.

"Yes," he said.

Somewhere, he knew, droves of white men soon would also be searching, yelling, looking yet not seeing, Worst of all, their clumsy boots would be destroying Alma Lee's tracks. Charlie Moon Sky was not a wolf who hunted in a wolfpack. Instead, he was a panther, a lone stalker, and the obvious shouts of hair and toes would beckon his ears and eyes.

As the ground became blacker, closer to the crick and the swamp that lay beyond, the trees changed from low-growing palmetto and scrub oak to cypress, red maple, fig. He passed beneath a gumbo-limbo which stood as a quiet sentinel guarding a small slough to his right. A scorpion crouched on a flat limestone rock. Beneath his bare feet, the earth felt damp, rich, moist, softer now than velvet, almost touchable like the gray, hairy back of a wolf spider.

He walked on.

The sounds also changed. Earlier, he had listened to woodpeckers, starlings, wrens, and sparrows, but now the chorus from the leafy canopy above was sung by water birds, waders, those who hunted on longer, thinner legs. He heard an anhinga, the bird that dived for fish and then fanned her black wings open to dry her feathers. His father, John Moon Sky, had called the anhinga a water turkey. Frogs and cicadas became louder, increasing in number, and he saw a white ibis standing one-legged, her beak curving from her head like a hungry arc of light.

The water in the sloughs looked deeper here, blacker, thicker even than the air, which was so wet it could almost be sliced for parting by a machete or a cane knife.

Slowly, following Alma Lee's trail, he slipped through the vine-tangled greenery, stepping near the scat droppings of quail. There were raccoon droppings too, larger, yet drying and crisp with the crunched shells of crawdads, freshwater mussels, and snails.

Everything spoke to him, telling him true stories of what events had happened here, and who had passed this way.

Coming to the crick, Charlie Moon Sky had a decision to make. Upstream, or down? To be true, Glory and Lot lived upstream on the island, here unseen. But would Alma Lee know this? No, he concluded, she would not know.

Looking down, he saw where the two small feet had ventured to the water's edge, perhaps stood to throw a pebble or two, and then waded forward. Here, her tracks melted away, washed away by the crick's gentle, yet insistent current. Far to his left, he heard noises, shoutings and callings of one white man to another, as they had gone to the shack island, or closer. No, he decided, he would not search there. Water flowed to his right, downstream, and it would be there he would continue his search. Besides, the white men would be drifting their search this way, and he had no desire to join them.

Glancing to his right, downstream, Charlie Moon Sky could see very little. The water, yes, and the swampy jungle across the crick. To improve his view, he cautiously stepped around the bell-like trunk of a cypress, touching its grayish bark, which was mottled like the scales of a swamp lizard. He came to several more cypress trees, the bases of their trunks swollen like a hanging clump of pears.

"Ah," he said.

An idea had come to him.

Were he to cross the crick, continuing to follow it downstream, then he could easily observe this near shore. And he was almost certain that Alma Lee, being so small, would not have dared to cross the crick. Wading dowstream, Charlie came to where the crick widened, three times wider, and here he crossed where the water would be much shallower.

Now, on the swamp side of the crick, it was like standing in another world. Here the foliage hung thicker than Miss Sellie's porridge, the ground neither land nor water, only swamp, the small lagoons and inlets surrounded by green battalions of ferns, all lace. In the swamp, Charlie knew no patch of land or water remained uninhabited. Fungus, vines, armies of small insects, mounds of moss, round as emerald breasts, sprouted from every fallen log. Thick air, drenching to stand in, large pumping hearts as well as small ones, gators or gnats, and everywhere played an orchestra of insects. Near his ear, a lonely mosquito was bowing his tiny fiddle. All was claimed, nothing wasted, including the blood of his ear as his hand began to shoo away the biting pest.

He moved through the swamp ankle-deep in water, eyes constantly examining the far shore, the shore closet to Miss Sellie's place, and the MacHughs, nearest to Hallapoosa.

Moving almost slower than a slugsnail, Charlie also glanced to his left, toward the depths of the swamp. The walking would be easier, he knew, were this winter instead of summer. During the dry season, in winter, rain rarely fell, and this black land hardened, turning grayer than an old mother's hair, then wrinkled like her skin, and cracked like her cackling laughter. But this was still August, the time of rain and growing, and the swamp was evergreen. Around him, dead brown fronds of fanpalms hung like the exhausted hands of witches that had once applauded life, but had now become still, and cold.

A male wood duck, exhibiting his rainbow of plumage, darted through a stand of cattails and out of Charlie's sight.

He walked on, always downstream.

"Where are you, Alma Lee?"

Down through the breezy canopy of cypress lace, tiny prisms of evening sunlight waltzed with fragments of shadow. Near the water, however, there was no wind. None. Only the smell of wild coffee and muscadine berries, which were tart when beyond ripeness. A redjacket hornet feasted on one. Around his constantly wading feet and ankles, fingerlings of bass and bream swarmed frantically to attack the disturbed mosquito larvae, darting their sleek silvery hulls through the small clouds of aroused silt.

A tiny green treefrog quacked five times, ducklike, then remained silent.

Moving downstream, Charlie crossed a narrow custard-apple swamp, wading through thick water. A large black fox squirrel scolded from atop a fallen cypress, watched Charlie with dark, curious eyes, its cheeks abulge with berries and cypress buds. The vines became thicker. Tendrils of hydrilla weed clutched to claim his ankles, and woven everywhere on the water's surface lay shawls of hyacinth—bulbous, leafy, irregular, a green goiter of pond nature. All above him, he could hear the subtle soft lisping of unfallen leaves, perhaps bickering as to which leaf would survive to nurse the lifegiving sap of its twig mother. As he moved through the swamp, Charlie's hands constantly had to part the hanging strands of Spanish moss as his feet punctured hole after hole in the surface's green carpet of frogspit algae.

From somewhere, a long way off, a swamp fox barked his

highpitched yappy taunt, perhaps as a threat or a cry of alarm
. . . and Charlie Moon Sky remembered, in that one barking
sound, so much of his boyhood. But there was no going back
to the Seminoles, no longer a swamp, and without his Miss
Sellie, no home. Someday, he promised, he would take Glory
and Lot and travel in a dugout canoe, poling it slowly, softly,
fleeing far to the south where the mangroves almost abruptly
displaced the waving sea of sawgrass. There he would hunt
for them, feed them, and make both Glory and Lot his own.

"Soon," he sighed.

Yet now was a poor time for dreams, he thought, because a
child loved by Miss Sellie was lost and must be found. So, he
would press on, and if necessary wade through snakes—cotton
mocs and diamondbacks—in order to find Alma Lee Mac-
Hugh. Alone, like a panther stalks, he would find her.

"Alma Lee," he yelled through cupped hands.

Waiting for the echo of his shout to die within its green
swamp grave, Charlie heard no answer, no little girl's voice
chirping a reply. All he could hear now was the scraping
screech of marsh hawk, one which might flush a wide-eyed
rodent from the haven of matted vegetation. As he looked to
his right, toward the crick, a flash of color caught Charlie's
eye. It seemed to be snagged on a thorn vine that looped, low
and sagging, into the water. In little more than a breath of
time, Charlie reached out and snared it with his hand.

It was a doll. The one he had repaired.

Charlie Moon Sky smiled.

Bending low, he studied the soft shore dirt for any telltale
footprints, carefully sifting each sight and sound, every bent
clump of swamp grass or open patch of soil. Finally his care
was rewarded. Stooping he saw a child's footmark, plain as
could be. But he saw far more.

The tracks of a very large man.

· *Thirty* ·

It was almost dawn.

Lifting his head from the kitchen table, Thane Mac-Hugh saw Vestavia sitting in the other chair, eyes closed and head nodding.

During the evening and most of the night, their telephone rang persistently, callers asking for news or informing whoever answered where they would be continuing to search for his sister. Vestavia had brewed coffee and tea, so that both of them could force themselves to keep awake, hour after hour. No, Thane told everyone who had called, there was no news at all, neither good nor bad.

Blinking his eyes, Thane stared down at the map of Halla-poosa that he had taken from his uncle's bedroom, unfolded, and then stuck with pins. As people called, offering assistance, Thane had directed each person to a different area, marking it on the map with a pin, in order to extend the search. As he studied the map, the Kalipsa Crick basin was thoroughly fastened to the table top by a company of little silver soldiers, representing searchers. Thane felt pleased that he had thought of using the map by himself, without any instruction from his uncle, the constable, or from Vestavia.

Eyes closed for a moment, hands and fingers knotted together, he whispered, "God, please help them find her."

Answering the phone had been frustrating, as Thane Mac-Hugh had wanted instead to be a part of the searching party. Several times he had told Vestavia, "I can't stay here any longer. I want to go down to the crick, with the others, and look for Alma Lee."

Vestavia had shaken her head.

"Mr. Thane," she had informed him, "I don't have no right to order you about. But you said you'd stay close. I heard you promise Mr. Hiram, so best you keep to your duty." With a long skinny black finger, Vestavia had pointed at the telephone, giving one brief but final nod with her gray head.

Thane kept remembering his uncle's face. How white he had turned when realizing that his niece had disappeared. And when the crick had been finally mentioned, by Thane himself, how he read the sudden terror that raged in Uncle Hiram's eyes. There had been, Thane MacHugh had earlier concluded, something going on down at the crick. It must have happened on Sunday morning. Because when he and Alma Lee had returned from church with Miss Sellie, he'd noticed the unusual mud on his uncle's shoe. A very strange kind of dirt, quite unlike the sandy soil near the house.

Rising from the kitchen table, being very careful not to disturb a dozing Vestavia, Thane tiptoed across the kitchen to stare out through the screen of the open door. To the east he could detect a slight lightening in the sky, a promise of dawn and a fresh Florida day.

"Rats," he said.

Looking over his shoulder, he could see the telephone in the parlor. Well, if it rang, Vestavia certainly could and would answer it. So there really wasn't much of a purpose in wasting himself here, when he could be out yonder, helping to find Alma Lee.

Slowly, as if testing the spring and the weight of the screen door, Thane pushed it slightly open, using only one finger. The door opened wider, as though it were agreeing to his leaving the house. His more-or-less commitment to stay by the telephone plagued him. How, he wondered, could anyone respect him were he to shirk his specific duty at the command post? Perhaps they had only called it that to make his staying behind with Vestavia seem more important.

With a nod of his head, Thane MacHugh stepped outside onto the squeaky boards of the back stoop, then eased the screen door to a closed position. Alma Lee usually banged it, he recalled, and the thought of his sister caused him to swallow. What if she never came home? *Home?* Thane sighed. This old Hallapoosa house wasn't really a home for him, or for Alma Lee. All it was was Uncle Hiram's house, and even more Vestavia's than his or his sister's.

As he was preparing to tiptoe down the back steps, he heard the telephone ring.

"Nuts," he said.

Bounding back up the stairs with a hurried one-legged leap, he did bang the screen door in his haste to reach the telephone, which was about to sound its third signal.

"Hello."

"Thane, it's only me." He recognized his uncle's deep judicial tone. At the other end of the line, his uncle sounded somewhat out of breath. "Is Vestavia still there with you?"

"Yes, she's right here."

He didn't bother to mention the fact that Vestavia had not been awakened by the telephone. Instead, he told his uncle how he had been using the Hallapoosa map.

"Good. Stay right where you are, like a good lad. We need somebody there, Thane."

"But I want to come help."

"You are helping, much more than you realize. Using the map and pins is a brilliant stroke. Now then, if anyone else calls, send them downcrick, toward Kalipsa Ferry way. Hear?"

"Yes, I will."

"There's no use looking upcrick. That's where everyone else is. No sign of her. " He heard his uncle's voice crack. "No sign at all. If there were any tracks at all, they've been stampeded over by dozens of good people who were merely attempting to be helpful."

Vestavia slowly opened her eyes and her face was immediately asking the only question on her mind. Thane shook his head to her, then took a deep breath.

"Vestavia's here, and wide awake. But there's no use of two of us hanging around, because we're wasting manpower."

For a moment, nothing but silence at his uncle's end of the wire. "Thane, whatever you do, you mustn't come to the crick. There's been some serious trouble, but it's in the past and I don't really have time to explain, certainly not over the telephone. Yet it all adds up to this. You cannot leave the house and endanger yourself. There are too many Callisters."

Thane frowned. The only Callisters he knew were Glory and Lot, and both of them seemed nicer than pie. But whoever had beaten up Glory and frightened Lot couldn't be too decent. Uncle Hiram hadn't told the complete story. As he worried about it all, a pressing uncontrollable question somehow popped from his mouth.

"Who hurt Glory?"

"We all have. Our family as well as hers. It's a long sad story, my boy." Thane heard a sigh. "However, now is hardly the time to explain it all."

As a number of questions had been asked during the night, several of which had only served confusion, Thane now knew possibly more than his uncle realized, a fact which somehow prompted the boy's next question.

"Who are those prisoners down at the jail?"

He had to pull the telephone away from his ear, because of Uncle Hiram's unexpected hollering. "*No,* stay away from there! You're never to come anywhere near the courthouse without my permission. Is that understood?"

"Yes, sir."

"Besides," his uncle's voice was slightly softening, "none of this business concerns you, my dear nephew, so keep out of it. I can understand that naturally you've become inquisitive, as Hallapoosa's a quiet town, compared to Jacksonville, and nothing much happens around here."

"If you'd ask me," Thane said, "there's an awful lot happening. Plenty in the last couple of days."

Over the telephone, he could hear the old Judge's cane rapping on somebody's floor. One irate blow. Something, he suspected, was odd about that cane, because on Sunday evening last, he had observed Hiram's staring at the heavy knob of the handle, as though his cane was almost some evil entity.

"True enough, boy. But it will all die down. I'm too exhausted to elaborate. We've got to find Alma Lee . . . before . . . " His voice trailed off into some mysterious unspoken horror.

"Before what?"

"Nothing. I have to go. Has Carney called?"

"Twice. He said that he hasn't seen you since he dropped you off at the fire station."

"Well, at least we're not all looking in one place. I'm sure we'll find Alma Lee. She couldn't have gone too far."

To Thane, he wasn't sounding too convinced that she would be found. Or found alive.

"I'll call you in a few more hours, Thane. And if Carney again calls, I'm with old Benson Higg. He's as lame as I am, and the two of us can search at our own speed, without holding up the others."

"Where will you be? If Constable Ransom calls, he'll probable ask me where you are. So what'll I tell him?"

"Tell him we'll be south of Wilowby Road, beyond the stilt house. He'll know."

"Okay."

"And . . . and Thane . . . "

"Yes?"

Silence. Then finally, "If anything tragic happens, some horrible news, you are not alone in the world. Because I . . . because you'll be all that . . . " Hiram's voice cracked and he was unable to continue. The only sound that followed was the distant click of a telephone receiver replaced on its hook, and the lonely humming of a discontinued conversation.

"Yes, I know," Thane said. "Me too."

As he hung up, Vestavia seemed to understand what had been said. As she held out her arms to him, he came to her, feeling her rough dress and her gentle hands, smelling her good-cooking smell.

"There, there now, Mr. Thane," he heard her whispering. Her fingers gently found his eyes and wiped their outside corners. "I'm right here. Right here."

On his knees, Thane was clinging to Vestavia, very hard, unable to say any words at all, because losing a mother and a father was enough. Thane didn't know if he could stand up to losing Alma Lee. He couldn't hold so much hurt. It was a long time before he could talk to Vestavia.

"You don't have to call me Mr. Thane. I don't guess I'm quite ready."

· *Thirty-One* ·

Big Callister smiled in the night.

As he sloshed through the heavy jungle of palmetto and wild grape vines, he carried the little girl over his shoulder as though she weighed no more than a ragdoll, his bare feet splashing through warm swamp water. For a while, the child had been screaming and crying, but now, much to Big's relief, she was quieter and made little sound except for a soft whimper.

"Hush," he told her. "You ain't hurting."

"I want to go home," the child said.

Big stopped. Slowly he lowered her to her feet, keeping a firm hold on both her pigtails. Looking down at her little upturned face, Big Callister couldn't believe his good fortune. The fates had certain smiled at him this night, sending him a MacHugh.

"Sure," he said, "I'm fixing to take you home."

Little girls brought more money than boys, Big knew. But lately, the secret trading of children had nearly dried up. Business was bad. Nobody made offers or placed orders because there wasn't a dollar to pass from one hand to another. The whiskey business was near as sorry. But on this particular night, Big could count at least one blessing, a surprise, a gift from the gods or the devils that determined a man's luck. His own MacHugh.

Big figured that some MacHugh blood ought to spill to even the score for Kelby, even though Cousin Kelby weren't better than a one-eared rat. Yet blood wasn't profitable. Nor was revenge.

This little girlchild would bring money.

MacHugh money.

Leaning against the curving trunk of a cypress tree, Big squeezed the pigtails in his hand, not feeling hair. He felt cash. It was a warm touch, alive, like whiskey, and his gut flooded with greed.

"I want to go home *now*."

"Quiet," he said, yanking her hair. "I got to cogitate a mite. So's I can figure up just how to get a message to that old Justice of the Peace in Hallapoosa."

"You know my Uncle Hiram?"

"Oh yes. Everybody know the Judge. And he'll fork over a fat ransom for you, honey. A tidy sum. He'll cough up the scratch for any ransom I demand on him."

"Ransom? You mean Constable Ransom?"

Big yanked her hair. "Naw, not *him*. I don't guess you learnt too much in school, or maybe you be too young to go. How old be you, girl?"

"Seven." She held up seven fingers.

"And your name is MacHugh?"

"Honest is. I want to go home. Let me lie down somewhere. Or take me back to Hallapoosa, please."

"In time. In due time."

Big looked around in the night. It made not a lick of sense to haul this child to his shack, on account he wasn't living there by himself right now. A couple of hot little hussies were there too. Dallie and Marleen. Dull as they both were, it'd be fooly to let either girl know that he was just about fixing to be handed a bundle of cash money. They'd have the whole wad spent in under a week and Big's pockets would again be hollow.

Whipping off the rope that belted his pants, Big lashed the child to the slender trunk of a scrub oak. "It's too tight," she said.

"Hush," he said, giving her cheek a slap. "I got thinking to do, and nobody can think with you wailing all the while. So shut it up, unless you maybe want another."

Bending down, he stared the little girl full in the face,

cocking back his hand. Turning her head, she closed her eyes, as though preparing to be struck again. "No, please don't."

"Now hush."

"I want to go home."

"Go to sleep. Like I said, I got me some thinking to do. So shut your mouth and still it."

How, he was wondering, would he send a ransom note to MacHugh? As he pondered the question, he swatted a bug, then another. Finding some dry tinder in a fallen cedar tree, he struck a match to it, then added plenty of green leaves so that the resulting smoke would keep away all the biter bugs. Some of the smoke blew up into the little girl's face, causing her to cough. She shook her head from side to side, glaring at him in the moonlight, reminding him of who she was by her uppity ways.

"You're a MacHugh all right."

"Yes, I certain am. And I'm glad I'm not like you because you're so smelly and mean."

"How come you don't live with your mama and your daddy?"

"They're dead."

"Is that straight?" Big sneezed. The smoke from the green fire was worrying his eyes and nose. "Is that true you don't have no people?"

"All I have is my brother. I had a doll, but I lost her in the crick back yonder. Her name's Claudine."

Big grunted. "Go to sleep."

"I can't go to sleep without my dolly. And I don't like being tied up in this old rope. It's all rough and prickly."

Big squatted, his back to a pine. Women, he thought, were a pain in the hinder, even at the tender age of seven. Always wanting, and never content. Whatever she had, a woman usual had a hanker for something else, fresh new. Marleen and Dallie, for example, certain acted up thataway, even in the stores over at Kalipsa Ferry. Neither one of them wanted something until the other one picked it up, then the battle began in earnest, spitting and yelling, raising ruck.

"Women," he snorted.

"I want to go home."

He threw a pine cone at her, but she voiced her complaint again, griping about not having her dolly, and that the rope was cutting into her.

"If you was fourteen," Big said, pointing at her, "instead of seven, I would silence you proper, the only way a female understands."

How much, Big Callister was silently asking himself, would he ask for? To be within reason, the figure ought to go along with the amount of money that old Judge MacHugh could skim as a Justice of the Peace. A salary, plus plenty of under-the-table graft, Big imagined. He almost rubbed his hands together, thinking about having his pockets crackling with crisp new bills.

He'd take a trip to Kalipsa Ferry and treat himself to a time. No, instead he'd go to Naples, maybe even stay at a hotel and lay up with a fancy lady or two. It was too far to Miami, and besides, that place was nothing except trouble. Too many sharpies from northern cities like New York and Chicago. Miami was a place to stay clear of, unless a man hankers to wake up naked and broke because some slut run off with everything during the night.

"You better take me home. Right now."

"Hush, I told ya."

"I don't like it here. I don't like all these bugs or the smoke, and I certain don't like *you*. Because you don't ever wash."

Big chuckled.

This little gal sure wasn't lacking in the spunk department. She'd grow up to be a regular hellcat, a scratcher and a biter, the kind worth taming and then training to tend a shack and fix eats. A man didn't dare turn his back on her breed of a hotspitter, not even in bed, on account all these hellcats would turn treacherous quicker than a blink. Couldn't trust a one.

"What's your name again, missy?"

"I won't tell you."

"Then I reckon I'll beat it out ya."

"I am Miss Alma Lee MacHugh, and I happen to be growing up into becoming a proper person. And if Vestavia comes to find me, she'll give *you* a what-for."

Big picked his teeth with the sharp edge of a pine seed. "Well now, ain't you the fancy one. If'n you be so doggone uppity and smart, little missy, tell me how I can git word to the Judge that I got you here, and hogtied to a tree."

"You won't have to," she said.

"Won't I?"

"No, because my Uncle Hiram has got everyone in Hallapoosa looking for me by this time. And if *they* don't find me, my *brother* will. His name is Thane Hiram MacHugh and he knows near to everything because he's thirteen. And soon he's going to the *world*."

Holding his sides, Big laughed until his belly was starting to hurt. Doggone, if this here little tyke wasn't fair company, a lot more fun than either Dallie or Marleen.

"Ain't nobody around here who knows this swamp like I do," Big told her. "I'm a old swamp rat, a Cricker born and bred, and nobody in Hallapoosa could even dare to dream about wading through a swamp wet. They be so afraid of all them snakes and gators and snapper turtles, why they might even quit breathing even to ponder on it."

He continued to laugh. The little MacHugh was spunky, for certain, but spunk didn't always go along equal with brains. There was city smart and swamp smart. Two kinds. Big figured he wasn't too city smart, not after Miami women had taken his poke, but he sure was smart in the swamp. Smart enough to hide in here for days, weeks even, where nobody from Hallapoosa would set foot.

"Yeah," he said, "I'm a old swamp hound."

Throwing back his head he faced the moon and closed his eyes to let out a long bay, like a coondog that's treed his find.

"I don't think you're a dog at all," the child said, even though tied tight to a tree. "All you are is . . . *un-proper*."

Everything this kid said struck him funny, and he giggled again, chin high, calling to the moon. Lowering his head, Big Callister expected only to see one face, that of his captive. Instead he saw two. Behind the child stood a young Seminole. A twisted rag circled his head and long black hair fell freely to his naked shoulders. He didn't quite see the Seminole's hand moving, yet one moment the hand was empty, then full, as a knife blade flashed and pointed directly at the girl. In a second the rope was cut.

The little girl looked up at the Seminole, then smiled, held up her arms with her fingers all extended and spoke a name.

"Charlie!"

"Come," the Seminole said, "and I will take you home." The Indian smiled at her. "I also found your doll. In a way, she told me where you were."

Nearby, where Big Callister watched openmouthed, stood a long slender knee of cypress, sprouting upward in the shape of a club. Snatching it, Big heard it crack free. Then he was charging forward, the cypress club above his head, intent on keeping the child, even if he had to kill to do it. Nobody was going to rob Big Callister. Surely not some dirty Seminole called Charlie.

As he swung the club, he felt a sudden burning across his belly, a sharp piercing slash of heat that seemed to slice him into two pieces. He could smell his own blood.

"Come," the man called Charlie said to the little girl, and through glazed eyes he saw them disappear into the darkness of the swamp.

Big was alone with his pain. Looking down at the wide bleeding slash across his belly, he was deciding that there was a curse on those MacHughs, nothing but bad luck, and he never wanted to see another MacHugh.

Large or small.

· *Thirty-Two* ·

People were everywhere.

All along the crick, Bobby MacHugh noticed, the citizens of Hallapoosa had voluntarily turned out to join the search for his daughter. Torches and flashlights were shining everywhere. Good folks, he silently thought.

"Spread out," Constable Carney Ransom was telling them, waving his arms and trying to organize his volunteers into some degree of order.

A person Bobby had casually known almost all of his early life, a man whose name was Diller Smith, was standing nearby, ankle deep in the crick water and dutifully poking around in a loose pile of crickside brush that had collected in an eddy. Shrugging, the man looked casually at Bobby and said, "Well, she certain ain't in here." Again he shrugged, holding out both hands in a momentary gesture of futility. "What did they say that kid's name was?"

"Alma Lee." Bobby almost choked on the words. Before saying his daughter's full name, he had to pause for a rasping breath, biting his lower lip. "They said her name is Alma Lee MacHugh," he said, disguising his voice as best he could.

Diller Smith squinted. Then with half a grin and an abandoning shake of head, he said, "For a second there, I thought I knowed you from somewhere. Don't guess I do. You a stranger in town?"

Bobby nodded. "In a way. I'm just passing through, you might say, sort of looking for work."

The man snorted. "Work? You an' everybody else, these days. Well, you certain won't turn up even a lick of it around Hallapoosa."

Diller turned away.

Slowly, without making his purpose seem obvious to any of the other searchers, Bobby worked his way downstream. On his ankles and through his worn-out shoes, the crick water felt cooling, welcoming, bringing back so many times in his boyhood that he had come to this very spot, to fish, to swim, or merely to enjoy the isolated beauty of Kalipsa Crick.

"Okay," Carney Ransom was still hollering, "y'all fan out. It don't make a smack of sense for us all to congregate here in one area."

To be honest about it, what Bobby really ached to do was go upstream, just to see Glory Callister. Not to love her, but merely to catch one last glimpse of her. He longed to touch her hair. It was like Della's had been, in a way, flowing and flaxen, only his wife's had been a shade or two darker.

Bobby felt thankful that nobody, thus far, had recognized him. Probable because their minds weren't on identifying a stranger, but locating a lost child. Again and again, he could hear a variety of voices calling her name. "Alma Lee! Alma Lee!" It hurt to hear it, as he was the only searcher who wasn't calling out the name of his daughter. It made him pause to wonder what kind of a man he had become. He felt like a used, crushed-out cigarette, bent and without any flame of life. Diller Smith, a few minutes ago, had viewed him as some outsider, and so a phantom stranger he was, even to himself.

Moving downstream, more alone with every step he took, Bobby realized that it had been a grave mistake, his returning a second time to Hallapoosa.

Seven years or so ago, the first time he had come back to Hallapoosa, Alma Lee hadn't yet been born. They only had Thane. Yet he hadn't gone to visit Hiram. He had come here to the crick and had loved Glory Callister. Same as three days ago. Again he had come here, upstream to the island, hoping to see Glory, but instead he had discovered that Hiram had taken a cane to Glory's pa, Kelby Callister, and had bludgeoned him to death. *Why?* The thought was gnawing at his insides. Hiram never went around seeking trouble. To be sure, not many people in Hallapoosa ever took much of a shine to any of that Callister tribe, and surely that one-eared Kelby was one of the least likable. It was said often enough that few of the other Callisters could stand Kelby.

Bobby sighed. "But old Kelby sure did sire one beauty of a Glory."

Why was he thinking these thoughts? The guilt of it suddenly plagued him. He was supposed to be searching for his daughter. *His daughter!* Alma Lee was lost, perhaps dead by drowning in the very crick waters in which he now stood. Bending, he splashed some of the cooling water into both eyes, washing his face, hoping that the jolt of its wetness would rekindle some semblance of reason.

"I have to think," he said softly, "so I might final do the right thing, for my children and for faithful old High."

The one thing he couldn't do, Bobby knew, was shock his children by appearing and announcing to them that he wasn't really dead.

"Is Mama alive too?"

The question haunting his mind might be asked him by Alma Lee, in her sweet-little-angel voice, abrim with hope. How, he wondered, could he begin to tell her the truth, the full and sordid story of their lives and their shattering marriage?

Yes, he wanted to find his daughter, to hold her and comfort her, then return her to the safety and stability of Hiram's home. More than finding her himself, he wanted her found. Then he could disappear. All the Hallapoosa minds would be centered on Alma Lee's return, and he could slip away and ease out of town forever.

Stumbling along over the fallen trees and sharp rocks, the memories of his schooldays all came back in vivid rushes of recollection . . . the athletic triumphs, the girls. But then graduation, which was followed by one disappointment after another, failure upon failure. Hired because of the high-school hero he had been, then discharged for incompetence or his lack of interest or industry.

The last straw was when some funds, only a few lousy dollars, were missing from the accounts at the Produce Mart, and accusing fingers had pointed his way. Although nothing had been proven, he was fired, and then he had begged for more school. Out of town. At Rollins College, up north in Orlando, he again failed, cut classes, and also was caught cheating on an examination.

Bobby looked at the moonless sky.

Visions of Alma Lee's being alone, perhaps frightened or threatened, were hot rapiers through his mind and body. Worry, he thought, is truly pain. His mother had been correct when she had once said that, about her worrying. Now he knew it was true. He wouldn't be able to leave Hallapoosa until he knew for certain that Alma Lee had been found.

"Damn," he said, cursing the darkness.

The night did pass, and with it the constant choir of bugs and frogs from along the crick, and from the swamp beyond the far shore.

In spite of himself, Bobby was now calling out his daughter's name. "Alma Lee!" And once, at an unguarded moment of panic, he even said, "Where are you, Alma Lee? It's me. It's your *daddy!*"

The word seemed to echo in the dampening night air, resounding again and again in his ears, lashing his remorse with its full meaning. What a rotten father he had been. A failure as a man, a husband, and as a parent. If his wife and children could have fired him for incompetence, or for indifference, surely they would have so done. But now Della was dead, because he had killed her, accidentally, yet by his own impetuous jealousy.

Was his daughter also dead, or dying?

"Alma Lee!" he was shouting. "It's . . . "

No, he must not say *daddy* again, even though he longed to, hungered to tell her that both of them were alive, and safe, and going home to Hiram. *Home?* There again was another forbidden term, because he had no home. No longer. But both Thane and Alma Lee could have one, with their wise and goodhearted uncle in his rumpled white suit, leaning on his cane. Well, that cane was the only thing that Hiram MacHugh had ever leaned on.

"I'm proud of you, High. I'm so damn proud to be your brother."

Having no watch, Bobby could only estimate how many hours of the night had passed. His bones ached. And the soles of his feet were throbbing, even though he soaked them frequently in the crick water. It must be almost four or five o'clock in the morning, yet no promise of dawn.

"Alma Lee," he called hoarsely.

For hours now, he had been working his way downstream, shouting her name, but always avoiding the other volunteers, of which he'd encountered only a few along the way.

Alone now, he wanted to stop and rest, and to get something to eat, realizing that he had eaten little or nothing in days. A man had to be alive in order to eat, and Bobby MacHugh was no longer alive. Instead he was playacting a charade, some dark-of-the-moon melodrama in which he was posing in the role of a stranger *just passing through*. He didn't actual live in Hallapoosa, or anywhere, because he officially had died in a burning car, his own, with his wife in Jacksonville.

He was legally, and spiritually, dead.

Voices!

They came from downstream. In the darkness, a silhouette of a man, carrying something, was approaching slowly. Closer now, Bobby could see that the man carried a child, piggyback, her little arms encircling his neck. He could hear his daughter's voice.

"I like you, Charlie."

He saw white teeth flashing in the dark as the man smiled, holding a little girl who, in turn, held a doll.

"Claudine likes you too."

Standing motionless in the shadows, he watched them pass, a young Seminole carrying his daughter straight as a dye in the direction of Hiram's place. Toward home. Mentally, he reached out for a final time to touch his daughter and to kiss the freckles on her face, feeling her little arms around *his* neck, instead of Charlie's, dreaming one last forbidden dream.

"Good-bye," he whispered. "This is my gift to you and to your brother. Yes, and to Hiram."

Looking at the moonless cloudy sky, Bobby MacHugh cursed the God who had not created him strong enough.

He was too weak for such pain.

· *Thirty-Three* ·

September arrived.
Even though the weather was blessing everyone cooler, Alma Lee was not quite sure that she was going to enjoy going to school, and first grade, but as it turned out, she had taken to Miss Biddeford a whole lot.

Early that morning, both Vestavia and Miss Sellie had appeared even before Uncle Hiram was out of bed, and the two old ladies had fussed with her school dress for most an hour. They even heated the iron and pressed the light blue trim ribbons several times. But then, just as she and Thane were leaving the house for school, both Vestavia and Miss Sellie stood waving on the front porch, holding one another and blinking very fast.

Alma Lee thought she knew why, and knowing it made her even a mite happier.

Today, the first day of school, had been a long one with plenty of excitement. More baseball at noon than she could quite keep up with. As she lay in bed, listening to Uncle Hiram's old clock striking the hour of nine, she sort of wanted to sneak into Thane's room, yet couldn't quite lift her head from the pillow. So she merely curled herself on a hip, knees up, and held Claudine closer, so her dolly wouldn't be afraid of the dark. And she was trying very hard not to remember Big Callister.

She heard someone coming. Opening her eyes, lifting her head from the pillow, Alma Lee saw her brother.

· 211 ·

"If you're fixing to stay," she said, "you'd better be grave-yard quiet, on account I'm just about all used up." For some reason, it always pleased her to say things exactly the way Vestavia put them. "My first day of school wore me plum through the heel."

In the moonlight, Thane grinned. Her bedsprings creaked some as he sat on the corner near the footpost.

"S'matter," she asked, "can't you sleep?"

He shook his head. "Not really. I was feeling sort of sad, lying there and listening to the whippoorwills. You know, we never heard a single whippoorwill when we lived in the city, in Jacksonville." He sighed. "Maybe we're going to like Halla-poosa a lot more than we dreamed."

"Maybe so." Alma Lee was quiet for a minute. Then, as she felt herself nearing sleep, she fought the urge and sat up to look at her brother. "What's that in your hand?"

He tossed it up and caught it. "It's just my Ty Cobb baseball, the one Miss Sellie gave me. I thought you might want to sleep with it under your pillow, just once, so it'll help turn you into a famous baseballer."

Thane handed her his baseball. The white horsehide felt smooth and warm, and only a few of the threads had worked loose.

"Thanks. I won't keep it, on account you favor it so much."

He touched her foot which was beneath the bedsheet. "You did okay at baseball this noon, over at school. In fact, I told some of the guys that you were my sister."

"*Okay*? I struck out! And I never hit the ball even once, or even gave it a scare."

Thane squeezed her toe. "Yes, but at least you were swing-ing the bat. Most of the kids just stood there closing their eyes whenever the ball would come. That's all I came over to your room to say." He stood up.

"Don't leave."

"We've got school again tomorrow. The school year isn't only one day, you know. We best get sleeping."

"I know. But if you stay for a while, maybe I'll tell you again about mean old Big Callister."

Flopping down beside her, Thane supported his head with a bent arm. "Weren't you scared?"

"Sort of. I was the mostest scared when Charlie came

sneaking up behind me with his knife and the fight started. And I actual did close my eyes and missed it all. Next thing I knew, old Big was bleeding something fearful from a long gash clear across his stomach. Charlie scooped me up and toted me home. But do you really want to know the part I liked best?"

"Tell me."

"Charlie found Claudine."

Both of them laughed and Thane tickled her to make it worse. As she saw her brothers's in-the-dark grin widen, Alma Lee heard a strange noise that seemed to be coming from out in the upstairs hall.

"It's Uncle Hiram," she hissed. "I can hear his cane. So we're caught now, for sure and for certain. He'll be sore we were making so much noise."

Sure enough, it was their next of kin. He stood in the doorway to her room, his bulk filling the gap. As he had taken his suit coat off, a white shirt and white trousers appeared like billowing clouds. On business days, her uncle always seemed to be a white overstuffed pillow, held from bursting by belt or suspenders.

He rapped his cane on the floor. "Well," he said, "the pair of you are making enough racket up here." Slowly he entered her bedroom. "So I merely came upstairs to join the fun."

Alma Lee and Thane looked at each other, then quickly back to their uncle.

"You're not mad?" she asked.

The Judge shook his head. "No. All I'm feeling these days is—is thankful." He cleared his throat of what he sometimes called a judicial frog. Raising his cane to point, he asked, "Do you think there might be room on that bed for three Mac-Hughs, even though one of us is far too large to cuddle?"

Without another word her uncle joined them on the bed, and for some reason, possibly because it was dark, Alma Lee leaned close to him and rested her head on his shoulder, inhaling the clean starchy smell that Vestavia always added to his shirts. Her uncle raised his other arm. "You too," he told Thane. "I want to hold both of you."

To Alma Lee, it felt good feeling Uncle Hiram's big arm around her shoulders. Leaning close, he kissed her temple. Then he did the same to Thane.

• 213 •

"You never did that before," she said, still aware of the touch of his lips on her face, as though his kiss wanted to tarry.

"No," he said, "but if you both will allow, I shall do it rather often from now on. At least once a month." She felt his big body chuckling at his own joke, but then he squirmed as if in sudden discomfort. "Good grief," he said, "I was lying on a baseball."

"Thane let me borrow it for under my pillow," Alma Lee said, "so it'll make me hit a homer."

"Good," he said. Their uncle was silent for a moment. "I never hit a home run. But I surely once knew someone who could." Again, he was quiet, this time for a longer period, but then he finally spoke. "So here we all are, my dears. You and I, Ty Cobb, and our dear Claudine. And we still have Vestavia and Miss Sellie next door, and Carney. By thunder, I'm one heck of a rich fellow."

There was a joy in his voice that Alma Lee had never before heard. It pleased her. "Are you still feeling sad, Thane?" Alma Lee asked her brother in a sleepy whisper.

She heard Thane sigh. "A bit."

"Why?" her uncle asked.

"Oh," Thane said, "because Miss Sellie told me that Charlie Moon Sky would be leaving soon, and that he'd be taking Glory and Lot along too. According to Miss Sellie, they're going to be a new family." Thane sighed. "That's what made me feel so doggone blue. Because I wanted to marry Glory."

"Well now," said Uncle Hiram, "that's quite a coincidence. I guess Carney Ransom was right when he said, Thane, that you certainly are a genuine MacHugh."

Eyes closed, holding tight to Claudline and Thane's baseball, Alma Lee was trying to say how much she would be missing Charlie and Glory and Lot. But the words wouldn't come. For now, it was enough just to lay her head close to Uncle Hiram and know that she was also a MacHugh. Again she heard her brother's voice.

"Miss Sellie was also saying that she was rather glad to see Julia Blount come to sit on our porch, now that we added an extra chair. Mrs. Blount comes almost every evening, Miss Sellie said, after we kids go to bed. Is that true?"

Hiram nodded.

"Does she come to hear the whippoorwills?" Alma Lee asked.

"Yes, that's quite right," her uncle said.

"I like Mrs. Blount," Thane said.

"Do you? And may I please inquire why?"

"Because she likes you. I can tell by the way she looks at you, and sometimes uses her own hanky to polish your eyeglasses when they're lying on a table."

Alma Lee heard her Uncle Hiram inhale a deep breath, then let it out in a contented rush, as though he suddenly felt very happy to be living right here in Hallapoosa. Turning her head slightly, she kissed the back of her uncle's hand, feeling his gentle hug in return. Somewhere in the room, she could hear Thane breathing his strong boy breath into the mimosa night air, and more.

Alma Lee heard the whippoorwills.